DANGEROUS DESIRES

RESCUE & REDEMPTION #5

MORGAN JAMES

ONE

SIENNA

The flashing red and blue lights strobed in my rearview mirror, and I bit back a groan. Damn it. I was already running late; I didn't need this on top of everything else.

"Hey, Soph?" I let off the accelerator and steered the car to the side of the road. "I'll have to call you back."

I hung up with my sister, then hit the hazard lights and put the car in park. The police cruiser pulled in behind me, and I drummed an impatient rhythm on the steering wheel as I waited for him to approach.

One minute passed, then two. What the hell was he doing? I tossed a quick look at the clock, and a grimace pulled at my mouth. No way was I going to make it to my showing in time now. This client had been particularly difficult, and I'd shown him sixteen houses over the past two and a half months. I was hoping today would be lucky number seventeen. But I had to get there first.

Movement in the rearview mirror drew my attention, and I straightened in my seat as I watched the door of the police cruiser swing open. A tall man unfolded from the seat, and my breath caught. Damn.

I craned my neck toward the side mirror, trying to get a better glimpse of him. He ambled toward me as if he had nothing better to do, and as much as it aggravated me, it gave me time to drink him in. The man was the epitome of tall, dark, and handsome with his deeply tanned skin and dark hair. His broad shoulders took up the majority of the mirror, and I felt my stomach do a funny little flip as he stopped next to my door.

My gaze slowly swept up his body until I found myself suspended in an icy gray gaze, and the butterflies in my stomach battered my ribcage wildly. He raised his brows and made a little motion with his hand. The back of my neck prickled as the heat of embarrassment raced over my skin. I'd been so preoccupied watching him that I'd completely forgotten to roll down my window.

I punched the button and offered a smile as I peered up at him. "Hi."

His expression remained blank as he stared at me. "License and registration, please."

I blinked. "What?"

His eyes narrowed, sweeping over my face, seemingly searching for something. What, I wasn't entirely sure, but I had a feeling it wasn't good.

"I need your driver's license and registration."

My spine stiffened at his brusque tone. No one had ever pulled me over before—probably because of my father—but I wasn't one to look a gift horse in the mouth. "Oh, I just—"

"Ma'am, I'll need you to step out of the car."

I jerked at his words, shock spreading through me. "What?"

His silvery gaze was unyielding as he stared at me. "Step out of the car, please."

My motions were jerky as I turned off the ignition, then opened the door, my fingers fumbling with the handle before finally managing to shove it open. The officer stepped back, watching me warily as I climbed from the car. I stood there awkwardly, every nerve ending on edge, as he studied me.

Finally, he spoke. "Have you been drinking?"

My mouth dropped open. "It's eleven o'clock."

He didn't even blink as he gestured toward his cruiser. "Ever used a breathalyzer before?"

"Wait!" I held my hands up in front of me, shock sending my thoughts scattering around my brain. "I'm not drunk."

His expression clearly told me he didn't believe me. "Ma'am, I—"

"I swear." I started to take a step forward, but his defensive posture stopped me in my tracks, and I dropped my hands to my sides. "I've never been pulled over before."

The officer snorted, and I thought I heard him murmur something to the effect of "Imagine that," before shaking his head. "Do you know why I pulled you over?"

I was almost certain I was speeding, but I figured I should probably keep that to myself. He already seemed to not like me. I seriously doubted that admitting my guilt would help my case.

I shook my head, and he pulled in a deep, aggrieved breath. "You were doing 72 in a 55."

Okay, so maybe I'd been going faster than I thought. I opened my mouth to speak, but he continued. "Standard protocol when you get pulled over is to provide proof of registration and your driver's license. Do you have either?"

I bristled at his tone. "Of course I do."

He gestured toward my car, and I took that to mean I should retrieve the documents. I bit back the urge to sigh and hurry things along as I grabbed my purse from where it rested on the passenger seat. I passed over the required documents and waited impatiently as he scanned them.

"Any reason you were going so fast?"

"I was on the phone, and—"

His hard look stopped the flow of words. *Shit.*

"You shouldn't be talking on the phone while driving."

I bit my tongue before spilling the first thing that sprang to my lips. Instead, I swallowed down the retort and smoothed my face into a complacent expression. "I wasn't actually using my phone." I pointed to the screen in the dash. "I was using the Bluetooth function."

His impassive gaze never changed. "Didn't seem to stop you from speeding."

My entire body went rigid at his words. He was by the far the most hardheaded person I'd ever had to deal with, and some of my clients gave Satan a run for their money. I opened my mouth to speak but was cut off by the ringing of my phone. Speak of the devil. Literally.

The officer's dark brow winged upward and his head tipped mockingly to one side. "Need to get that?"

Never tearing my gaze from his, I shook my head as I dropped back into the driver seat and grabbed my phone from where it rested in the cupholder, then tapped the button to silence it. For several seconds neither of us moved. Finally, he nodded. "Now, if—"

My phone chirped again, and I closed my eyes briefly, wishing I could crawl into a hole somewhere. *Damn it, Ashton.*

When I opened my eyes again, the officer's stare had hardened further, and he crossed his arms over his chest as he stared down at me. "Why don't you go ahead and get that?"

His intense scrutiny made me want to squirm like a little kid, and I hated it. "It's fine."

"No, really." He smirked, but it held no humor. "I wouldn't want to hold up such an important conversation."

A combination of anger and humiliation rolled through me, and I reluctantly swiped the screen to answer the call. Infusing as much politeness into my voice as possible, I greeted the man on the other end. "Ashton. I'm so sorry, I—"

"Where are you?"

I gritted my teeth at his hard tone, and my gaze flicked to the officer in front of me as I responded. "I apologize for the delay. I've been... momentarily detained."

"I don't have all day," he snapped on the other end. "If you can't handle this—"

"It's no problem at all," I assured him, keeping my tone as even as possible. "I'll be there just as soon as possible."

Silence filtered through the line, and I glanced at the screen. The asshole had hung up on me. Anger roiled like acid in my stomach, and I tossed my phone toward my purse before directing my gaze to the officer in front of me once more. "I'm supposed to be showing a client a house right now, and I'm running late."

Something flashed across his expression but disappeared just as quickly. "Can't have that, now can we?" Before I could respond, he continued. "Stay here for a moment. I'll be right back."

I slumped in my seat as he retreated to the cruiser to do whatever he needed to do. A few moments later, he returned and passed me my license and registration. Relief rolled through me. Finally. Now I could get the hell out of here and show that asshole Ashton the house.

"Thank you," I said to the officer. "I—"

My words stalled as he ripped a piece of paper from a pad and stuck it through the window. I stared stupidly at it for a moment before I managed to close my fingers around it. The words swam before my eyes, and I lifted my gaze to his. "What's this?"

"A ticket. For speeding," he clarified, his words slow and drawn out. "Have a nice day, ma'am."

It felt like every cell of my body had frozen in place as I watched him retreat to his vehicle. He'd given me a ticket. I'd never even been pulled over before, and he'd given me a ticket. Granted, I knew I'd been speeding, but wasn't there such a thing as a warning? My driving record was impeccable. One mistake shouldn't cost me...

My eyes drifted downward and widened. "$135?"

Shock rippled through me, my voice several octaves higher than normal as I practically shrieked the number. Tossing a look in the rearview mirror, I caught a glimpse of the man climbing into his cruiser. My eyes narrowed as he dropped his sunglasses into place and slid effortlessly into the seat. Damn him.

I knew exactly what this was. He was punishing me for who I was—the daughter of one of the wealthiest men in Cedar Springs. Though his expression had given no indication that he recognized me, he certainly could have found out when he ran my name.

I fumed silently for a moment before tucking the ticket into my handbag and starting the car. I didn't have time for this right now. I had Ashton waiting on me, and if he got impatient, he was bound to find another realtor. It was bad form, but a man like Ashton didn't care about that. Ashton cared about only one thing—and that was himself.

Shifting into gear, I tossed a quick look at the road to make sure no traffic was coming before steering onto the highway once more. The cruiser still sat there, the flashing lights mocking me as I pulled away.

I made sure to keep to the speed limit, my blood pulsing impatiently through my veins with every second that passed. By the time I finally pulled into Ridgewood Estates, I was vibrating with nervous energy. I pulled into the long, curving driveway of the house and parked next to Ashton's dark Mercedes. Ahead of him sat two unfamiliar sedans, and my brows drew together.

Who the hell...?

The dread in my gut congealed as the front door of the huge home swung open and Calvin Christensen stepped out. My mouth dropped open a fraction, and I clawed at the door handle in my attempt to scramble from the vehicle.

Calvin's gaze swung toward me, and even from here I could see the haughty arrogance carved into his features. I gritted my molars together as I approached, schooling my face into the most pleasant expression I could muster. Which, at the moment, probably resembled a rabid raccoon. Calvin and I had never gotten along, and he'd been needling me more and more recently.

I forced a smile, more a baring of my teeth than anything else. "I didn't know you had a showing here this morning, too."

My words were barbed, but his condescending smile only grew. "It was a last-minute thing."

My gaze narrowed. I was supposed to be made aware of any showings so clients didn't overlap. Like now. Of course, I knew that was precisely why he'd shown up now. He'd probably seen that I was showing the house and scheduled a last-minute viewing. The man was absolutely infuriating.

A well-dressed couple exited the home, and I stepped aside with a polite smile. "Excuse me."

The gentleman shook Calvin's outstretched hand. "Thank you for showing us on such short notice."

I tried to repress my eye roll and failed.

"It was no trouble at all, I assure you." Calvin nodded toward the woman. "Margaret, it was lovely to see you."

She smiled. "We'll let you know what we decide."

"Take your time," Calvin soothed, and I wondered if anyone else could hear the insincerity in his tone.

The couple disappeared down the steps toward their BMW, and I shot a dirty look Calvin's way. Before I could say anything, though, Ashton appeared in the doorway, his disapproving gaze fixed on me. He threw a pointed look at this watch, his mouth turned down at the corners. "Sienna."

"Mr. Reeves. I apologize, I—"

"Mr. Christensen was kind enough to allow me to look around while I was waiting." Again, that pointed gaze landed on me, and my shoulders tightened.

It took every ounce of effort I possessed to turn toward Calvin. "Thank you for assisting my client."

He grinned widely. "It was my pleasure. After all, I was already here."

God, I hated this man with a passion. I turned back to Ashton, who shook Calvin's hand. "Appreciate it."

He started down the steps, and I tripped after him in my four-inch heels. "Mr. Reeves, if you'd like to take a bit longer to look over the home, I'd be more than happy to—"

"That won't be necessary." The Mercedes chirped as he tapped the button to unlock the doors. "I'll be in touch."

I watched helplessly as he climbed inside and cranked the engine, then pulled out of the drive. Calvin sauntered down the stairs, and I threw an angry look his way. "You've pulled some underhanded stunts before, but this..." I pointed to the house. "This is ridiculous."

"Perhaps you should have been here on time." He lifted one shoulder. "I can't help it that you weren't here to help your client."

With that, he unlocked his car door and shot me a condescending grin. "See you around, Sienna."

A litany of curse words rolled around my head as I watched him pull away. Damn the man. Damn this awful morning. This was already the day from hell—and I hadn't even gotten to the worst part yet.

TWO

VAUGHN

Spoiled brat. I watched the taillights of the Audi as she shifted into gear then pulled away. Despite the fact that she didn't seem to recognize me, I knew exactly who Sienna was.

The pretty blonde was basically Cedar Springs royalty. Some long-dead relative of hers had been one of the first men to settle in the small town and had established the first bank. The Holts were prosperous back then and had grown even wealthier over the years.

Spencer Holt, Sienna's father and oil baron, sat on the city council. There was no doubt in my mind that he'd be in the station next week waving this in my face, but I didn't give a fuck. She'd broken the law; I gave her a ticket. Maybe if he'd raised his daughter to be more than a self-absorbed brat this could have been avoided.

It was disappointing to see her real personality emerge. I typically had pretty good instincts, but Sienna had thrown me for a loop. Though her father was brash and overbearing, I'd always thought Sienna to be more sweet-tempered.

Served me right for making assumptions. It was a shame, too, because she was the kind of beautiful that inspired men to do stupid things—like throw themselves at her feet. Or let her out of a speeding ticket.

In a town of less than four thousand people it was inevitable that we'd eventually cross paths. One night, several weeks ago, I found myself in Mason's Tavern, throwing back a few beers and discussing a case with the guys. The door opened and in stepped the gorgeous blonde. It was like lightning had struck. I still remembered the way my heart had stopped, my lungs seizing in my chest at the sight of her.

Sienna glanced around, looking more than a little insecure, before finding her friend and settling at the bar for a drink. I'd considered going up to her but decided against it. She was the kind of woman every man noticed but few had the balls to approach—myself included. I was ashamed to admit that I'd looked for her at Mason's every time since then. But she hadn't been back.

Not that it mattered. Women like Sienna didn't belong with guys like me. Now I was grateful I hadn't made a move. I had enough going on in my life; I didn't need her kind of drama on top of it.

My radio crackled to life, jerking my attention from the small sedan fading into the distance. "Code twelve in progress," came the dispatcher's voice.

I listened as she rattled off the address, then touched the button to respond. "Dispatch, this is 3006. I'm en route."

Mac chimed in a moment later, letting me know he'd be right behind me. Quickly checking the rearview mirror, I pulled a K-turn, then headed toward the residential area where the 911 call had come in.

A bystander lifted a hand in greeting when he saw me, and I pulled to a stop in front of him. I parked and climbed out of the cruiser, then approached the older man. "Are you the one who called in the breaking and entering?"

"Yes, sir." He pointed to a house across the street and two doors down. "I came out to get the mail and noticed the door was standing wide open."

I nodded a little. "Have you seen the owner?"

He shook his head. "I normally see her leave about the time I'm drinking my coffee. But I wasn't feeling well this morning and I overslept. Guessing somebody broke in after she left."

"Thank you..." I trailed off, and he extended a hand.

"Lionel Bancroft."

I gave his hand a quick shake. "I'll check it out. Will you be home if I have any other questions?"

"Anything you need, I'm right here." He hitched a thumb over his shoulder toward a well-kept brick ranch.

"Thanks." I dipped my chin in acknowledgment just as Mac's cruiser pulled in behind mine.

I met his gaze as he climbed out. "Neighbor says he noticed the door was wide open. Thinks someone broke in after the woman left for work."

Mac fell into step beside me as I cut across the street. The front door still stood wide open, but I didn't hear anything from inside. Keeping my back pressed close to the side of the house, I risked a quick peek around the doorjamb. The house opened into a large living area, but there was no movement that I could see.

I knocked loudly. "Police."

When no one responded, I knocked again. Whoever had broken in was either hunkered down somewhere deep inside the house or had already fled. Tossing a look at Mac, we drew our pistols, keeping them at the ready. I went first, scanning the corners of the room as I stepped cautiously inside.

The place had definitely been tossed. There were papers everywhere, and stuffing from pillows and couch cushions littered the floor. The curio cabinet had been emptied, the dishes beneath it a jagged, broken mess.

Mac and I quickly cleared the bottom floor, and I began to climb the stairs. Halfway up, the scent of death assaulted me.

"Shit."

Mac and I shared a quick look, and he grimaced. We checked the rooms as we passed, the smell growing stronger as we made our way down the hall. I found the body in the master bedroom. The woman lay face down on the floor, still clad in her pajamas. I reached for my radio just as a photograph across the room drew my attention. I knew this woman—had just handled a break-in at her bookstore a few weeks ago.

"Is that...?"

I glanced over to where he stood just outside the doorway and nodded. "Beverly Reynolds."

"Damn."

I dug a pair of nitrile gloves from my back pocket, then checked the woman's pulse. Nothing. Damn it.

My lips pressed into a firm line as I drew my phone from my back pocket and hit speed dial. Our detective answered a second later. "What's up?"

"We've got something you need to see." I rattled off the address.

"The breaking and entering?"

"Burglary," I corrected. "And a homicide."

On the other end, Finn swore. "I'll be there in ten."

Eight minutes passed before I watched his unmarked car turn onto the street, then park behind my cruiser. His gaze swept the area, and he gave an almost imperceptible nod when he noticed me. His long stride ate up the pavement as he crossed to me. "Have you called it in yet?"

"No." I shook my head. "I wanted you to know first."

His brows dipped in question, and I jerked my head toward the house. "I'll show you."

He snorted when he saw the house in shambles. "Assholes."

I nodded in commiseration but didn't say a word as I led the way up the stairs. I stopped just inside the bedroom, and it only took a few seconds for him to make the connection.

"Fuck." He wiped a hand over his face. "I assume you checked for a pulse?"

I nodded grimly, my expression conveying my answer. He swore beneath his breath again, then shook his head. "Call it in. We need to get the guys in here to process the scene."

"You got it." I called dispatch and requested extra officers at the scene while Finn went outside to retrieve his bag.

"Any idea where they entered?" he asked as he pulled on a pair of gloves. "This door looks fine."

"I'm guessing the back door." I spoke as I led him down the hallway to the large, sunny kitchen and the door that overlooked the fenced-in backyard. "It was closed when we got here, but..."

Mac pointed to a spot on the doorjamb. "Definitely forced entry."

Finn examined the cracked wood and nodded. "No security system?"

I shook my head. People who lived in a small town took their safety for granted and often neglected to even lock their doors.

From the direction of the front door came the sound of

another officer arriving. Our lieutenant glanced around the kitchen, taking in the destruction. "What happened?"

"Neighbor says the front door was wide open when he went out to get the mail," I relayed to Aiden. "He thought the victim had already left for work, and he never saw anyone in or around the house."

Aiden nodded slowly. "B&E gone wrong?"

"Maybe." Beverly was still dressed in her pajamas, so it was possible the intruders had expected her to be gone when they'd broken in.

"But you don't think so."

I glanced at Finn. "After the break-in at the bookstore... Timing is a little too coincidental."

"Agreed." He gave a terse nod, then turned to Mac. "See if you can lift any prints. I need to speak with Adrian."

Beverly's son, Adrian, was currently being held at the county jail pending charges for attempted manslaughter. He'd broken into the bookstore while Finn's girlfriend, Harper, was working and held her at knifepoint, demanding she show him where the safe was.

Mac sent a sympathetic look his way. "We'll take care of it."

He began to mark off the crime scene while Aiden gathered his things to begin the painstaking process of lifting prints.

"Mind if I come with you?" I asked Finn. There were a lot of details to his story that didn't add up, and I was very interested to see what Adrian had to say.

THREE

SIENNA

"Please don't make me do this."

Eden's tinkling laugh filtered through the headpiece of the phone. "It won't be that bad," she replied, her voice far more confident than I was feeling.

With a groan, I flopped backward to sprawl dramatically across the bed. "What if he's a giant douche?"

"Harper says he's a really good guy. I promise," she tacked on. "I wouldn't set you up with just anyone."

"Hmmm..." I stared up at the ceiling fan, studying the light layer of dust that had accumulated near the edges. My house could really use a good cleaning—the kind that took all night long.

I bit my lip. Tempting as it was, I couldn't do that to Eden. She and Harper had been nice enough to set me up on this date, and I was going to make the most of it. Even if I was dreading it.

"I hope he's not shorter than me." I didn't really care about that—not really. As soon as the words left my mouth,

I knew exactly what I was doing. I was finding things wrong with this guy before I'd even given him a chance. Damn it.

A sigh escaped before I could stop it, and several beats passed before Eden spoke again. "Do you really not want to go? I can tell her to cancel it," she said softly.

Truth be told, I had no idea what I wanted. My heart still felt tender and bruised from the last man who had broken it. I wanted to move on—*needed* to move on—but I wasn't sure how. Part of me was terrified to put myself back out there again, especially with someone I'd never met.

Five months ago, my boyfriend had made reservations for us at a restaurant. And not just any restaurant—the one where we'd had our first date. Our four-year anniversary was just a few weeks away, and I couldn't help the giddy excitement that had bubbled up as we sat down at the secluded table in the dimly-lit back corner.

Everything was stunningly perfect for the wedding proposal I was expecting—amazing food, soft candlelight, sweet red wine. But despite my eager anticipation, Derrick had been awkward and uneasy throughout the meal. Naïvely I chalked it up to nerves, not once considering that I'd misconstrued the entire situation. He dropped the bomb over coffee and tiramisu.

He wasn't proposing. In fact, he'd found someone else. A month prior he'd been scrolling Instagram and commented on a model's photo. One comment led to two, and eventually they'd begun to chat regularly. At some point, he'd fallen in love.

I sat there in stunned horror as he relayed every detail of their whirlwind love affair. He gushed over how sweet and wonderful she was, as if that were supposed to be some sort of consolation.

The model—Veronica—happened to be a brand ambassador for a popular clothing line, and using her connections, Derrick had contacted the company and begun to model as well. He'd turned in his two-weeks' notice at work with the plan to move to Australia so he and Veronica could finally be together.

His words twisted the knife of betrayal a little deeper. The man who refused to move in with me had decided to move halfway around the world to be with a woman he'd just met.

He stared at me over the coffee, begging me to understand. But I couldn't. When I asked why he'd brought me here, to this exact restaurant, he'd merely shrugged and said he knew I wouldn't make a scene in public.

Heart shattered, I left the restaurant a broken, single woman. A tiny sliver of me hoped that he would come around, that he would realize what he'd done and come back to me. But that didn't happen, either. Two weeks later, he boarded the plane for Australia and was gone. He hadn't even said goodbye.

Then again, what was left to say?

"Am I doing the right thing?" The question came out tinged with more vulnerability than I would've liked, but I couldn't call the words back.

On the other end, Eden was silent, and I could picture her sitting there in her office, gathering her thoughts before speaking. "I'm probably not the best person to give advice," she began, "but I do understand where you're coming from."

Eden had been through a horrific divorce herself, but for as long as I'd known her, she'd never dated anyone serious.

"I know how badly Derrick hurt you," she continued, "and when something like that happens, it affects the way you view your self-worth. No one will ever know why he did what he did, but you need to understand that you had nothing to do with his choice to leave. I know you don't believe that now, but maybe going out with someone new will bring you one step closer to getting the closure you need."

Tears burned across the bridge of my nose, and I blinked them back. Eden was truly one of the sweetest people I'd ever met, and I desperately hoped that she would find someone just as wonderful of her own one day.

"Thank you," I murmured. "I didn't mean for this to be a giant pity party."

"I know," she replied easily. "And it's not pity. You had your heart broken by someone you trusted. It's only natural that you grieve the loss."

She was right. I'd spent the past several months moping around, feeling sorry for myself. Even if nothing came of tonight's date, at least I was taking a step forward.

"You're right." I rolled to a sitting position, then popped to my feet. From here on out, I was manifesting only good things. "I'm actually excited to be going out again. And I know it's going to be great. I'll keep you posted."

"Good luck! And I want to hear all about it!" came Eden's response. "I have a good feeling about this."

God, I hoped so. I could use some good luck for once. "I'll call you tomorrow."

With that, I hung up and tossed my phone on the bed before striding toward the closet. I sifted through the racks before pulling out my favorite suit. It was a little formal for a date, but the cut of the fabric never failed to make me feel better.

I quickly stripped off the stark black power suit I'd worn this morning and pulled the soft taupe fabric from the hanger. The fabric glided over my bare legs as I stepped into the skirt, then zipped it into place. I selected a teal top that brought out the blue in my eyes, and tugged it on, tucking it into place.

In the bathroom, I touched up my makeup, adding a tiny bit of liner to give my eyes a more sultry look. Once I was done, I spritzed on some perfume and slipped into my jacket. I stepped into my favorite pair of nude heels, turned toward the mirror, and gave myself a critical once-over.

The suit hugged my body, making my minimal curves look more pronounced. I'd been blessed with my mother's fair genes, so I stood a couple of inches taller than the average woman. I'd hated my willowy figure in high school, but I'd come to appreciate my high metabolism as I passed twenty-five and crept closer to thirty.

I knew I should probably ditch the heels just in case my date was short, but I couldn't bring myself to do it. These were my absolute favorite; they matched the suit perfectly and made my legs look even longer. While that wasn't necessarily a good thing, it would give me a first impression of my date. If he complained about me being taller than him, I knew I could cross him off my list.

Pleased with my outfit, I headed downstairs and swiped my car keys and purse off the small console table in the hallway. I snuck one last look in the mirror hanging on the wall, then headed toward the back door. I swung it open, already locking it with one hand, when I was brought up short by the sight of the fluffy gray creature near my feet.

"What the..."

The cat peered up at me and meowed plaintively.

"Oh, no." I shook my head. "Go away. Shoo."

I waved my hands at the cat, but it only meowed again, then brushed against my legs.

I shifted, trying to move away from it. "Sorry, kitty. You can't stay here. And I have to go, so..."

I trailed off, hoping the cat would magically take the hint and go seek refuge at the neighbors' house. It paused near my ankles and peered inside the house, then lifted its gaze to mine once more.

Meow. The cat cocked its head, those yellow eyes locked on mine, and I felt my resolve waver.

Damn it. "Fine. I'll feed you." I pointed at the cat. "But you are *not* coming inside."

Closing the door, I stomped off toward the kitchen and dug a can of tuna out from the pantry. I still wasn't even entirely sure why I was taking care of a cat that didn't belong to me as I peeled open the can and scraped the fish into a shallow bowl. I was almost to the door when something occurred to me. The cat would probably need water, too.

With a shake of my head, I retraced my steps and filled a small bowl with tap water. The cat was sitting in the same spot, seemingly waiting on me as I stepped outside.

"Don't get used to this," I warned the animal as I set the bowls down on the corner of the deck. "This is a one-time deal. You eat, then you leave. Got it?"

Meow. The cat blinked up at me, and I rolled my eyes. Right. It more than likely didn't understand a word I was saying. "All right, then."

I pushed to my feet and straightened my skirt. "Hope you find a nice, warm home. Somewhere else."

The cat waited until I'd stepped away, then cautiously approached the bowl. It sniffed the tuna, flicked a quick look my way, then began to eat with voracious intent. I couldn't help but smile. The animal seemed fairly tame, though it didn't wear a collar.

Pushing the thought away, I retrieved my things from the house, then made my way to the car. I tossed one last look at the cat as I backed out of the drive. It would be long gone by the time I got back—and I'd be alone once more.

FOUR

VAUGHN

The walls of the conference room were gray, dingy from years of use, and they lent a serious, bleak vibe to our surroundings.

The door swung open, pulling my attention to Adrian as he was escorted into the room by another officer. His expression was guarded as he studied us. Finn waited until the officer was gone before speaking. "There's something we need to discuss with you."

"I told you I have nothing else to say," Adrian said by way of greeting.

"Why don't you have a seat?" I suggested.

"I don't—"

"It's about your mother," Finn replied.

Adrian visibly jolted. "What about her?"

"Sit, please."

Warily, he dropped into the chair across from us, his gaze bouncing between Finn and myself. "What's going on?"

Finn rested his forearms on the table and gazed steadily at Adrian. "I'm sorry to be the one to tell you this, but someone broke into your mother's house late last night. Apparently she surprised the intruder, and she was knocked unconscious."

The color drained from Adrian's face, his mouth going slack. "Is she... Is she all right?"

Finn slowly shook his head. "I'm sorry. She didn't make it."

Adrian dropped his head into his hands. "Fuck!"

I slid a quick look at Finn. It was the only time I'd seen any real emotion from the man; maybe he really did care for his mother. We allowed him a few moments to grieve, and Adrian finally sat up, eyes red as he stared at the wall behind us.

"We should discuss arrangements," Finn said gently.

Adrian was quiet so long I wondered if he was still in shock. When he broke the silence, his words surprised me. "I didn't think they'd go after her."

His expression didn't change despite the cryptic words, but they piqued my interest. "What do you mean? Who went after her?"

Adrian closed his eyes and shook his head. "I should've known better. I should've known they wouldn't let it go."

I felt Finn's gaze on me as I stared at Adrian. "Mr. Hughes, what did you mean when you said someone went after your mother?"

He swallowed hard, the remnants of tears glittering in his eyes. "I... I don't know who." He dragged in a ragged breath. "He... he called me a few weeks ago, asking for help."

"Who called you?" I pressed.

Adrian swiped at his face. "My father. He—he sounded scared."

"Mhmm..." Finn hummed a noncommittal sound. "And where is your father now?"

"I don't know." Adrian shook his head. "He wouldn't say. He hung up before I could find out."

I turned his words over in my mind. "You said he asked for help. What did he say?"

"He asked me to get something for him—a book. My father used to keep a book on the corner of his desk—a beat up old copy of *The Count of Monte Cristo*."

"A book?" Suspicion tinged Finn's voice. "What's so special about a book?"

Adrian rubbed his temples. "It doesn't look like much. That was the point. But inside, it was hollow—just a small space. He mentioned a flash drive, which I suspect was inside the book."

I tamped down the urge to shake my head. Smart people did some of the stupidest shit. If the man was on the run—which it sounded like he was—whatever was inside the book must be damn important. To keep it out in the open where anyone could find it was either brazenly stupid or incredibly ingenious.

I glanced at Adrian. "Where's the book now?"

"I don't know." Adrian's face fell. "Dad thought my mom may have ended up with it by mistake."

"Did your mother know about the false pages?"

Adrian shook his head. "If she did, she never mentioned it. I checked her house, but the book wasn't there. I assumed she'd put it in the safe at the store."

"Why didn't you ask her about it?"

"I did." His voice was tinged with exasperation. "She claimed she didn't know where it was. Maybe she was trying to cover for him."

"So instead you broke in and tried to kill an innocent woman."

Adrian blanched at Finn's hard tone. "I wasn't going to hurt her—I swear. I just... I needed to find the book. I wanted to scare her a little. Once she gave in, I was going to pay her off, make her go away."

Finn glared at the man, still furious that Adrian had put Harper's life in jeopardy. "Didn't work out for you, did it?"

Time for me to intervene. "Now that we know what to look for, maybe we'll find the book at the house." Adrian looked stricken at the reminder of his mother's death, and I gentled my tone. "I want to help you. But I can't do that if you're not telling us the truth. Is there anything else you know about what your father's involved in?"

"No." His eyes were glassy with tears as he shook his head. "I need you to find them. For her. She didn't deserve this."

"We'll do our best," I promised. "Do you have any idea where your father might have gone? Any favorite vacation spots? Friends or family he could stay with?"

Adrian contemplated that for a moment. "No. We vacationed all over the states, but he never seemed to have a preference for any one place in particular. And most of our family is gone. He might have a friend willing to let him stay, but he didn't mention anything."

"Okay. We'll see what we can do."

"What about Mom's services? Can I..." He trailed off, his face drawn. "I know it's a lot to ask."

I threw a quick look at Finn, whose eyes still burned with anger. "We'll speak with your lawyer," I finally said.

Adrian nodded dejectedly as he pushed back from the table, then knocked on the door to get the guard's attention. The door swung open, and he started to step forward before turning back to Finn. "I'm sorry. For what happened at the store that day. Will you tell Harper for me?"

After a long moment Finn finally nodded, and Adrian

disappeared, leaving the two of us alone. I turned to our detective. "What do you think about all that?"

"I don't know." He crossed his arms over his chest, looking conflicted. "Part of me thinks the asshole's full of shit. He's always been a smooth talker. But..." He shook his head. "Something about this whole thing just doesn't feel right."

On that point, I agreed wholeheartedly. Finn stood, and I followed him from the room, my mind whirling with possibilities. If what Adrian said was true, we were in for a shitstorm of trouble.

My ass had just hit the seat of the cruiser when Finn's question jerked me from my thoughts. "You ready?"

I blinked at him. "For what?"

He rolled his eyes as he cranked the engine. "Your date."

I dropped my head back on a groan. "Damn. That's tonight?"

"Sure is." He grinned.

"Sorry." I shook my head, not feeling the least bit apologetic. "With all the shit we've got going on, I'm—"

"Don't fucking start," Finn cut me off. "Drew and Mac have the scene handled, and I'll deal with Hughes."

"But—"

"Your ass is going on a date." He took a curve a little faster than he should have, and I gritted my molars together as I grabbed the handle over the door.

"I can't believe I let you assholes do this to me."

"You'll like her," Finn replied.

"Do you know her?"

"Not personally. Harper says she's nice, though."

"Nice?" I made a face, and he laughed.

"Harp says she's pretty too, so don't worry. That wasn't a euphemism."

I was only slightly mollified by his confirmation. I hated

blind dates. I hated dating in general, and I'd been burned more than once by women who thought they were better than me. It was so much easier to keep affairs short and sweet. Or dirty.

I preferred to keep things simple—stick to sex and no one got hurt. It was mutually gratifying for both parties, and no one had to worry about any of the messy emotional attachment.

I'd come to the conclusion that maybe I wasn't the forever type of guy women wanted. The few I'd dated had bolted as soon as they met my mother, which pissed me off more than anything. If they couldn't get along with her, they weren't worth keeping.

"How'd you find this girl again?"

"She's a friend of a friend," he explained.

Goddamn it. This was sounding worse by the minute.

"Just give her a chance," Finn said. "You never know, you might really hit it off. Harper's hoping you do so we can double date."

Fucking fantastic. "Can't wait."

FIVE

SIENNA

"You." The word escaped before I could stop it, sending my pulse into a wild tailspin. I blinked once more, but the man remained.

No. Freaking. Way.

His eyes widened as they met mine, and a startled laugh fell from his lips. "Well, well. If it isn't Danica Patrick."

Oblivious to the discord between us, the hostess who'd seated me made herself scarce, and I glared at the officer who'd pulled me over this morning. "What are you doing here?" I demanded.

"Same as you, I would assume. I'm guessing you're my date." He didn't look happy about that, and I bristled at his tone. How the hell could they have set me up with this guy?

He lifted a brow. "Are you going to sit, or do you have somewhere else to speed off to?"

I bit back a retort as I dropped into the chair across from him. A waitress appeared next to the table, a bright smile on her face. "Can I get you something to drink?"

"Do you have anything with arsenic?" I quipped.

Across the table *Officer Hard Ass* snorted, and the waitress's smile dimmed. "Um..."

"Never mind." I waved her off, immediately feeling guilty for exercising my sarcasm from my bad mood on her. I tossed a look at my date. "Are you drinking tonight?"

"I will be now," he muttered before taking a sip of his water and averting his gaze.

I glared his way before turning back to the waitress. "Just a glass of your house red for me, please."

She offered an uncertain smile before glancing his way. "Anything for you, sir?"

"I'll take a whiskey, neat."

With a tiny nod, the waitress gratefully disappeared toward the bar. An uncomfortable silence descended over the table. I took my time studying the menu even though I'd eaten here many times.

Finally, he cleared his throat. "Sienna, right?"

I blinked at him, trying to figure out how he knew my name.

"I saw it on your, uh..." He lifted a shoulder, and it clicked. Of course. He ran my name when he pulled me over.

I smiled tightly. "That's me."

He slid a look my way, and the intensity of his bright pewter eyes stole my breath for a second. Everything else aside, he really was incredibly handsome. Too bad he was such a jerk. I offered a tight smile. "I never did ask your name. I've just been referring to you as *Officer Hard Ass* all day."

A tic ran along his jaw and annoyance flashed in his eyes. "Vaughn," he bit out.

Vaughn. As a realtor, I knew a lot of people in Cedar Springs, but his name didn't sound familiar, and I knew I'd never seen him before. "How long have you worked for the police department?"

He stared at me for a long moment, as if debating whether to answer. "Next spring makes twelve years."

The information stunned me. How had we never run into each other before? Not only that, but my father sat on the city council, and he'd never mentioned Vaughn before. Maybe he was the type of person who kept to himself, though I seriously doubted it considering his attitude this morning. He struck me as the type of person who liked to control a situation. Every city had one of those cops—apparently Vaughn was Cedar Springs' overzealous enforcer.

The thought piqued my curiosity, but I wasn't quite done needling him yet. "And what do you like to do for fun, Vaughn—besides ticket innocent women?"

"Innocent, my ass." He scoffed. "You were seventeen miles per hour over the speed limit."

"On a straight stretch of road without a single car in sight," I snapped back. "It's not like I was putting anyone in danger."

"Always nice to see people take responsibility for their actions." He shook his head. "Not that I should be surprised, coming from you."

My hackles rose. "What does that mean?"

He cast a look of disdain my way. "You rich girls always get whatever you want."

"I certainly do when it's unreasonable. Did it make you feel more important?" I goaded him. "You hit your quota or whatever?"

He rolled his eyes heavenward. "Why do people always think that?"

"Um, because I know for a fact that that's one way the town generates money," I pointed out.

He looked annoyed. "While that may be true, it's not

like I spend every waking minute tracking people down and finding them at fault for something."

God, this man was infuriating. I grabbed up my purse. "You know, I think this was a mistake."

I started to stand, and he scrubbed a hand over his face before gesturing for me to stop. "Sit. Please," he added. "We're already here."

I sank into my seat and regarded him dubiously. "You don't have anything better to do than fight with me?"

"Are you asking if I have more important things to do? Because the answer is yes," he snapped. "I know you're way above the rest of us in that ivory tower of yours, but you may have heard about the recent string of rapes we've had recently."

His comment about living in an ivory tower stung. I'd worked damn hard to get out of my father's house and buy a place of my own, despite his insistence otherwise. And I wasn't ignorant. I'd heard about the several women who'd come forward after having been drugged and raped. But they'd caught the man, and he was now dead.

I opened my mouth to speak, but Vaughn lifted a challenging brow my way. "Not to mention the murders."

There was that. Several men had been killed recently, and I knew the police were struggling to find a connection between the victims. The most recent victim had been discovered just a few days ago. It hadn't occurred to me that Vaughn might be stressed from the situation.

Shame washed over me, and I felt like a little girl again as I peered across the table at him. I needed to apologize. I opened my mouth to do so, but he spoke again before I got the chance.

"But... if you're asking if I have better plans for dinner, then the answer is no. It was this or a frozen dinner." He offered a tight smile. "Let's just... get through this so we can tell Harper and Finn we tried, but it didn't work out."

I swallowed hard at the sting of rejection spiraling through my heart. Irrational as it was, his words hurt. Derrick had walked away, and Vaughn was already counting down the minutes until he could escape. What was it that drove every man away?

The only answer I could come up with was... Me.

SIX

VAUGHN

I should have kept my mouth shut. At my words, her gaze shuttered and her shoulders twitched, almost like her body was trying to close in on itself. I immediately regretted saying anything. It was evident she didn't like me, but it was just as apparent that I'd hurt her by pointing out the obvious.

While Sienna studiously avoided me, I took my time studying her. She was pretty—in a prissy, stuck up, rich girl kind of way. Especially when she was angry. A delicate pink flush had swept over her face, filling her cheeks and lighting her eyes.

There was a reason Finn and Harper had hooked us up. Why, I didn't know, and I had half a mind to throttle him when I saw him again. Her chest rose and fell on a deep breath, her elegant neck elongating and drawing my focus to her throat. Her collarbones peeked out from beneath the teal dress shirt, and I bit back a smile.

Who wore a suit on a date? I'd seen her only a few hours

ago, so I knew she'd changed into it this afternoon. It was fitting that she was dressed more for an interview than a date. She was far too buttoned up, and it made me want to rile her all the more. I wanted to pull that clip from her hair and shake the golden locks loose. The fire in her eyes struck a chord deep within me, and I had the sudden feeling that there might be more to her than met the eye.

Before I could say anything, the waitress delivered our drinks, and Sienna offered a tiny smile. I watched the transformation, the way her eyes glowed and the lines of her face softened. It made her look even prettier, the tilt of her stubborn little chin less severe in profile.

The waitress turned to Sienna. "Are you ready to order?"

She closed the menu and handed it to the younger woman. "I'll have the seafood Alfredo, please."

"Good choice." The waitress jotted down Sienna's order then looked to me. "And for you, sir?"

I tipped my head toward Sienna. "That sounds good. I'll have the same, please."

"I'll get that right in for you."

The young woman disappeared, and I gazed across the table at my date. The soft overhead lighting made her porcelain skin look even more delicate and doll-like as her watchful gaze scanned the room, taking in everything around her. Her fingers wrapped effortlessly around the stem of the wineglass, and I watched as she brought it to her lips. She sipped daintily at the red liquid, her throat moving under the motion, and my stomach twisted into a knot at the sight.

She lowered the glass and her tongue flicked out, licking up a tiny drop of red wine that clung to her pretty lips. Maybe I'd been too hard on her today. Yes, she'd technically broken the law, but I'd reacted based on my assumption of her. She'd put me on edge, and I'd been far harsher than necessary.

I was just about to apologize for my behavior when her cerulean gaze snapped to mine, and her brows pulled into a glare. "What?"

Or not. I refrained from rolling my eyes at her defensive tone and instead shook my head. "Not a damn thing."

I picked up my drink and drained half of it, acutely aware of her gaze on me the entire time. Her eyes followed my movements as I set the glass on the table between us, then she lifted her eyes to mine. "Do you drink often?"

"Tonight I do," I snapped back, unable to help myself.

She made a little face, then turned away again. A growl threatened to escape. Damn, this woman was a pain in the ass. But I'd promised to stay, and I never went back on my word. No matter how badly I wanted to leave the brat here all by herself.

The silence stretched between us, painfully tense, and I'd never been so happy to see another human in my life as the waitress delivered the food to the table. Sienna smiled her thanks, then tentatively picked at her pasta. I had no such reservations. I wanted to eat and get the hell out of this place.

By the time I finished my pasta, Sienna had worked her way through nearly one third of hers. I pushed my plate aside, and she did the same. "Good?" I asked.

She nodded. "It's one of my favorites. Mario's Alfredo sauce is the best."

"Do you come here often?"

"Once in a while," she acknowledged with a little shrug.

"We could have gone somewhere else," I offered, though I was beginning to regret this whole blind date.

"It's fine. I like it." She offered a polite smile, and I nodded. Her phone buzzed in her purse, and she shot me a quick look. I couldn't help but smile, and I was certain she was remembering this morning.

"Popular, aren't you?"

She scowled as she dug the phone from the bag. Her eyes flew across the screen, and a relieved breath rushed from her lungs. "Thank God."

"Good news?"

She nodded. "My client finally decided to put in an offer on a house."

"That's... good," I said lamely, not really giving a shit one way or the other.

"It is," she agreed. "Lucky seventeen. I'd better get the paperwork started before he changes his mind."

And that was my cue to get the hell out. I tipped my head. "I'm ready if you are."

Her brows lifted slightly before she nodded. "Okay."

I waved at the waitress. Sienna began to dig in her bag for her wallet, but I waved her off. "You're not paying," I said. "If you come out with me, I'll take care of it."

Her lips twisted. "How... gentlemanly."

"You're welcome," I said before she could start up again. I passed the waitress money for the food and tip, then stood. Sienna started toward the door, and I fell into step behind her. My gaze automatically swept the room, and my eyes caught on a man at the corner of the bar. I followed his intense stare—right to the woman in front of me.

There was something about that look I didn't like, and I lengthened my stride to catch up to her. I settled a hand on her lower back as I pushed the door open, and her eyes widened a fraction as she stepped past me and onto the wide sidewalk. She paused. "Thanks for dinner."

"You're welcome."

"Well... Enjoy your evening."

With that, she turned on her heel and started to walk

away. I bit the inside of my cheek, agitation warring with the need to see her safe. Goddamn it. I hated having to do the right thing sometimes. I reluctantly fell into step beside her, and she stopped.

Her gaze narrowed as she studied me. "What are you doing?"

"Walking you to your car."

She blinked like it was the first time she'd ever heard of it. I didn't give her time to think it over. I wanted to get her settled and put this whole debacle behind me. "Where are you parked?"

She pointed wordlessly toward the lot on the corner, and I loped along beside her. She finally got inside the small Audi and offered a little wave. "See you later."

I lifted a hand, and a strange combination of relief and regret welled up inside me as I watched her drive away. "See you… never."

SEVEN

SIENNA

Never again. I was officially done with blind dates. The next man I dated would be fully vetted with a background check and everything.

A shudder rippled down my spine at the memory of my dinner with Vaughn two nights prior. In an effort to forget about the dumpster fire that had been my blind date, I'd thrown myself into work, preparing paperwork for clients and showing a half dozen houses. I'd gotten Ashton's offer submitted and, after a counteroffer, we'd decided to split the difference.

Ashton was a little disgruntled, most likely because he wasn't able to bully the buyer into accepting his lowball offer. The second the home had moved into contingent status I'd breathed a sigh of relief. At least now I wouldn't have to deal with Ashton again until he was ready to sign the paperwork. I mentally crossed my fingers, hoping everything went well with the inspection.

Exhaustion pulled at me as I turned into my driveway

and slowed to a stop. A sense of pride welled up inside me, and I couldn't help the bittersweet smile that curved my lips. It was supposed to be a home—a place for a family to grow. Instead, it was just me and a bunch of empty rooms.

Still, I refused to regret it. Buying this house was the first thing I'd done after Derrick left. My father disapproved of me moving in with anyone I wasn't engaged or married to—rightly so, I could now acknowledge—so I'd continued to live at home with my father and sister while I planned for the future.

After nearly four years, I had stupidly assumed my future would include Derrick—getting married, settling down and starting a family. But each time I'd brought up taking the next step, Derrick would balk. I wasn't sure what hurt worse—the thought that he couldn't see himself settling down with me, or that he'd left me for some woman he barely knew.

It didn't matter now. My father was upset when I moved out, but he understood that I needed my own space, especially now. At twenty-six I most certainly wasn't some naïve schoolgirl any longer, and I had exactly zero prospects in my dating queue. As evidenced by the disaster with *Officer Hard Ass* the other night.

Movement from the deck caught my eyes as I put the car in park, and my smile grew. The cat never left. For the past two days it had been milling around the house, and it came running each time it saw me. I thought by now the cat would have found its way home to its owners, but it was lingering by the door each morning when I left for work and was waiting for me each night when I got home.

It appeared relatively tame despite the fact that it didn't have a collar, and I worried that someone might be missing him. Though I'd checked in town, no one seemed to be missing a cat matching his description. Maybe his owners had dropped him off, no longer willing or able to take care of him. The thought made me sad.

I'd been feeding it tuna, but I decided today that it needed real food so I'd stopped by the store on my way home.

The cat meowed from its perch on the railing, greeting me as I climbed from the car. "Still here, huh?"

The cat tipped its head at me in question, and I mentally smacked myself. I couldn't believe I was carrying on a conversation with a cat. I retrieved the litter box and bag of food from the back seat, along with the small bag of assorted toys and treats the owner of the pet shop had recommended for me.

The cat hopped down from the railing when I climbed the wide steps of the deck, but it stuck close by as if it knew all the purchases were for it. I had no idea whether it was a male or female; if it stuck around I would need to find out.

I unlocked the door, then held it open. "Coming?"

The cat hesitated for a moment before darting through the open doorway, and I chuckled. It obviously had no qualms about entering a strange place. While the cat sniffed around, I tripped toward the laundry room, lugging the heavy bags along. Inside, I set the litter box on the floor, then poured some litter into it. Next came the food and water bowls, which I filled up and set in the corner.

The cat came closer, investigating all of the new stuff before digging into the crunchy morsels of food. "That's better, isn't it?"

I tentatively ran a hand down the cat's back, and it arched into my touch. I wasn't entirely sure when I had made the decision to keep the cat, but here we were. I'd never owned an animal before; now I had a stray cat running rampant through my new house. How far I had fallen.

With a shake of my head, I pushed to my feet and retraced my steps through the house. I gathered my purse and cell phone from the car, then headed upstairs to change into a pair of comfy sweats. By the time I got back downstairs, the cat was apparently done eating and waiting for me in the kitchen.

"You had your food for the night," I quietly admonished it. "Now it's my turn."

I poured myself a bowl of cereal, then retreated to the living room to watch TV while I ate. It would have been a huge no-no in my father's house, and I briefly relished the ability to do anything I wanted in my own home. After my mother passed, he wanted to keep his daughters close. And his number one priority was to make sure that we were safe and had a set routine so my mother's absence wouldn't disrupt our lives.

The family dinners in the formal dining room had extended into our college years, and I couldn't help but be grateful that I no longer had to endure them. As much as I loved my family, I enjoyed quiet time of my own with no pressure after a long day of work. The TV played in the background as I ate, and I was almost finished when my phone rang.

I couldn't help the prickle of aggravation. So help me, if Ashton was calling again...

I retrieved my phone from the end table, and a different sensation twisted my stomach as I saw my sister's name on the screen. "Hey, Soph. What's up?"

"Hey!" came her jubilant response. "I'm not bothering you, am I?"

"Not at all." I set my nearly empty bowl on the table, then turned down the volume on the TV. "What's up?"

"I was wondering if I could get your help with something. I know it sounds so silly, considering I do this all the time, but I just can't decide on what colors to use for the wedding."

I sank back against the couch, a dull throb immediately taking up residence behind my eyes. My baby sister, Sophia, was currently trying to juggle her business as a wedding planner while planning a wedding of her own. Recently, she'd been asking for my help more and more with invitations and other wedding-related things. I knew she was trying to include me, but talk of wedding stuff was just depressing.

In a way, I envied her. I thought by now I would be planning a wedding of my own; instead, I was offering guidance to my baby sister, who wasn't even twenty-four. But she was head over heels in love with her fiancé, Ethan, and I couldn't find it in myself to tell her no.

"What do you need?"

"I was hoping you could meet me at the country club tomorrow morning so we could take a look at the ballroom and see which colors would work best."

I tipped my head back to stare at the ceiling. As if I didn't already have enough going on. "What time?"

I turned my head just in time to see the cat jump up on the end table and begin to lap at the bowl of milk. "No! Get down." I scooped the cat up and gently set him on the floor.

"Who are you talking to?" Sophia's voice was tinged with curiosity.

I let out a frustrated sigh as the cat jumped right back up. "The cat."

"You have a cat?" my sister practically shrieked.

"I know," I muttered, grimacing as I angled the speaker away from my ear. "I can't believe it either. But every single woman needs a cat, right?"

My snippy remark was met with silence, and guilt assailed me. Before Sophia had the chance to take pity on me, I quickly recovered, telling her all about how the cat had shown up a few days ago. "He acts like this is his home, so I figured it's better than him running around getting hurt."

"If you say so," came her dubious reply.

I quickly steered the conversation back to the topic at hand. "So, you said you wanted to meet at the country club. What time?"

"Is one o'clock okay with you?"

I quickly scrolled through my calendar to check my appointments for tomorrow. "I can make that work."

"Perfect!"

I could practically see her bouncing in her seat, and I smiled. "See you tomorrow."

I ended the call, my appetite gone, and carried my bowl to the sink. I took my time showering and getting ready for bed, and by the time I climbed under the covers, exhaustion pulled at me. I snuggled in, pulling the blankets up to my neck. I was almost asleep when I felt something land on the bed near my feet.

Levering myself up onto my elbow, I glared at the cat. "You can't sleep here."

Meow.

The cat turned around twice, then curled into a tight ball next to my feet.

Damn it. I stared at the cat for another moment. "Fine. But only for tonight."

Even as I said the words, I knew they were a lie.

EIGHT

VAUGHN

Official cause of death was blunt force trauma to the back of the head. The medical examiner handling Beverly's case suspected that she had been killed sometime between midnight and four in the morning, which certainly put a darker spin on things.

With conclusive evidence that she'd been killed sometime during the night, that almost completely eliminated the possibility of Beverly's presence catching the intruders by surprise. According to both Harper and Adrian, Bev had no plans to go anywhere. She was a creature of habit, traveling mostly between her bookstore and home. Anyone watching her carefully would have known she would be home that night.

She hadn't dated since her divorce, and aside from her ex-husband, we had no suspects on our list. Ever since Adrian had admitted that his father was embroiled in something, we'd been trying in vain to reach the man. He wasn't at home, and he had quit his job several weeks prior.

Robert Hughes was currently in the wind, unless his "employer" had somehow managed to track him down. If the man had killed Beverly, as Adrian was certain had happened, they would be looking for Robert next.

I'd been keeping an eye on death certificates, but so far Robert's name hadn't shown up. That was good news, at least. We just needed to figure out where he might go to lie low, then flush him out.

Over the past several days, I had questioned his previous coworkers, all of whom had nothing but good things to say about the man. According to them, he was diligent and hard-working. He had told his employer that he was leaving to start a firm of his own.

The information that we got back from the lab wasn't much help, either. They confirmed that the prints found at Beverly's house belonged to Beverly herself, as well as Adrian. There were no other fingerprints to speak of, nothing so far that seemed out of the ordinary. It was quite evident from the state of the house, though, that the intruders had, in fact, been looking for something. Possibly the flash drive that Adrian had mentioned.

So far, there were no leads, and the case was quickly running cold. As if that weren't bad enough, we'd made no progress on the recent string of murders, either. A third victim, Johnathon Forsythe, had been found dumped in the woods a couple of weeks ago, his body covered in dozens of cuts. In his hand we found the teeth of a second victim. For the past two weeks we'd been running down every lead to try to ID the second victim and find Forsythe's killer.

The killer was trying to make a statement, though what his intentions were, I couldn't begin to imagine. The man had continued to escalate over the last couple of months, but we had jack shit for evidence. I had a feeling that all of the recent deaths were tied together somehow, I just wasn't sure of the connection.

Andrew Thorne, Gray's middle brother, had arrested Seth Stratton last month after he'd drugged and raped several women, leaving one dead. When the man escaped from jail, he'd kidnapped Drew's girlfriend, Emery, and held her hostage.

According to Emery, a second man had arrived at the cabin and had shot Stratton before coming after her. Thank God, she had managed to escape before he'd reached the room where she was being held. After she managed to escape, she'd relayed the location to the police who'd immediately descended on the small cabin tucked into the woods.

By the time they got there, the place was clean as a whistle. Testing confirmed an immense amount of blood had been present in the kitchen where Emery reported Stratton had been shot. But there was nothing to officially confirm either man having ever been in the cabin—no prints, no fibers, no shell casing... Nothing.

Stratton's body had been found nearly a week later. He'd sustained a single gunshot wound to the head, exactly as Emery speculated. Unfortunately, whoever killed Stratton had been incredibly meticulous, and the portion of his brain where the bullet had entered had been removed to eliminate any evidence.

On all fronts, it seemed like whoever had killed Stratton hadn't approved of his actions. In a strange way, the man had done us a favor by taking justice into his own hands. While it would have been better to let the police handle it, I was glad no more women were at risk. Stratton was gone, and that was all that mattered.

We thought that was the end of it. We were wrong.

A few days after Stratton's body was discovered, our

department received an envelope with two photos inside: one of Stratton postmortem, the other of a man we'd identified as Diego Perez, who had a list of priors a mile long, including battery, assault, and distribution of an illegal substance. A robbery had put him in jail for the past couple of years, but there hadn't been much on him since his release two months ago.

Stratton had been murdered before we'd been able to determine exactly how he'd drugged his victims, but it was entirely possible he'd been working with Perez. Despite sustaining multiple stab wounds, no blood had been found at the scene. From what we could tell, the man had been killed elsewhere and dumped for us to find. The same was true of Forsythe, who was found just a few weeks later.

We needed to figure out how the victims were connected. It seemed that all four men had been involved in something, though I wasn't entirely sure what. Drugs, more than likely. Stratton had used a GHB-like substance to drug his victims prior to raping them. Perez and Forsythe both had criminal records, including trafficking. I suspected we'd find the same of our fourth victim.

Most concerning, though, was that Stratton had escaped from jail, seemingly without notice. Though all of the guards on duty had been questioned, it was as if he'd disappeared into thin air. We could only speculate that he'd bribed a guard, but so far there was no conclusive evidence.

The warden, Frank Darwin, had tightened security since then, but we needed to know how Stratton had managed to slip past everyone without being caught. Someone else was most certainly involved, and we needed to find out who.

While Stratton's death had been quick, the killer had taken his time with Perez and Forsythe. It took an inordinate amount of time and rage to stab someone twenty-three times. Not to mention pulling teeth. The thought made me sick. I hoped to hell the man was dead when it happened, but I seriously doubted it. It seemed like the killer wanted to wreak havoc, to punish the men, but why?

The pieces of the puzzle didn't fit. Most killers used the same method, but it was possible Stratton had been shot out of convenience. Perhaps he hadn't wanted to waste the time doing so, or maybe the killer was testing different methods. If that were the case, we'd need to be extra vigilant. We would need to check all recent violent deaths to see if there was any kind of crossover so we didn't miss anything.

Between the drugs, the string of rapes, and subsequent murders, Cedar Springs had its hands full.

I had no idea how it was all tied together, but I was damn well going to find out.

NINE

SIENNA

I was going to strangle him.

My phone buzzed again where it lay in the corner of my desk, and I gritted my teeth at the sight of Ashton's name lighting up the screen.

Again.

With a beleaguered sigh, I swiped up the device and smoothed my face into a smile. I'd heard once that just by smiling, you could transform the tone of your voice to sound more pleasant. I certainly hoped that was the case, because otherwise my disdain for the man would be obvious.

The cat lifted its head and meowed from its spot on the floor in a shaft of light warmed by the sun. It shifted, turning its back toward me as if offended that the phone call had ruined its nap.

"I don't like him either," I muttered before tapping the button to answer the call. "Hello, Ashton."

"Any news on the inspection yet?" I gritted my molars together and inhaled deeply.

"Not yet. It usually takes a few days for the inspector to turn the results over to the county."

"What the hell's taking so long?" he groused. "I thought paying cash expedited these things."

"It does," I soothed, "but these are steps that can't be avoided. If you take ownership then find something wrong, you'll have no legal recourse. It's best to be patient and try to be proactive."

On the other end Ashton let out a little growl. "Fine. Keep me updated."

I hesitated for a moment before glancing at my phone. The home screen was visible once more, indicating he'd hung up on me, and I rolled my eyes. "Jerk."

I threw a quick look at the clock. One hour until I had to leave to meet Sophia at the country club. I was still dreading it, but it was better to just get it over with. The sooner her wedding came, the sooner I could breathe easier. My single status hung like a black cloud over me, and I hated feeling jealous of my little sister.

Pushing thoughts of weddings and asshole ex-boyfriends to the back of my mind, I focused on work until the alarm on my phone announced that it was time to go. I looked at the cat, who hadn't moved from its warm spot in the sunlight, and a smile tugged at my lips.

"If you're going to stick around, you'll need a name."

The cat blinked at me and yawned sleepily.

"Are you a boy or a girl?" The cat hadn't gotten close enough to let me look, but I guessed from glimpses that it was a male. "Maybe we'll be safe with something neutral, like..." My gaze swept over the cat, taking in its gray fur and white-tipped paws. "Mittens?"

The cat stared at me. "You're right. Too overused. Socks?"

The cat yawned, and I felt a flush of warmth sweep over me. I couldn't believe I was talking to a cat. I shook off the thought and stared at the feline. "How about... Boots?"

The cat meowed, then stood and turned in a circle, like it was preening.

"Well, all right, then." I slapped my thighs and stood. "Boots it is. Behave."

I wagged a finger at the cat who had settled in the sunlight once again. "Don't tear anything up while I'm away."

It seemed to be one of the most docile animals I'd ever encountered. Though the cat wasn't the cuddly type, he was incredibly well-behaved, content just to lie in the sun or play with the few toys I'd picked up at the store. I closed the lid of my laptop, then quickly changed into a dress before grabbing my phone and heading downstairs for my keys and purse. Satisfied I had everything I needed, I locked up and headed to my car.

The engine had just turned over when my phone rang. I glanced at the unknown number on the screen, then tapped the speakerphone function as I shifted the car into gear. "This is Sienna, how can I help you?"

Waiting for the person on the other end to respond, I flicked a look in the rearview mirror before backing out of the driveway. Silence greeted me, and I tried again. "This is Sienna."

I rolled my eyes as I shifted into drive, then headed down the street. This wasn't the first time I'd gotten hang-ups. People sometimes saw my signs around town and called the number out of curiosity, just to see if someone would answer.

I'd also had more than one man see my photo on the

signs and try to contact me for a date. Derrick had joked about me being in high demand, but I knew it made him a little jealous when that happened. I always did my best never to lead anyone on, and I kept all of my business dealings incredibly professional. I tapped the screen to end the call, then glanced at the clock. I had just enough time to stop for a coffee at the Daily Grind before meeting my sister.

The drive was quiet, and I didn't see a single car as I made my way toward Cedar Springs. I was mentally checking things off my list of things to do this evening when my engine gave a cough. Automatically, my foot lifted off the accelerator and my ears perked up.

The sound was entirely foreign to me. The car was less than a year old, and I made sure to take care of routine maintenance as promptly as possible. The engine gave another rough cough, then sputtered, and I clenched my hands around the wheel before slowly steering it to the side of the road.

Safely out of the way, I parked then hit the button to turn on my hazard lights, my gaze fixed on the hood. There was no steam, nothing to give any sort of indication there was something wrong with the engine. My eyes dropped my gauges, and I sucked in a breath when I saw the needle dipped below the empty light on the gas gauge. "What the hell?"

I'd filled up just a few days ago, and though I'd shown a few homes since then, it wasn't nearly enough to burn off an entire tank of gas.

Crap. What was I going to do now?

TEN

VAUGHN

I wasn't sure what I had done in a past life to deserve this, but I must've pissed someone off.

I barely repressed a groan when the small Audi pulled to the side of the road caught my attention. If I hadn't recognized the license plate, I most certainly wouldn't have been able to deny the leggy blonde standing next to the left front fender.

I slowed to a stop, then parked just a few feet behind the navy sedan. I couldn't read her expression behind the giant lenses of her expensive sunglasses, but I could feel the surprise rolling off of her in waves as I climbed from the driver seat. A moment later, her full pink lips parted in shock as recognition dawned. She muttered something beneath her breath, but from this far away, I couldn't make out what it was.

I lifted a brow her way as I approached. "Car trouble?"

"I'm beginning to think I'm cursed," she shot back.

I couldn't help but chuckle. "Seems like we're in agreement there."

I gestured with my chin toward the car. "What happened?"

She crossed her arms over her chest and stared at me defiantly. "I think I ran out of gas."

I blinked, desperately trying to keep my expression under control. She was damn near thirty years old and couldn't remember to check her fuel?

"I know how it sounds," she said tersely. "But it's not my fault. At least, I don't think it is."

I regarded her for a second, before gathering my words and saying as tactfully as possible, "You don't think it's your fault you ran out of gas?"

I could picture her eyes narrowing behind the lens of the giant sunglasses as she straightened, pulling her shoulders back tight. "I just filled up a couple days ago. I showed a few houses, but I don't think there's any way I could've used an entire tank of gas."

"When was the last time you went somewhere?"

"Yesterday," she replied matter-of-factly. "I showed a house yesterday afternoon in Apple Grove."

The small village lay about fifteen miles west of Cedar Springs, but she was right; it wasn't nearly far enough to burn that much fuel going there and back. "Do you remember looking at the fuel gauge any time yesterday?"

She nodded. "I had almost half a tank before I left the office."

"You went there and back, and that's all?" I clarified.

She nodded again. "I stopped by a couple stores on the way home, but they were right there in town."

I bent and peered under the car. "And you haven't noticed anything else? No strange sounds or smells?"

"Not until just now." She shook her head. "I worked

from home all morning, then left about ten minutes ago. I had just passed the bridge when the engine made a funny sound."

I didn't see any fluid coming from under the car, but that didn't mean she didn't have a leak somewhere. "Did it sound like the engine wasn't getting enough fuel?"

She lifted one shoulder. "It went *kerchunk*, then kind of stalled."

I pressed my lips together, trying not to laugh. "How did that go again?"

She opened her mouth to repeat herself, then snapped it shut when she saw my expression. The corners of her lips turned down in disdain. "Very funny."

"I have my moments." I smirked, then sobered. "So you pulled the car over as soon as you heard the sound?"

She regarded me warily, as if making sure I wasn't going to tease her anymore. Personally, I thought she could stand to have a little more fun, but it wasn't up to me to make that happen. "That's right," she finally said. "I thought it might be the engine, and I didn't want to do any damage."

"Good idea," I replied. "Let me take a closer look to see if anything seems to be out of place."

The situation was a little strange. From what I remembered of her address, Sienna lived in a fairly affluent community. It wasn't like the people there needed to steal things to get by, especially gasoline. But kids often did stupid things, and I wondered if a teen in her area had siphoned the gas from the tank.

"Let's move to the other side." I held out one hand, gesturing for her to precede me, and she tipped her head to one side.

"Why?"

Did this woman seriously have to challenge everything I said? "The pavement is hot, so I prefer to lay in the grass.

Besides that, I don't want you standing on the side of the road."

She looked both ways before meeting my eyes again. "There's no traffic."

I clenched my molars together. "Humor me."

I could practically feel her roll her eyes, but she did as I asked and rounded the car. Kneeling down in the grass, I peeked underneath. A quick survey of the fuel lines showed that they were still intact, and I ran my fingers over them just to be sure. Aside from a little road dirt, they came away dry, and I wiped my hands on my pants as I stood.

"No damage to the fuel line. My guess is some kid probably drained the gas from your tank."

Her brows drew together. "Why?"

I help up my hands in supplication. "I can't answer that. Maybe to be a nuisance, or maybe they just needed the fuel and didn't want to ask their parents."

Her lips pressed together in a tight frown. "Damn it. Now I'm going to have to wait for it to be towed all the way into town."

She started to root through her purse, probably to look for her phone, but I held her hand to stop her. "Hold off on that for just a second."

I pulled my phone from my pocket, then dialed Finn. He answered on the second ring. "Hey, man. What's up?"

"I need a favor," I said without preamble. "I have a motorist stranded on the side of the road. Looks like she ran out of gas. Could you send one of the guys over with some fuel so she can get into town?"

"No problem," he replied easily. "I'll do it myself. I'm actually near the gas station right now. Where are you?"

I rattled off the location, then hung up. Sienna stared at me, her teeth buried in her lower lip, looking perplexed. "Why did you do that? I could've had it towed."

"That'll take longer," I said. "This will save you some time and money."

She continued to stare at me like she didn't understand. I felt the need to elaborate. "It's not a big deal, Sienna. There's no sense in you spending money on the tow truck when we can get you up and running in just a few minutes."

She nodded haltingly. "Thank you."

I didn't tell her that I didn't want her standing alone on the side of the road while she waited on the tow truck. This was both faster and safer. "Finn should be here in about ten minutes."

She nodded again but didn't say anything else, and an intense silence descended over us. She shifted awkwardly, and my gaze was drawn down her long legs to the pair of impossibly high heels she sported. I tipped my chin at her. "If you don't want to stand, we can wait in the cruiser. At least we'll have A/C in there."

She offered a tiny smile but shook her head. "I'm okay."

I had a feeling she would've turned me down no matter what I offered, so I brushed off my aggravation.

She rested one hip on the trunk of her car and pulled out her phone. "I suppose I should let my sister know I'm running late."

"Are you hanging out with her today?" I asked as I leaned against the brush guard on the front of the cruiser.

"We're supposed to meet at the country club to work on wedding stuff."

Her tone changed, and I sensed it was a sore subject, so I let it drop.

The sound of an approaching car drew my attention, and I glanced over my shoulder at it. The engine accelerated, and the car seemed to pick up speed the closer it got.

Who the hell thought it was a good idea to speed right in

front of an officer? I didn't want to leave Sienna alone to wait on Finn, but this guy was going entirely way too fast.

I opened my mouth to tell Sienna as much when the roar of the engine increased. Instead of swerving out around us, the tires crossed the white fog line. My breath halted in my lungs as the car barreled right toward us.

ELEVEN

SIENNA

The screech of metal filled the air as something hard slammed into me. The ground disappeared from beneath my feet and all of a sudden I was flying. It felt like I was suspended in the air forever as the world slowed and I became hyperaware of everything happening at once.

Before I could blink, the ground came rushing up, and I braced my hands in front of my face. I landed hard, and my teeth gnashed together as my shoulder hit first, the momentum of the fall carrying me over. My body flopped like a rag doll, and I was dimly aware of something pulling at me.

As quickly as it had started, my body came to an abrupt stop. The stiff grass tickled my nose where I landed facedown, and my lungs ached from having the air knocked out of them. My ears buzzed, and my vision swirled for a moment. Closing my eyes, I drew in a breath.

It had all happened so fast. One second I was standing there with Vaughn, the next a car seemed to be heading straight toward us. Before I could even think to move, he'd pushed me out of the way just a split second before the car had made impact.

Ice slid down my spine. I didn't want to consider what would have happened had Vaughn not reacted as quickly as he had.

I forced my muscles to move, placing my palms flat on the ground and lifting my torso. Tears sprang to my eyes as I shifted to a sitting position. Next to me, I saw Vaughn was already on his feet, his back to me as he looked after the driver who'd nearly hit us.

"Shit!" He whirled around, anger carved into his handsome face. His furious gaze landed on me, quickly turning to concern as he dropped to a knee. "Are you okay?"

"I'll be fine." I slowly clambered to my feet, and I winced as I tried to put pressure on my left leg. I staggered awkwardly, shifting all of my weight to my right foot and stumbling in the process.

One arm immediately banded around my back to support me. "Are you hurt?"

"My ankle." I bit my lip against the pain shooting up my leg.

"Hold on, I've got you." He swept me off my feet and carried me toward the back of my car where he set me on the trunk.

One black heel had come off in the scuffle, and it lay discarded in the grass. "Can you...? My shoe came off."

I pointed toward it, and Vaughn nodded. With three long strides he reached the shoe and scooped it up, then stalked back toward me. He set the shoe next to me, then immediately reached for my leg, his long fingers sliding over my flesh as he inspected the injury.

"You twist your ankle when you fell?"

The feel of his fingers touching me so intimately made

me tingle, and I licked my lips. He didn't wait for a response as he resumed his examination, sweeping his hands over my ankle bone, gently flexing my foot back and forth. He lowered my foot, but his fingers trailed up the outside of my leg, up to my knee. A dark bruise was beginning to form, and he tenderly touched the area.

I nodded but couldn't form words, and his gaze darted up to mine. "That was a pretty hard fall. You sure you're okay?"

I nodded shakily, still acutely aware of his fingers tracing light circles over my skin. "Fine," I managed to croak out. "Just... surprised, I think."

"Understandable," he murmured, his gaze fixed on my leg. "You'll need to get some ice on this."

Now that I could focus, I noticed the deep scratch he'd been fixated on. The skin had peeled away, and a few faint lines of blood began to well to the surface. His thumb lightly stroked along the inside of my knee, and the soft caress sent my heart pattering wildly in my chest. My stomach tightened, and I barely resisted the urge to squeeze my legs together to quell the ache that had formed in my center.

I watched in rapt fascination as his fingers drifted over my skin, my pulse still galloping a thousand beats per minute. But this time it wasn't from fear. I liked the way he touched me; and from the look on his face, he was enjoying it, too. Gaze locked on mine, Vaughn stepped in close and studied me, those bright gray eyes sweeping over my face. "Do you want to go to the hospital?"

I swallowed hard, pushing the ridiculous thoughts away. I rotated my foot a bit, testing the muscle. It was starting to feel better already. "I'll be okay. It's just sore."

"You sure?"

His voice was gruff, harsher than I'd ever heard before,

but I knew it wasn't directed at me. I nodded, and some of the tension seeped from his muscles. One hand lifted, and he gently swept a stray lock hair off my forehead.

"Thank you."

My voice cracked, and his hold tightened the tiniest bit. "Hopefully the dash cam caught something. We'll find the guy."

He sounded so sure of it that I couldn't help but trust him. I bit my lower lip, choppy breaths escaping in shallow pants as I watched him drink in every inch of me. Was he going to kiss me? What would he taste like? What would his lips feel like against mine? My gaze dropped to his mouth, and I felt myself sway toward him just as the sound of an engine cut through my heated thoughts.

I snapped my head around, looking for the approaching car. Vaughn was instantly alert, his hands clenching around my waist like he could physically carry me away from the threat to protect me. I wasn't entirely sure how it happened, but I found my arms looped around his shoulders, my torso pressed firmly up against his.

"It's okay," he murmured, his breath stirring the wispy strands of hair near my ear. "It's just Finn."

Swallowing hard, I slowly retracted my hands from where they were curled around his neck. He swept one hand up and down my spine in a comforting motion but didn't release me right away. His skin was warm, and a woodsy, masculine smell wafted up into my nostrils, making me dizzy.

With Vaughn, I felt... safe. He'd wrapped those strong arms around me, holding me close, protecting me from harm. He was attractive and strong, and he had saved me from the reckless driver. Like he... cared about me.

No. I immediately pushed the thought away. Vaughn was only doing his job. He didn't like me—he'd made that abundantly clear. And I didn't like him, either. Except the tingling awareness in my belly told me otherwise. Maybe I had a concussion. It had to be the stress of the situation, because there was no way I could be getting lightheaded over the uptight cop. And had I really almost kissed him?

Good God, what was wrong with me? I'd only known him for a few days, and here I was practically throwing myself at him. I didn't need to go all gooey around him like some damsel in distress.

Pressing my palms against the trunk of the car, I scooted backwards, putting distance between us. His hands dropped to his sides immediately, and his face shifted into an emotionless mask as Finn pulled to a stop on the opposite side of the road.

As he climbed from his cruiser, he glanced curiously at the damaged vehicles. "What happened?"

"Someone sideswiped us," Vaughn said before I could respond. "We were both standing right here when it happened. Luckily she didn't get hurt."

Finn turned to me. "Glad you're okay. We'll pull footage from the dash cam and find out who it was."

"That's what Vaughn said," I replied shakily, still reeling from the accident, but mostly from the feel of his hands on me.

As if just remembering that I was perched on the trunk of the car, Vaughn turned back to me. Instead of wrapping me in his arms, this time, he extended one hand to help me down. An irrational surge of disappointment slammed into me, but I shook it off.

He watched me carefully as I climbed down from the trunk, then moved off to the side as Finn carried over a red plastic jug and began to pour the fuel into the tank.

"Thanks for your help," I said once he was finished.

"No problem," he returned. "Do you need one of us to follow you home to make sure you get there okay?"

I shook my head. "No, thanks. I'm good."

I guess I'd be dealing with the insurance company today instead of wedding plans. I couldn't begin to explain how relieved I felt, and guilt rose up, along with a familiar pang of hurt. I was going to have to get over this sooner or later and move on with my life. But that was easier said than done.

TWELVE

VAUGHN

Anger surged through me, and I swore aloud as I turned into the parking lot behind the station. Chief was already outside, and he lifted his chin in greeting as I pulled to a stop in front of him and climbed from the car.

His gaze skimmed the left front fender, raking over the deep scratches and broken marker light. "Not too bad," he commented. "We'll have Mick get it fixed up."

The damage to the car wasn't terrible; I was far more concerned about the fact that Sienna had been put in danger.

Grayson rested a foot on the brush guard and stared at me. "You okay?"

"I'm fine." I had a couple scratches, but nothing to bitch about. "Sienna twisted her ankle when I pulled her out of the way, but she seemed to be fine when she left."

"What happened?"

I recounted what had transpired after I found Sienna stranded on the side of the road. "I could tell the driver was distracted when I saw the car swerving all over the road. I'd already called Finn, and I was getting ready to pull him over when it accelerated and slammed right into the cruiser."

Gray lifted a brow. "Intentional?"

"Yeah." I nodded grimly. Not only had the asshole never slowed down, I distinctly remembered the sound of the engine accelerating as the driver got closer.

Gray studied me. "I have the dash cam footage pulled up, but I figured you'd want to take a look at it, too."

"Damn right." I couldn't wait to see who the fuck had been ballsy enough to sideswipe an officer then flee.

I fell into step next to Gray as he entered the station through the back door, then strode toward his office. He took a seat behind the computer and gestured for me to pull up a seat.

The footage on the screen was a frozen image of Sienna's car pulled to the side of the road. She stood next to the vehicle, and I knew this was the moment I'd pulled up behind her. As soon as we were both situated, he started rolling the video. I talked as it played. "She ran out of gas and was getting ready to call Mick for a tow. I knew Finn was working, so I called him, had him bring enough to get her by."

Gray nodded, eyes glued to the screen, and I breathed a silent sigh of relief when he didn't question me. It was a plausible enough excuse—after all, we lived in a small town and often did favors for our neighbors. But I still wasn't entirely sure why I'd done so for Sienna. She was already prepared to call for a tow, so it wouldn't have mattered. But for some reason I felt bad for her.

It felt strange to watch myself, so I focused on Sienna, taking in the tense set of her shoulders and remembering vividly the way she'd watched me warily, muscles rigid, every emotional wall firmly in place. What the hell had made her so defensive? She was like an onion. A little bitter, a tad spicy, but deep down I knew she would be well worth the time it took to peel back every layer.

On the screen, I watched myself turn, and I knew the tan car was approaching. I shoved Sienna out of the way a second before the cruiser jolted, making the camera jump wildly. We fell out of focus for a moment, and I spoke aloud, walking Gray through everything.

"She hurt her ankle when she fell. It didn't look broken though, and she didn't want to go to the hospital."

A moment later, we entered the camera's field of vision, Sienna in my arms. My mouth went dry as I watched her settle on the trunk of the car, those long legs draped over the edge. My fingers tingled at the memory of her soft skin beneath my touch, and I clenched my hand into a fist. The image on the screen wasn't great, but her face was obviously pale, her eyes wide. I watched as I checked for injuries, and then... I saw it.

I thought I'd imagined it, but her expression changed the tiniest bit. Just for a second. Her mouth parted the tiniest bit and she swayed toward me before she caught herself. Had she felt the same spark of attraction? Or was it just the stress of the situation that caused her to reach for me?

Ridiculous as it was, I'd wanted to kiss her in that moment. She looked scared yet so damn brave at the same time. I'd wanted to slip my arms around her, pull her close and taste that smart mouth of hers.

Beside me, Gray cleared his throat. I stiffened, shoving the thought away.

"Recognize the car?"

I was so preoccupied watching Sienna that I'd forgotten the true purpose of watching the video. I quickly recalled the tan sedan I'd seen as it fled, and I shook my head. "Not that I can think of."

He tapped a button and the footage rewound until just after impact. He hit another button to slow the playback, and after a few seconds the car appeared on the left side of the screen. I scowled when I saw the rear of the car—minus a license plate.

Shit.

Gray nodded. "I was afraid of that. Think he was aiming at you or her?"

I turned toward Chief as I considered the question. "There are enough people out there who hate cops. She's a realtor, and the town princess. She's spoiled and kind of a snob, but is that enough for someone to try to run her down?"

Gray lifted a brow. "So you think he was aiming for you?"

"Possibly." Maybe someone I'd pissed off, or a disgruntled family member.

"I'm inclined to believe the same. Watch your ass while you're out." Gray printed off a still shot that captured the make and model. "Get a rough year on that and run it through the system, see if we get any hits from the last couple of months."

"Will do." I grabbed the photo off the printer and headed back to my desk to narrow down who the hell had tried to run us down.

As she had often over the past couple of days, Sienna came to mind again and I wondered how she was feeling... and whether she would find it odd if I stopped by to check in on her. For professional reasons, of course.

THIRTEEN

SIENNA

I wanted to scoop my eyeballs out with the serving spoon. Glancing across the table at my baby sister and her fiancé, I barely managed to hold back the grimace pulling at my lips. They were so disgustingly in love that it was sickening.

"Don't you think we should do a video like that?" she asked him.

One of her recent clients had commissioned a choreographer, and the bride and her attendants danced down the aisle to the couple's favorite song. Sophia had seen it and fallen in love. I thought it was horrendously tacky, but I would never say as much.

"Whatever you want, sweetheart." Ethan leaned forward and brushed his nose against my sister's, making my stomach flip violently.

God. I really was going to throw up all over the immaculately set table if I didn't get out of here soon. My father caught my eye from his space at the head of the table, and he sent me 'The Look'. The one that said *this could have been you if you hadn't ruined it.*

I was well aware of my shortcomings, and if I ever forgot, I was certain he'd be right there to remind me. To say he was displeased when Derrick left me was an understatement. Despite the fact that I'd had absolutely no say in the matter, my father seemed to believe I should have begged Derrick not to leave me.

Of course, he wasn't exactly happy that Derrick had made a huge career change and was now working as an influencer for social media, but as he often said—you have to go where the money is. And apparently I was the idiot for not following him.

I loved my father—I did. But I often felt like I never measured up to his exacting standards. He seemed to think he knew exactly how I should feel, what kind of job I needed, and what was best for me. Moving out was the best thing I'd ever done. Thank God for my sister, Sophia. Even though the wedding planning was a giant pain, it took some of the focus off me for the time being.

As the baby, Sophia was the apple of my father's eye. He'd never been able to deny her anything. She looked so much like our mother that I sometimes thought he doted on her in an effort to relive the past. Our mother had been gone for decades now, but my father had never remarried. Instead, he'd turned his full attention to us. He'd ensured we had a good education, but he encouraged us endlessly to settle down.

At least one of us would make him proud in that regard. Over the past couple of months, he'd tried to hook me up with his friends' sons, but I'd refused. My father had dictated the rest of my life; I wouldn't let him choose my spouse, too. I'd put him off by insisting that we should focus on Sophia until after the wedding.

Thankfully, she took up enough attention for both of us. I loved my sister, but she was incredibly flighty and full of dreams. Though she'd opened her event coordinator business two years ago, I seriously doubted she would continue it after she was married. She was perfectly content to be a kept woman, spending her lunch hour at the country club when she wasn't with her husband or children.

That life would never be for me. Oh, I eventually wanted to get married and settle down, have a few kids. But I wanted a career, too. I wanted to be successful, to have something for myself. I wanted this promotion not only because I felt like I deserved it, but to prove to myself and my father that I could do it. I didn't need a man to take care of me.

There seemed to be a definitive line for women. We could either work or have families, but not both. And I refused to choose. I wasn't going to settle down with a man who didn't love me just for security, no matter how lonely I felt sometimes.

I glanced at the empty seat next to me where Derrick had sat for every holiday over the past four years, and my heart ached at the reminder of his betrayal. No, I wouldn't go through that again.

"Sienna?"

My head jerked up at the sound of my name, and I swiveled toward Ethan. "I'm sorry, I didn't hear you."

"I asked how you were feeling." His concerned blue eyes settled on me. "I heard about the accident. And I saw the rental in the driveway."

I offered a little smile. "I'm fine, thanks for asking. My knee is still a little sore, but it's nothing major."

"The police need to find that driver and get him off the road."

I glanced at my father. "I'm sure they're working on it."

"Well, they need to do it soon, before this happens to someone else."

Instead of responding, I took a fortifying sip of wine. Better to let him bluster about it and get it over with.

Ethan clapped his hands together. "Is everyone ready for dessert?"

I threw him a grateful look from behind my wine glass, and he sent a quick wink my way. My father's maid, Elsie, hearing his pronouncement, quietly entered the dining room and began to gather the dishes. Waving her off, I stood and collected my plate. "I saw a beautiful pie in there."

"Ooh, yes!" My sister's eyes widened. "It's from Lettie's, so you know it's going to be heavenly."

"I do love their pies," my father responded with a smile. "We used to buy your birthday cakes there every year."

Lettie's was a staple in Cedar Springs, and the ancient baker had been around for decades. She made some of the best pastries I'd ever tasted.

"I really shouldn't have any." My sister pouted prettily. "After all, I have to worry about fitting into my dress."

I barely resisted the urge to roll my eyes. The wedding was still several months away. "I'm sure a small piece won't hurt."

"Maybe you're right." She grinned. "I'll have to put in an extra hour on the Peloton in the morning, but it will be worth it!"

"You're going to be a beautiful bride," Ethan said, a sappy smile on his face.

Bile crept up my throat, and I immediately whisked the plates out to the kitchen. Inside, Elsie slid a look my way. "You okay, miss?"

I forced a smile. "I'm fine, Elsie. Thanks."

She passed me the pie, and I carried it to the dining room. "Here you go."

My father glanced expectantly at me. "Did you bring the whipped cream?"

"I'll be right back." I dashed back into the kitchen. "Elsie, do we have any whipped cream for the pie?"

"No, miss." She made a face. "I'm sorry."

"No problem." I strode back into the dining room. "Looks like we're out. I can just run to the store and—"

"No, no." Ethan pushed back his chair. "You sit and relax. I'll take care of it."

"But you're a guest." And I desperately needed to get away from them for a minute.

"It's no trouble at all," he assured me.

"Oh! Let Ethan take care of it," Sophia piped up. "I wanted to run a few more ideas by you since you didn't make it to the country club."

Her words were condescending, like it was my fault some crazy driver had rammed into my car. I swallowed my retort and smiled tightly. "I'd love to help."

Ethan gave Sophia a quick kiss on the cheek, then disappeared. Less than a minute later, he popped back into the dining room. "Sienna, I forgot you're parked behind me. Do you mind if I take your car?"

The rental had insurance, and I was only going to make things worse if I tried to get out of discussing the wedding again. I dug the keys from my purse and passed them to Ethan, who smiled. "Perfect, thanks."

He disappeared once more, and my sister launched into a debate about whether teal or aquamarine would look best in the reception hall. My eyes had begun to glaze over by the time Ethan reappeared. "Sorry that took so long. The first place didn't have any."

The topic soon changed to talk of my father's upcoming trip to Europe, and I silently thanked every deity known to man that I wouldn't have to suffer through any more wedding plans for the day. Dad was flying out tomorrow, and for the next hour he regaled us with tales of his plans for the continent.

After we'd finished, Ethan approached and handed me my keys. "Thanks again. For everything." His voice lowered. "I know Sophia is a little crazy about the wedding, but she just wants it to be perfect."

"It will be," I assured him. "And I'll help however I can."

He leaned in and gave me a light kiss on the cheek. "You're a lifesaver. I don't know what we'd do without you."

I felt my anger begin to drain away. "It's no problem, really. I just want you two to be happy."

"We will. And forget about Derrick. You'll find someone who truly cares about you and treats you like the amazing person you are."

Ethan and I didn't often talk, but it was one of the nicest things he'd ever said to me. "Thanks, Ethan. I appreciate it."

He squeezed my shoulder, then moved next to his fiancée. I watched the two of them together, desperately in love, and a pang ricocheted through my heart. The truth was, I did want what they had. I just wasn't sure I was ever going to find it.

FOURTEEN

VAUGHN

Finn's name lit the screen, and I tapped the button to answer the call. "What's up?"

"ID just came back on the Vic from the field. You free?"

"Yep. Just finished a traffic stop," I told our detective. "You need me on the scene?"

"Yeah. Mac pulled last known address, so I'm sending it to you now."

"You got it." I shifted into gear as I hung up, and Finn's message beeped through seconds later. I mentally calculated the quickest route, then tossed a quick look behind me before pulling a U-turn and heading toward the west side of town.

Since Forsythe's prints were in our system, he'd been identified almost immediately. Though we had the second victim's teeth, it had taken them time to pull dental records. We still didn't have a body, but hopefully this would bring us one step closer.

I arrived at the scene first and took a moment to scan the

house while I waited for backup. The paint on the small duplex was peeling, and dirt caked the windows. The grass was dried and brittle, and debris littered the yard.

It wasn't the best section of town, and the hairs on the back of my neck lifted, prompting me to check my surroundings once again. Nothing seemed out of place, but I remained vigilant until Finn pulled up a couple of minutes later, followed by a second cruiser.

Climbing from the car, I met Mac and Finn on the sidewalk. "Name?"

"Chester Davies."

I lifted a brow and Finn smirked. "Goes by Blaze. Served time for larceny and possession."

Figured. Drugs weren't extremely common in Cedar Springs, but every town had their problems. We'd seen a recent spike in a homemade substance that had popped up at several crime scenes.

I nodded before moving toward the front door. Using the side of my fist, I gave three hard knocks. "Police," I called out. "Anyone in there?"

According to Finn's report, there was no wife or family member listed at this residence, but it wasn't out of the realm of possibility. I gave another hard triple knock, then counted to twenty. When no one responded, I glanced at Finn, who nodded in response. We had probable cause to enter the premises, so we were good to breach entry. I tried the door handle, which turned surprisingly easily beneath my fingertips.

I glanced at the men behind me, brows raised. This wasn't the type of neighborhood where you left your doors unlocked. Each of us in turn drew our weapons as we prepared to enter the house. The door creaked as it swung open, and I held my pistol in front of me as I cleared the corners.

The house was a mess. Old food and beer cans littered every surface, and clothing had been strewn about the room. I couldn't tell if the place had been tossed, or if Davies had left it like this prior to his death.

I moved farther into the house, the two men flanking me as we moved from room to room. I checked the kitchen, which was equally disgusting, but I found nothing of value. "Clear," I called out. Mac and Finn echoed similar confirmations within a few seconds of each other, and I followed their voices toward the bedroom.

"He's not here," Finn said unnecessarily as he reholstered his weapon.

I glanced around. "Pulling that many teeth would definitely have caused some bleeding. I don't see anything to indicate it happened here."

Finn shrugged. "I'm guessing he was held elsewhere."

Davies didn't have a job since he had recently been released from jail, and he obviously hadn't been home for some time. Although it wasn't likely considering what had happened to Perez, it was entirely possible that Davies was still alive. We needed to find him sooner rather than later.

"Let's contact next of kin," Finn stated. "Mac, see if he was dating anyone, or if he had any close acquaintances. Also, check with the neighbors and see what they can tell you. Vaughn and I will check with his mother."

Goddamn it. I always hated delivering news like this, especially when the victim wasn't present.

It was a short drive to Marion Davies's house on the outskirts of town. The house was small and run-down, the lawn overgrown with weeds and dotted with discarded trash. The sidewalk was broken, lifted up in places, and I picked my way across the concrete to the small front porch that looked more than a little worse for wear.

Avoiding the broken, rotting boards, I punched the

button for the doorbell. I wasn't surprised when no sound came from inside the house. I gave a hard triple knock, then waited. A moment later, the door swung open, revealing a diminutive woman.

She squinted at me through the ripped screen of the door. "Yeah?"

"Marion Davies?"

She glanced over my shoulder at Finn and scowled. "Whatdya want?"

Ignoring her hostility, I drew in a calming breath. "Mrs. Davies, I'm here in regard to your son, Chester."

The lines bracketing her eyes and mouth deepened. "Boy's always gettin' into trouble. What'd he do now?"

"Ma'am, when was the last time you saw Chester?"

"Dunno." She shrugged. "Before he got locked up. Shouldn't have let him out."

Apparently there was no love lost between Chester and his mother. "You haven't seen him since he was released?"

"He's not welcome here. Last time he came home, he stole $200 from me." Her scowl intensified. "Reported it to you, not that you did a damn thing."

"I apologize for that, ma'am," I said, attempting to steer the conversation back to the topic at hand. "The reason I'm here is because your son appears to be missing."

She snorted. "No doubt holed up somewhere with one of his friends. They're all bad news."

"We recently responded to a call at the duplex where Chester lived most recently. His belongings are there, but he seems to have left in a hurry. If you could tell me where he might be, it would be helpful. We believe he's involved in a related crime."

"More than likely." She shook her head. "Take him back to jail where he belongs."

"He may be in danger," I warned. "We found—"

"Officer, what my son does is none of my business. I hope you find him and put him behind bars where he belongs."

Before I could say another word, the door slammed in my face. I turned to meet Finn's wry gaze. "Guess she's a dead end."

He tipped his head. "Come on. Let's check with the landlord. Maybe he'll be able to tell us something."

FIFTEEN

SIENNA

My steps faltered, and I bit back a groan when I saw Calvin's hip propped on the front fender of my car. Between the car accident the other day and Ashton hounding me, getting into an altercation with Cal was the last thing I wanted to do today.

I forced my lips into a polite smile as I strode forward. "Can I help you with something?"

I could feel the weight of his gaze burning into me even from behind the dark lenses of his expensive sunglasses. He didn't move, and for a long moment, he didn't say a word. He just stared at me, an almost imperceptible sneer twisting his handsome face. "This promotion should be mine," he finally said.

I fought the urge to sigh. Tristan Starling, the owner of TriStar, had made it perfectly clear that the promotion for partnership was between Cal and myself. He seemed determined to do anything to keep me from getting the position.

I smiled sweetly. "You've already tried to steal my client. Are you going to steal the partnership, too?"

His lips pressed into a firm line. "We both know I deserve it."

I shook my head. "No, I don't know that. I work just as hard as you do. In fact, I bring in more commissions every year than you do on average. So I would say that, of the two of us, I'm the one who deserves it."

He pushed to his full height and took a step forward. The move was so sudden that I had to lock my muscles into place to keep from stepping backward and putting distance between us. Cal glared at me. "The only reason you're here is because of your daddy."

My mouth dropped open. "What?"

"You heard me. The only reason you're here is because Mr. Starling didn't want to piss off your father."

A twinge of doubt moved through my heart. That couldn't be true. I shook my head, clearing the thought away. "If that were the case, how do you explain all my sales?"

"Please." Cal scoffed. "Haven't you ever noticed how Mr. Starling offers you all the most expensive properties?" I opened my mouth to speak, but he cut me off. "Those places practically sell themselves, you know that. The only reason he would just hand them over to you on a silver platter is because he knows you couldn't move anything else."

The heat of humiliation burned over my skin, and I clenched my fist around the handle of my handbag to hide my trembling fingers. "I'm going home now. You need to move."

"Or what?" His head tipped slightly to one side, his face a mask of hate. "Are you going to try to get me fired? Make it even easier for you to get the partnership."

I swallowed hard and forced myself to meet his gaze. "Please move."

He stared at me for a full three seconds before taking a step backward. "You just don't want to face the truth, do you, Sienna?"

Blocking out his ugly words, I used the key fob to unlock the door, then quickly slid inside. I cranked the engine, acutely aware of Cal's eyes on me as I put the car into gear and reversed out of the spot. He was still standing there when I pulled out onto the main drive.

I gripped the steering wheel hard, my knuckles turning white under the strain. Asshole. There was no way what he said was true.

Anger and unease churned in my stomach as I drove, expanding with each passing moment. I wasn't oblivious to my father's clout in Cedar Springs. My great-great-great grandfather was one of the first settlers and had used his money to develop the town. No one wanted to piss off the founders' kin. Damn it.

I swore out loud as I pulled into my garage and climbed from the car. My father was technically on vacation, but this was worth disrupting his little jaunt around Europe. I dug my phone from my bag as I pushed open the door to the house and stepped into the small room lined with storage shelves.

Dropping my bag in its place, I glanced around, my attention momentarily diverted. A strange smell lilted on the air, and I scrunched up my nose. The litter box definitely needed to be changed.

Boots hadn't greeted me yet, and I called out his name as I headed toward the kitchen. The oxygen was sucked from my lungs, and I jolted to a halt at the sight that greeted me. On the pristine white cabinets someone had written the words DIE BITCH in huge letters. The reddish brown paint was splashed over the walls and windows, and...

Oh, God.

Bile rose up when I saw the small bundle lying on the floor, the fur matted and dark with blood. My stomach pitched violently, swiftly losing the battle to contain its contents. I retched until there was nothing left, my empty stomach twisting painfully.

I lifted a shaky hand to my mouth as I slowly backed away from the grotesque scene. I needed to call for help, needed...

I glanced at the phone still clutched in my hand.

I needed *him*.

SIXTEEN

VAUGHN

I'd never seen anything so grotesque. The rust-colored liquid spattered the walls like they had been painted with it, and slightly darker splotches had pooled next to the mangled body of the small animal lying in the middle of the floor.

It looked like something out of a horror film, and the potent iron-tangy smell clogged my nose and mouth. Christ. What the fuck had happened here?

I turned abruptly away from the gory scene and made my way into the living room. I'd called for backup as soon as I got the call from Sienna, and now Drew Thorne was here working the scene, freeing me up to check on Sienna.

The woman in question sat perched on the edge of the couch, her face completely devoid of color. Though I'd settled her in here half an hour ago when I first arrived, I wasn't sure my pulse had begun to slow. That phone call had stopped my heart, sending stark fear all the way down into the marrow of my bones. She'd sounded terrified, and

I'd never felt a stronger sense of relief when I saw her standing on the front porch, shaken but unhurt.

She was still rattled; not that I blamed her. She'd witnessed something absolutely horrific and lost something she'd been attached to. I could see her trembling even from where I stood in the archway that separated the room from the rest of the downstairs.

Sitting on the plush ottoman across from her, Finn eyed her shrewdly as he attempted to question her. "Is there anyone you can think of who might be upset with you?"

She gave an abbreviated shake of her head but didn't say a word.

"If there's anything you can think of, it might help us narrow it down," he pressed gently.

Sienna blinked at him. "I... I don't..."

Finn glanced my way and I shook my head, indicating for him to stop. She'd been through enough today.

"We'll figure this out," he offered gently. Sienna didn't bother to respond, just stared despondently at the floor.

Finn met my gaze as he made his way toward the doorway. I tipped my head toward the kitchen. "Why don't you help Drew?" I suggested in a low tone. "I'll take care of her."

"You sure?"

I nodded.

"Okay." I didn't miss the dubious way he looked at me, or the curiosity tingeing his voice. He lightly slapped my shoulder as he passed. "Good luck."

I dipped my chin in acknowledgment before crossing the room. Sienna had a pillow settled on her lap, and she picked errantly at a loose thread as she stared aimlessly at a spot by her feet. Stopping barely a foot away, I dropped to a knee in front of her. "Sienna?"

Her lashes fluttered at the sound of my voice, but she

didn't meet my gaze. "Drew and Finn will take care of everything," I said softly. "In the meantime, I'm going to need you to get your things together."

Ever so slowly, her chin lifted and her eyes met mine. "Why?"

Her house was officially a crime scene, at least for the next day or so. I was certain she hadn't even thought that far ahead, but even if she wanted to, she wouldn't be able to stay here tonight.

"You can't stay here." I shook my head. "We're still investigating."

At the reminder of what happened, a stricken expression moved across her face. It made me want to reach for her, and I curled my hands into fists to keep from doing so.

"Do you have a place where you can stay the night?"

She bit her lip and gave a jerky nod.

"Okay," I replied softly. "Let's go get some of your things packed up."

Her gaze drifted toward the stairs, but she didn't move. Five seconds passed, then ten. "Do you want me to take care of it?"

"N-no," she stammered. "I... I can do it."

She pressed her palms to the edge of the couch, then almost as if it pained her, levered to her feet. I watched her carefully, making sure she was steady before standing and gesturing toward the stairs. Sienna moved slowly, like she was on autopilot. Her high heels teetered on the thick carpet as we climbed the stairs, and she swayed on her feet.

I shot one arm out, grasping her bicep to keep her from faceplanting forward just as she caught herself on the banister. "You good?" I asked in a low tone.

She gave a brief nod, then continued upward. I placed one hand on the middle of her back, silently giving her strength and urging her forward. I trailed behind as Sienna led away to her room, and I paused in the doorway as she moved inside. Standing in the middle of the room, she hesitated, looking numb and lost.

"Sienna?"

The sound of her name seemed to jolt her out of her reverie, and she glanced over her shoulder at me. Her blue eyes were wide and filled with grief.

"Do you have a suitcase or a duffel bag?"

She nodded, then cleared her throat. I could practically see her pulling herself together, and her spine straightened as her chin inched upward. "How long?" she asked.

"Hopefully we'll be able to get you back in here by tomorrow or the next day."

She flinched a little bit but nodded. With that, she moved into the walk-in closet to retrieve a small suitcase, then began to methodically pull blouses and pants from their hangers. She folded and placed them inside the suitcase, then moved toward the dresser. She tossed a tiny look my way as she retrieved her lingerie, then packed that away as well.

Her next trip into the bathroom yielded what I assumed was makeup and toiletries. Once she had everything settled in the suitcase, she zipped it up and turned to me. I strode forward and picked it up off the bed.

"Anything else?"

"No. Thank you."

"For what?"

She lifted one shoulder. "For helping. For being nice."

"You're welcome," I said simply. "Unfortunately, this has been the easy part. Finn will probably have more questions for you tomorrow."

Her expression dimmed the tiniest bit. "Okay."

"Where will you be staying? Are you going to your dad's place?"

Her eyes widened a tiny fraction, and her hand landed on my forearm, like something had just occurred to her. "Please don't tell him."

I tipped my head to one side. "You don't want your father to know about this?"

She shook her head emphatically. It set off my protective instinct, and I stepped the tiniest bit closer to her. "Is everything okay? Has he done something...?"

She shook her head again. "It's not that. It's just... He's on vacation right now, and I don't want to ruin it for him. I don't want him to worry."

I bit back the urge to tell her that this was very much worth worrying about. "I can't guarantee he won't hear about it," I said. "I'll do my best to keep the details under wraps, but he's going to hear that your house was broken into."

She didn't look very happy about that, but I couldn't help it. "If you're not going to his place, you could stay at the bed and breakfast."

"Yeah. I'll give Eden a call," she said.

I couldn't begin to figure out why she didn't want him to know, but I bit my tongue. It was her choice; I just hoped she would tell me later.

"Why don't you call her now? I'll give you a ride over there."

Her gaze darted back to mine. "I can drive. I have the rental, and..."

She trailed off, her mind seemingly far away— probably on the accident. She'd had a rough couple of weeks, and I took pity on her. I dipped my chin, but I hated the idea of her being alone, even for a minute. "I'll follow you."

She studied me for a moment like she was trying to read between the lines. "Do you think I'm in danger?"

I debated what to tell her. "I think it's a possibility," I finally admitted. The person who had killed her cat was most certainly unbalanced, and I worried what would happen next. "I would feel better if you stayed with someone you trusted, maybe fly under the radar for the next couple days."

"But I need to work."

"How many showings do you have?"

"I'd have to check my calendar. Maybe two or three?"

"Have someone go with you. Ask a coworker or friend. You can't be too careful." The message written on the wall was threatening, but until we had something more solid, she was unfortunately left to her own devices. We didn't have the manpower to put someone on her full-time, but I'd make sure our patrolmen did a few extra drive-bys each shift to make sure she was safe.

Her fingers tightened briefly where they pressed against my forearm, then she dropped her hand away. "I'll be careful."

The color had come back to her cheeks and though she still looked exhausted and shocked, she was starting to rally. "We'll fix this," I promised.

I didn't need to elaborate, and she offered a sad smile. "Thanks."

She turned and headed out of the room then, and I trailed a few steps behind as she made her way down the stairs. Next to the front door, I briefly touched her elbow. "Wait for me. I'll be right back."

I popped into the kitchen to let the guys know I'd be right back, then joined Sienna again. She was quiet as she climbed into her rental car, then reversed out of the driveway. I followed her to Eden Snow's bed and breakfast, located just outside of Cedar Springs. I pulled to a stop in the driveway, watching as she made her way up the path.

The door opened and Eden vaulted outside before Sienna even reached the porch. I watched as the pretty blonde wrapped Sienna in a tight hug, and something flared to life in my chest. I didn't like what had happened this afternoon, and I had a horrible feeling it didn't bode well for Sienna. I was going to have to keep a close eye on her to make sure no one got this close to her again.

Eden gazed at me over Sienna's shoulder, and I lifted a hand in greeting before pulling away. I was glad that Sienna had friends like Eden to watch out for her.

When I returned to Sienna's house, I headed straight to the kitchen. "Find anything?"

"Knife's missing," Finn replied, pointing to an empty slot in the block on the island. "Guessing whoever did this took the weapon with them."

"No sign of forced entry?"

"Nope." He made a face. "I hate to say it, but... you don't think she had something to do with it, do you?"

Anger washed over me, turning my body to stone. "She didn't do it."

"We have to check—"

"I did." I was well aware that we needed to explore every angle. And even though I believed wholeheartedly that she was innocent, I knew I had to cross her off my list. "There wasn't a speck of blood on her when I got here. I even checked her hamper while I was upstairs. Nothing in there, either."

"Shit." He ran a hand through his hair. "Does she have any idea who might have done this?"

"Not that she could think of."

"Damn." He shook his head. "I don't like this."

Me, either. Not one damn bit.

SEVENTEEN

SIENNA

It was truly amazing what money could do. Ashton had somehow managed to grease the hands of the inspector, who had moved the house to the top of his schedule. He'd finished the inspection and turned in the paperwork in record time, and now all that was left to do was officially transfer the house into Ashton's name.

Though I'd dragged my feet all morning, I needed something to do to get my mind off what had happened at my house last night. Tearing my eyes away from Ashton's most recent text message, I glanced at Eden. "I think I'm going to go into the office for a little bit."

"Are you sure?" Her brows drew together. "Do you think that's a good idea?"

I lifted one shoulder and sighed. "I'm not sure. All I know is, the longer I sit here thinking about things, the more I drive myself crazy worrying over it."

"I can understand that," she said, her expression creased with sympathy. "I could go with you if you want."

I waved away her offer. "That's okay, you have things to do around here. Besides, the office is in the middle of town." It wasn't like anything would happen with so many people around all the time.

"And Ashton?" Eden lifted a brow as she stared at me. "Are you sure it's safe to be alone with him?"

No, I wasn't. I couldn't begin to imagine who had done something so heinous. He struck me as the direct type, the type of person who addressed things head-on when he had a problem. I couldn't imagine Ashton torturing an innocent animal because he had some sort of personal vendetta against me.

Of course, I wasn't the best judge of character. I've been wrong about the last man in my life, and I could be wrong about Ashton too. At the top of my list was Calvin. He'd been a royal pain lately, but I wasn't sure that even he could do something so evil.

I knew he was pissed off about the promotion. We'd started working together at almost the exact same time, and he no doubt saw it as a sort of slight that he would have to work under someone his own age. He resented the rapport I'd built with Tristan, and I knew he would never want to work for me if I was promoted to partner.

But I didn't know if that was enough for him to seek revenge. He could easily open his own brokerage, either in Cedar Springs or outside of Dallas. As far as motive, he currently topped my list.

Ashton was a close second, for no other reason than he was the only person I'd interacted with on a regular basis recently. Not to mention he was a giant pain in the ass.

My phone buzzed again, and I rolled my eyes as I glanced at the screen. Case in point.

I glanced at Eden. "I'm going to do it. The quicker I can get this over with, the better."

"Okay." A worried frown tugged at her lips. "Just be careful."

"I will." I pushed away from the table then headed upstairs to change. I hadn't been thinking clearly last night, so I'd grabbed only a handful of random outfits, none of which were appropriate business wear, but if Ashton insisted on doing this today, then he would just have to deal with it.

Back in my room, I pulled on a pair of black pants that ended just above my ankles then scoured the tops I'd brought. The least wrinkled was a white blouse with lacy, fluttering sleeves, so I tugged it on. After washing my face, I twisted my hair up and pinned it with a clip, then did the fastest makeup job in history.

In less than fifteen minutes I was on my way to TriStar. Much to my chagrin, Calvin was in the office when I arrived, and he offered a shark-like smile as I passed. "What brings you in today?"

"I'm finalizing the sale of the Waterman property."

"Right." His lip curled. "The one that should have been mine."

I bit down on my tongue to keep from snapping at him. It wasn't my fault Ashton had chosen me. Hell, I gladly would have given him to Calvin, but Mr. Starling had wanted me to handle it. Instead of replying, I offered a small smile. "Excuse me, I need to get ready."

While I waited for Ashton to arrive, I readied the necessary paperwork and placed it in the conference room. I heard Calvin on the phone, presumably speaking with another agent, when the front door opened with a soft jangle. Ashton strode inside, and I lifted a hand in greeting. "Come on back."

I led the way to the conference room and gestured for him to take a seat. "Can I get you anything to drink?"

"No thanks." He snatched up the pen and pointed to the sheaf of papers in front of him. "These ready?"

"Yep." I forced a smile I didn't feel and sank into the seat across from him.

He flipped through the papers, signing them with the familiarity of someone who did this on a regular basis. When he was finished, I gathered everything up to make copies. "I'll be right back."

He lifted his chin my way as he settled back in his seat, and I left the room. I passed Calvin's office, noticing with relief that the lights were off. Thank God, he'd left for the day. That was one less thing I'd have to deal with.

Once I had everything ready to be filed, I carried a copy of the paperwork back to Ashton. "Here you go."

He unfolded from his chair and accepted the outstretched folder. "Anything else?"

"That's all."

"Great." His tone was drenched in sarcasm. "Nice doing business with you." He turned on a heel and strode toward the lobby.

Barely repressing an eye roll I followed behind and saw him out. "Have a nice day!" Lowering my voice, I murmured, "Don't let the door hit you on the way out."

As soon as he had disappeared from sight, I locked the door with a relieved sigh and headed back to my office. I detoured briefly into the supply closet to grab more paper when a soft noise from the outer recesses of the offices made my ears prick up.

I froze in place, goosebumps sweeping over my skin as I listened intently. Creeping toward the doorway, I peeked my head around the doorjamb. "Hello?"

No one answered, and I shook off my unease with a soft laugh. I was obviously still on edge from yesterday, hearing things that weren't really there. Paper in hand, I turned toward my office. I had taken two steps when the sound of glass shattering ripped through the air and the window in the office to my left exploded. It was followed by a burst of orange and a billowing heat that knocked me off balance.

I hit the ground hard, flames bursting from the office and licking down the hallway. Heart in my throat, I scrambled to my feet. I couldn't make it back to the lobby— that way was blocked by flames and gathering smoke. Disoriented, I glanced around for a moment until an unobstructed doorway came into view. I hurled myself inside, slamming the door behind me.

Light filtered through the window, and I raced forward, desperate to get out of the building. My hands scrabbled over the sill, seeking a lock. There was none. The glass was a solid pane of tempered glass, and my heart sank. I was going to have to break it open. But with what?

I spun around, taking in the meager contents of the room. The office was empty except for a desk and filing cabinet. I lurched toward the metal filing cabinet, already reaching for the top drawer. I could use it to break out the glass, then climb out the window. Grasping the handle I yanked as hard as I could—but the drawer refused to budge.

My mind spun wildly as I stared at it. I pulled again to no avail. It was locked. A frantic cry welled up as I tried the other three drawers with the same result. Smoke began to billow in under the door, the thick, dark air gathering near the ceiling.

Oh, God. I was going to die in here.

My eyes stung and my lungs felt tight. Every cell of my body screamed as I jerked on the filing cabinet. It rocked up an inch or two before falling back into place. Adrenaline caused my pulse to spike, and I shifted the cabinet again, aiming it toward the window. I shoved hard and the metal edge hit the glass. It spiderwebbed then gave, and a triumphant whoop burst from my lips as blessed fresh air swelled into the room.

Lightheaded from the smoke, I swung a leg over the sill. Two arms wrapped around me as I collapsed and everything went black.

EIGHTEEN

VAUGHN

Heart beating furiously, I stormed forward. My gaze slid to the man standing in the corner, typing something into his cell phone. His eyes snapped to mine as I entered, and his mouth parted to speak. I didn't give him a chance. "Get out."

He took a step forward as if to intercept me, but I was already focused on Sienna. She sat on the edge of the hospital bed, her face pale and marred with soot, eyes wide. I stopped a foot away, scanning every inch of her from head to toe. Her right hand was bandaged, and her feet were bare, but otherwise she looked to be unhurt.

"Can you stand?" I could feel the other man watching, but I tuned him out as Sienna slowly slid off the bed. Without her sky-high heels she seemed so much shorter—more vulnerable and fragile. My chest constricted as I peered down into those big blue eyes. "Are you okay?"

She nodded but didn't say a word, and I slid my hands onto her hips. A moment later she leaned into me, giving me all of her weight, and I pulled her into my embrace. Keeping one arm locked around her lower back, I buried my free hand in her hair as she tucked her face into my chest.

Her body shook but she didn't cry, and neither of us said a word for what felt like forever. I was acutely aware of the man leaving the room. I would have questions about that later, but all that mattered right now was her.

The silky curtain of hair tickled my skin, and I slid my hand down to cup the back of her neck. Her face lifted, and I brushed a lock of hair away from her cheek. "Don't ever scare me like that again."

Even though it was completely out of her control, she licked her lips and nodded. The gesture was a testament to how scared she was. The Sienna I'd met before never would have acquiesced to such a request. She'd have made that adorably offended face and told me to go to hell.

I cupped her face in my hands, sliding my thumbs over her cheekbones. She stood so close I could feel the faint trembling of her muscles, and I grasped her biceps to steady her. "Have you been cleared to leave?"

"Not yet." She lifted her bandaged hand. "The nurse is getting the discharge paperwork ready."

"Good." I nodded. "I'll take you home."

She opened her mouth to say something, but a masculine voice had both of us turning toward the doorway. The man I'd seen earlier stood there, brows raised as he studied Sienna. "Everything good in here?"

I barely resisted the urge to grab Sienna and pull her to me, to show him she was mine. Thankfully, I didn't have to. Sienna shuffled a bit closer and nodded. "I'm okay. Thanks, Ashton."

I settled a hand on her hip as I regarded the other man. "Were you with her?"

His gaze moved to mine and he nodded. "Yeah. We were just leaving TriStar when I noticed the fire."

Releasing Sienna for a moment, I extended a hand to him. "Thank you."

He searched my eyes for a second before slipping his palm into mine for a firm shake. I could see the envy there, the resentment at having Sienna come to me, and it filled me with a fierce satisfaction.

I released him then settled my arm around her waist once more as I directed my question to the man in front of me. "You spoke with the police?"

"I did, but only for a second," he replied. "I wanted to come with her, make sure she was okay."

"I'm glad you were with her. If there's anything else you can think of, let me know."

"Will do." His gaze moved back to Sienna. "Hope you feel better."

"Thanks." She offered a wan smile that didn't reach her eyes.

Our attention was splintered when a nurse entered the room a moment later, his gaze immediately flicking to me and taking in my uniform, the way I stood protectively close to Sienna. I didn't miss the way his eyes roved hungrily over her for a moment before he cleared his expression and pasted on a smile.

Jesus Christ. There was way too much testosterone in this room. I needed to get her the hell out of here before I said something I would regret. Actually, that was a lie. I wouldn't regret a damn thing. I had no problem making it very clear to both of them that if a man was going to be part of her life, it was damn well going to be me.

I had a feeling, though, that Sienna wouldn't appreciate it, and it was only that tiny prick of my conscience that stopped me from showing both men that she belonged with me.

The male nurse strode forward and passed a clipboard to Sienna. "I'll just need you to sign this for me."

Before she could move, I extracted the clipboard from his hand and held it steady for her so she could fill out the discharge paperwork. She signed her name with her left hand in an awkward, jerky motion, then directed her focus to the nurse. "Anything else?"

"Just this."

He held out a typed set of aftercare instructions, which I took, folding it up and tucking it into my back pocket. "Keep the bandage on for forty-eight hours, and no heavy lifting for at least a week."

"Okay." Her voice was small, timid almost, and it tore at me.

I squeezed her waist. "Do you have your shoes?"

"Right here."

Ashton bent and hooked his fingers inside the toes of her shoes, then held them out to me. I nodded my thanks as I took them, then knelt to place them on the floor at her feet. She settled one hand on my shoulder, and I grasped her hips to steady her as she stepped into first one shoe, then the other. I climbed to my feet and nodded to the others. "Thanks for your help. I'm going to get her home."

I tipped my head for Ashton to proceed us from the room, but he held out a hand. "Ladies first."

I couldn't tell if he was trying to be polite, or if it was a slight. At the moment, I couldn't bring myself to care. I gently nudged Sienna into motion, then stepped behind her, blocking her from Ashton's view.

Didn't matter that she was hurt; I knew exactly what he'd be looking at as she left the room, because I would have done the same thing. And the last thing I wanted was some other guy's eyes roaming her ass.

Sienna's steps faltered in the hallway, and I settled a hand low on her back as I gestured toward the elevators. "Down the hall on your right."

We made our way to the elevator, and I jabbed the down arrow to summon the car. It arrived within a few moments, and I guided her inside as the doors slid open with a soft whoosh.

I leaned against the railing as the car began its descent, and I watched Sienna in the mirrored reflection across from me. Her eyes were closed, and her head tipped drowsily to one side. "Tired?"

She lifted her face to meet my gaze, then gave a tentative nod. "Adrenaline is wearing off."

I offered a small smile. "We'll get you to bed so you can rest."

She shook her head. "You don't need to do that. I can…"

Her words trailed off as I took a step closer, closing the distance between us. "It's exactly what I need to do."

Big blue eyes blinked up at me, filled with fatigue and tinged with confusion. I wanted so badly to kiss her, but I knew she wasn't ready for that yet, either. I brushed my fingers along her forearm. "Let me help, Sienna. You don't have to do everything by yourself."

She nibbled her lower lip for a moment before finally nodding. "Okay."

It was little more than a whisper, but the single word caused my chest to fill with hope and relief. The tension I'd been carrying with me for the past hour began to melt away. She was okay.

I squeezed her wrist lightly before stepping away again to give her space. I knew Sienna well enough by now to recognize when she was ready to run. And this was one of those times.

The elevator dinged our arrival at the parking garage, and I gently propelled her forward, steering her toward my truck. Using the key fob to unlock the door, I held it open and supported Sienna as she lifted herself into the seat. Once she was settled, I closed the door and rounded the hood, then slid behind the wheel.

As I drove, I snuck peeks at her from the corner of my eye. Gradually, her lids lowered and her head rolled slightly to one side as she drifted off to sleep. Twenty minutes later, I pulled into my garage, then turned to look at her. She'd only just recovered from her fall after the car accident; now she had new scratches and bruises to match.

Protectiveness welled up inside me, urging me to reach across the console, pull her into my arms and never let go. She wouldn't appreciate the gesture—at least, not yet. Despite the fact that she continued to deny it, I knew there was a connection between us, something special that I wanted to explore.

Sienna didn't stir when I cut the engine, then rounded the truck to open her door. Her breathing remained deep and even as I reached over and released her seatbelt. I slid one arm under her thighs, the other behind her upper back and gently lifted her from the seat. Arms curled tightly around her, I was shocked at how light she was.

When Sienna stood toe-to-toe with me, she seemed larger than life. Her fiery demeanor made her look every inch of her five-foot-eight frame, like her spine was made of steel, and molten iron flowed through her veins. Now, though, exhausted and hurt, she seemed so small and fragile.

A fierce possessiveness rushed over me, and I tightened my hold. I never wanted to let her go. Sienna was always so strong, so determined to do things on her own. I admired the hell out of her for that, but I hated it at the same time. I saw how much it cost her to put on a brave face each and every day, and I wanted to take that burden from her—I wanted to keep her close and shower her with affection, show her how good it could be between us.

It wouldn't be easy, but nothing worth having was ever easily obtained. I wasn't sure why she couldn't open herself up, but we had plenty of time for that. I'd give her the time and space she needed while keeping her close, and I would break down her walls brick by brick.

NINETEEN

SIENNA

In my dream, I was floating. I was wrapped up tight, cocooned in warmth, the slight pressure against my skin tender and reassuring.

I snuggled closer, loving the sensation, rubbing my cheek against the soft material and breathing deeply. A delicious scent filled my nostrils, and contentment seeped into my bones like warm honey. Consciousness returned by increments, and I realized with a start that I wasn't floating —I was being carried.

My eyes flew open, and I blinked in confusion. My brain was still fuzzy from sleep, but that didn't stop the memories from pouring in—Boots's mutilation, the explosion at the office...

Oh, God. Had the man come to finish me off?

Panic exploded in my brain, and my fight or flight mechanism automatically kicked in. Before I'd even fully considered what I was doing, my brain sent the message to my limbs to run, and I instinctively started to struggle against my captor. Instead of releasing me, the man's hold tightened, sending my pulse galloping in my veins.

"Shh, honey, I've got you." A deep, masculine voice reached my ears, and a combination of confusion and relief rushed through me as I blinked up at Vaughn.

The vise around my lungs loosened, and I dragged in a breath. Right. I wasn't being abducted. I'd been taken to the hospital after the explosion and Vaughn had showed up, then offered to take me home. Or, rather, Eden's bed and breakfast since all of my things were still there.

I opened my mouth to speak, but Vaughn shifted me in his arms and I grasped at his shirt to keep from falling. He angled me sideways through the doorway and into the narrow hallway, and I forced myself to release my hold on him.

Inside the house, he carefully set me on my feet. Hands planted on my hips, he waited until I was steady before releasing me. "Good?"

I nodded, my gaze scanning the bare walls. "Where are we?"

"My place."

I jerked around. "What?" Why were we at his place?

Those silvery eyes stared intently into mine, studying me for several long seconds before he spoke. "How are you feeling?"

I notched up my chin. "It's just a few cuts. Nothing I can't handle." That wasn't entirely true, though. My throat felt dry and itchy from the smoke, and my voice sounded hoarse, even to my own ears. Fatigue pulled at my brain, and my muscles felt drained from the events of the day.

"I'm sure you can handle it," he said softly. "But you didn't answer my question."

No, I hadn't. Because I didn't dare open myself up to him. I was afraid if I told him how I felt—angry, confused...

scared—I would want to throw myself back into his arms. I couldn't allow that to happen. "I'm fine. I can take care of myself."

Being so close to him was messing with my head. I needed to find a place to stay. The obvious answer was back to Eden's place. She wouldn't mind if I rented a room for a night... or ten.

I also needed to call my father and let him know what had happened, but I assumed Vaughn had my phone. I wanted to have a plan in place before we spoke so he wouldn't try to cut his vacation short and convince me to come home.

"Where's my phone? I need to call Eden."

"Why?" He lifted a brow, and I glared at him.

"So I can stay at the bed and breakfast."

"You're not staying there." He shook his head.

Excuse me? I blinked at him. "Why not?"

"It's not safe. Not for you or her. Until whoever started the fire is caught, we can't afford to put anyone else in jeopardy." He met my gaze. "From here on out, you'll be staying with me."

No, no, no. That wasn't possible. This couldn't be happening. "I can't stay here. Eden will be wondering—"

He shook his head, cutting me off. "I texted her a little bit ago and told her what happened."

My jaw went slack. This man knew no bounds. "You can't just tell me what to do!"

His lips flattened into a firm line. "What would you prefer? That I send you back out there unprotected?"

I'd never seen him so angry, and his fierce expression stole my words. "Some psychopath has a hard-on for you, and you continue to throw yourself right in front of him. Goddamn it, Sienna, you're smarter than that."

Cold washed over my skin at his words, my pride stung. "I'm not nearly as stupid as you seem to think I am."

He growled, his pewter eyes glinting. "I never said you were stupid."

"You implied it." I spun away, intending to storm off, before I realized I had no idea where I was going. The living room seemed as good a place as any, and I stormed toward the window.

Staring into the dark glass, studying him in the reflection, I wrapped my arms around my waist. He was absolutely infuriating. He was sorely mistaken if he thought he could just snap his fingers and I'd jump to do his bidding.

Anger pulsed through my body, causing me to tremble from head to toe. I tightened my hold on my waist to control the spasms. The last thing I needed was for him to think I was scared and try to come to my rescue.

Again.

Although, if I were being totally honest, I *was* scared. The fire had been terrifying. And on the heels of Boots's death, I couldn't deny that someone most definitely was after me. Could it have been Calvin or Ashton? Both had been at the office yesterday when the explosion had gone off.

I shook my head. All that mattered right now was that I figured out where to go. I had no desire to go home, and I certainly couldn't stay here with *him*. As much as I hated to admit that he was right, I couldn't stay with Eden and potentially put her in danger. Which left a hotel. There were plenty of places to stay in Dallas, but it was nearly an hour away. I would prefer to be closer to home in case I was needed for anything.

"I can go to a hotel," I suggested. "And my father gets back in a couple of days. I could go to his place." Even as I said the words, I dreaded the idea of admitting defeat and slinking back to my father's house with my tail between my legs.

"You'll be safe here," he said, his tone brooking no argument.

"I don't have any of my things," I pointed out.

Vaughn sighed. "I'll have someone get your stuff from Eden's tomorrow. Tonight, you'll just have to make do with something of mine."

I glared at him. So much for his concern. "What about my things for work? My laptop and—"

He stared at me incredulously. "Your building was just blown up and you're worried about work? Jesus Christ." He scrubbed a hand over his face. "When are you going to realize how serious this is? You're not going to Eden's, and you sure as hell aren't going to work until we find this asshole."

Red exploded across my vision, and I sucked in a breath at his high-handedness. "You can't—"

"Damn it, Sienna. No—" He cut me off when I started to speak. "Just listen for once. I'm not here to control you. I know you think you need to be strong every second of every day but believe me when I say that I want to help. I only want what's best for you. I will do everything in my power to keep you safe, and I don't give a damn if you hate me for it, but I will *not* put you in harm's way."

I knew he would say anything to get me to acquiesce, but his words were so honest that I couldn't help the little thump my heart gave in response.

My stomach fluttered at his vehemence. He truly sounded concerned about my safety, and my annoyance began to fade. For a full minute we stared at each other, neither of us daring to speak.

I was too exhausted to argue with him. Besides, what he said was true—I knew I would be safe here. Despite his obvious disdain toward me, Vaughn would never let me get hurt. He'd saved me once already and had come to my aid twice since then. I knew he cared about my well-being. But that begged another question: did he care about me, or was he just doing his job?

Heat swept over my skin as I recalled the sight of him storming into my room at the hospital. I'd been trying not to think about it too much, but now I couldn't help myself. His expression was fierce, though I knew it wasn't directed at me. He'd held me close, much like he'd done the day of the car accident. His stormy gray eyes were violent as they stared into mine, searching for... something.

Don't ever scare me like that again.

What did he mean by that?

I'd apparently been silent far too long, lost in my own thoughts, because Vaughn's question startled me. "Are you hungry?"

I blinked at him and, as if on cue, my stomach growled. I placed a hand over my midsection as a small grin curled his lips. "I'll take that as a yes."

My stomach flipped for an entirely different reason, and a tingly sensation swept over me. God, he was so handsome. Deeply tanned from the sun, his dark skin made his silvery eyes stand out, looking even more captivating in the low light of the dimly lit room. His broad shoulders filled my vision, and my fingers itched to trace the muscles that seemed to be carved from stone.

Was it my imagination, or was that woodsy smell even more potent now? It made me lightheaded, and I grabbed the windowsill to keep from swaying on my feet. Or straight into his arms.

I cleared my throat, shoving all of the incredibly inappropriate thoughts away. "Now that you mention it, I am kind of hungry."

He nodded. "What did you have for lunch?"

"Um…" Belatedly, I realized I hadn't eaten anything all day. I'd been too sick over Boots this morning to eat breakfast, and after the ordeal at the office…

I licked my lips. "I haven't eaten today yet."

His handsome face formed a dark scowl. "No wonder you're dead on your feet. You need some carbs for energy."

"Oh, I shouldn't—"

His silver gaze snapped to me, cutting off my words. The heat of embarrassment swept over my cheeks. Derrick had always made me feel bad about eating any kind of bread or pasta, but he wasn't here now. And Vaughn was right—I needed something of substance.

I tipped my head his way. "I'm good with whatever. Thank you."

He studied me intently before nodding. "Come on. Kitchen is this way."

I settled at the table while he moved seamlessly around the kitchen, gathering ingredients and preparing the meal. "Anything I can help with?" I wasn't very good in the kitchen, but I felt the need to offer.

"No, thanks. But you can help yourself to a drink if you'd like one."

My mouth suddenly felt dry, whether from the earlier smoke or from being in such close proximity to Vaughn, I wasn't sure. I pushed from the table and glanced around. "Where are your glasses?"

He flipped open a cupboard and grabbed one, then passed it to me. My fingers grazed his as I took it, and I immediately turned toward the sink where I filled the glass with water. "Sorry, I don't have any sparkling water or anything fancy."

I wrinkled my nose as I rested a hip on the counter and regarded him. "Sparkling water is gross anyway."

A tiny smile teased his lips as he turned the ground beef in the pan. "I'm not a fan, either."

He didn't say anything else, and we descended into silence as I watched him add sauce and noodles to the pan. He covered it with a lid, then turned to me. His brows drew together at the sight of blood and soot streaked across my white top. "Do you want to change while we wait for the noodles to cook?"

Some of my earlier annoyance flickered to life, and the Devil on my shoulder prompted me to poke the bear. "I would love to, but..." I narrowed my gaze at him. "Someone wouldn't let me get my clothes."

Vaughn just stared back impassively. "I'll get your things tomorrow."

I rolled my eyes. "I still don't understand why we couldn't have just stopped there on the way."

He snorted. "I'm not that stupid. You think I was about to take you to the bed and breakfast so you could dig in your heels and refuse to leave?"

Manipulative ass. My annoyance turned to anger. "So, you basically kidnapped me and brought me to your house without my knowledge."

Something that sounded suspiciously like a growl welled up his throat. "That's hardly kidnapping. And I explained my reasons for doing so already."

He had, but my anger at the situation had yet to fade. "Fine. Where can I change?"

Wordlessly he led the way upstairs to a single bedroom. He pulled a fresh T-shirt and pair of sweats from a drawer and tossed them on the bed. "Dinner should be ready by the time you're done."

He closed the door with a snap behind him, and something inside me twisted. As much as I resented the situation, I did appreciate his help, and I mourned the loss of our momentary truce. It was my fault; I'd ruined the easy camaraderie with my snarky comments, but I hadn't been able to help myself.

Dropping to the edge of the bed, I buried my face in my hands. What was wrong with me? Why did I have to sabotage everything?

Part of me still wanted to throw myself into Vaughn's arms the way I had at the hospital and soak up every bit of strength and comfort those hard muscles had to offer. The man was potent, and I had to constantly remind myself to stay on guard around him. He ripped away my defenses much too easily, stared into my eyes and read what I felt in my soul.

I was just so... confused. Part of me wanted so badly to give in, but I wasn't sure I could trust him yet—or myself. He could be so high-handed sometimes, and other times he was so incredibly sweet. He'd done nothing but try to help, yet I continued to push him away at every turn.

Deep down, I still hurt. I wasn't sure I was ready to put myself back out there, even casually. My heart felt too fragile; Derrick's betrayal had been bad enough, but I'd never felt about Derrick the way I did about Vaughn. There was just something between us—chemistry, hormones, something—that made my body come alive.

Over the past few weeks, he'd somehow managed to chip away at the wall I'd built around my heart. And I was terrified that one day he would break through. I couldn't let that happen.

Every man in my life had tried to control me in some way. First my father, then Derrick. While my father was more outspoken and brash, I knew he had good intentions. Derrick, however, was much more stealthy in his attacks.

It seemed like no matter what I did, it was never good enough. Derrick refused to move in with me, stating that *only loose women moved in with a man before marriage.* He'd constantly undermined my confidence, telling me what I should wear or what I should eat. If I ate too much, he was worried I'd get fat. If I ate too little, he'd complain that I wasn't curvy enough. He'd somehow managed to twist me into knots until my confidence had all but leached away.

I understood now that it had all been a lie, just a way for him to feel better about himself. Likely this new woman—Veronica—wasn't the first woman who'd turned his head. Looking back, I could see more clearly the holes in his lies, and I felt sick to my stomach knowing how easily I'd been manipulated.

When I moved out of my father's house, I'd promised myself I wouldn't let a man dictate my choices ever again. And being here with Vaughn was like jumping right back into the frying pan. I wasn't naïve enough to believe he did this all out of the goodness of his heart. He would lure me in, make me trust him, make me believe he cared. Then... Then he would change.

I hated myself for feeling vulnerable and weak. I was just going to have to ignore the feelings he invoked, fortify the walls around my heart, and move on. I might be alone, but being with someone who didn't love me...

I couldn't allow that to happen.

TWENTY

VAUGHN

Her attitude hadn't improved. If anything, it'd gotten progressively worse since our argument nearly half an hour ago. Dinner was a quiet affair, Sienna sitting in stony silence across from me, picking at the noodles.

Dark circles ringed her eyes, and exhaustion pulled at her pretty features. Despite her obvious anger, something else sparked deep in her eyes, something that looked like... sadness? It was the same look I'd seen on our date, even before she'd been targeted by a crazy psychopath.

I couldn't figure her out. One minute she was soft and sweet, the next she was prickly as a hedgehog. Each time we took a step forward, she immediately took two steps back. What the hell had happened to make her so damn defensive?

Normally I would assume she just didn't like me. And I would have accepted that. But I'd seen the glimmer of attraction that day of the accident. I'd *felt* it. I had a feeling the answer was tied to her past; I just wasn't sure I'd ever have the chance to find out exactly what it was.

Sienna set the fork on the edge of her plate and peered across the table at me, pulling me from my thoughts. "Do you mind if I use your bathroom? I smell like smoke, and I'd like to clean up."

I tried but failed to repress the image of her standing naked in the shower from my brain. My tongue felt too thick for my mouth, and I stumbled over my words. "Are you supposed to...? I mean..."

I gestured hopelessly toward her bandaged hand, and she shrugged. "I'll keep my hand out of the water. I just want to take a bath and get the grime off."

I rubbed the back of my neck. "I, uh... don't have a bathtub."

Big blue eyes blinked uncomprehendingly. "What?"

I lifted one shoulder. "I'm not a bath kind of guy. I have a big shower, though."

"That would be great, thanks." She bit her lip. "Do you have a plastic bag or something to put over it to keep the bandage from getting wet?"

"Good idea." I dug in a couple of drawers before finally unearthing a plastic grocery bag, and I passed it to her. "Here you go."

She took it with her good hand, absently fingering the slippery plastic. "I was wondering... Um..." She swallowed hard, her gaze reverted on the bag in her hand. "Could you help wash my hair?"

There was no other explanation. The woman was trying to kill me. I cleared my throat. "Sure."

After I'd cleared the table, I led her into the bathroom, then turned on the water in the shower until steam rose into the air. She struggled with the hem of my oversized shirt, and I kept my eyes locked on the wall behind her as I helped strip it over her head, followed by the pair of sweats I'd loaned her. They were much too big, and she'd had to roll them several times to make them stay on her slender hips.

The sight of her half-naked made my mouth water. She stood there in her bra and underwear, looking like the most delectable thing I'd ever seen. She shifted uncomfortably and gestured at her underwear. "Should I...?"

"No." The word came out too fast, too firm, and she startled a little.

Christ. The last thing I needed was her naked anywhere around me. As it was, I seriously doubted I would be able to control my reaction to her. I stripped down to my boxers, then held the shower door open for her. She had wrapped the grocery bag around her arm, but she kept it out of the water as she angled her head beneath the showerhead, saturating the long blonde strands.

I stepped inside and closed the door, sealing the heat in, then retrieved the shampoo where it rested on the ledge. I squeezed a bit into my palm, then moved behind her, blocking her from the spray as I lathered the thick soap into her hair. The action was incredibly intimate, and the feel of the delicate strands slipping through my fingers had my cock thickening where it pressed against the seam of my boxers.

I could just imagine those silky, flaxen locks spread over my pillow, those sultry blue eyes staring up at me as I slid deep inside her. Jesus. I needed to get a hold of myself.

"Tip your head back," I murmured. She did as I asked, and I stepped out of the way, allowing the water to rinse off soapy bubbles from her hair.

I dropped my hands and stepped away, but she wasn't taking pity on me yet. She glanced over her shoulder at me. "Could you wash my back?"

Fuck my life.

I forced a stiff smile. "No problem."

I poured a bit of body wash into my palms then rubbed

them together. Her skin felt velvety soft beneath my touch, and she moaned a little as I rubbed her back and shoulders in small circles. The sound reverberated through the space, and it felt like every bit of blood in my body flooded straight to my groin.

Her head tipped slightly to the side, exposing the arch of her neck, tempting me to run my teeth along the sensitive flesh. I traced a line down her spine until my thumbs brushed the top of her panties. The two small divots in her lower back called to me, and I massaged them before sweeping my palms along the curve of her waist.

Soapy bubbles slid over her skin, and though the masculine scent should have turned me off, it didn't. Knowing that she smelled like me made me harder than ever.

All of a sudden, Sienna stepped backwards, her body bumping into mine. I quickly grasped her hips and angled my body away so she wouldn't feel my erection pressing into her bottom. I thrust her away and let go as if the heat of her flesh had scalded me. "Can you handle the rest?"

The words came out more gruffly than I intended, and Sienna stiffened. "I'll be fine."

Without another word, I escaped from the shower, grabbing a towel from the cabinet before making a beeline for the bedroom.

I was going to hell. My dick was hard enough to pound nails, compounding the guilt already throbbing through my veins. Sienna was in a bad place, but here I was, getting turned on by the sight of her naked. Or mostly naked. I didn't think I could handle any more. If she asked me to help her dress I was going to cry.

As soon as she went to bed I was going to need to take a shower myself so I could work off the tension building in my muscles. Being so close to her was a serious strain on my resolve not to touch her. I wanted to push her up against the wall and kiss that sassy mouth, throw her over my shoulder and carry her to bed, then slide between those gorgeous legs.

But I would be the worst kind of asshole to take advantage of her like that. She needed help, she needed my protection, and I was going to make sure she was safe. Regardless of how much I wanted her. And if I needed another reason to keep my hands to myself, there were the giant red flags she was waving in my direction. She obviously wanted nothing to do with me.

My dick was still hard, and I grimaced as I quickly toweled off and yanked on a pair of boxers. The water in the bathroom cut off just as I finished dressing, and I set out an extra set of clothes for Sienna.

When she emerged from the bathroom a few moments later, she was mostly dry except for her hair, and water escaped from the long strands, dripping onto her shoulders and sliding down to the towel where it was wrapped around her breasts.

Heat swept through me as I stared at her. I wished I could peel the towel away, strip off the skimpy underwear, touch and taste every inch of her. Maybe it was just my imagination, but I could smell the soap even from here, and my cock thickened again.

Shoving the thought away, I gestured toward the clothes. "I put some fresh clothes out for you. Do you need help, or are you good?"

"I think I can handle it." She stood there, arms banded around her middle, looking incredibly vulnerable and unsure. Did she want me to take care of her? Something in her voice told me yes, but I wasn't sure. One second I thought we seemed to be making progress, the next she was the cold woman from the restaurant.

I watched her from where I stood next to the bed,

debating my options. I thought—I knew—I'd felt a spark between us, but maybe she wasn't ready to admit it. Or maybe she was an incredibly good actress, and I was reading more into it than was there.

Regardless, I did care about her, and I wasn't going to let her get hurt. She already meant too much to me, and I couldn't—wouldn't—let that happen.

TWENTY-ONE

VAUGHN

I approached slowly, keeping my steps measured and even, my gaze locked on her face the entire time. Her body tensed even as her lashes fluttered. It was almost like her body couldn't help but react, though her mind told her she shouldn't. One day I swore I would figure her out.

Sienna bit her lip. "What happens tomorrow?"

Tomorrow I was going to find out who the hell was after her, and why. Then I was going to make his life a living hell. "I'll take care of that."

She met my gaze and held for a moment before nodding. "Okay."

I squeezed her shoulder. "I'll be in the living room if you need me."

Her eyes darted toward the bed before meeting mine again. "You're not...?"

Was that disappointment or relief? I couldn't tell. "I'll be right downstairs." I shot her a tight smile. "Try to relax and get some sleep."

I left the bedroom, closing the door behind me, then dug my phone from my back pocket. Even though Sienna was safe here, her wounded hand would hamper her ability to take care of herself. And, if I were being honest, I didn't want to risk leaving her alone. I didn't think anyone would break into a cop's house to get to her, but I made it a point to never underestimate someone's stupidity.

I called in a favor for tomorrow, asking my mother to watch over Sienna while I was at work. Sienna's clothes were dirty and bloody, but I knew she'd be more comfortable in her own things instead of my sweats, so I threw them in the washer. In truth, I did feel a little bad for not getting her things from Eden's. But I wanted her here, under my roof, where I knew she was safe.

It was a little crazy to think that she was in my house. My gut tightened at the knowledge. She seemed so close, yet so far away. I reveled in those rare moments when she let her guard down and let me in. Unfortunately, they were few and far between. But Sienna was definitely worth it, and all I could do was be her shoulder to lean on until she trusted me enough to truly open her heart.

The washer finished its cycle, and I hung her clothes up to dry before settling down to sleep. My couch was comfortable but too small, and my legs ached from the cramped position. Overhead, I heard the soft scuffle of footsteps as Sienna settled in for the night. I closed my eyes but sleep refused to come.

Nearly an hour passed before I heard the footsteps resume. My eyes popped open, and I stared at the ceiling. I could practically see her pacing the bedroom, tense with anxiety and unable to sleep.

Should I go to her or not? I knew how difficult this was for her. I probably wasn't her favorite person at the moment, but I was the only anchor she had in this violent storm. Trying not to think too much about what I was doing, I pushed from the couch and climbed the stairs. I found myself in front of my bedroom door a moment later, staring at the slab of wood, a strange mix of sensations welling up in my chest.

I lifted my hand to knock just as the door swung open. Sienna's eyes flew open wide, and she let out a little squeak of surprise. "Vaughn!" She pressed a hand to her heart. "You scared me."

"Sorry." I rested my hand on the door frame. "I heard you moving around up here and just wanted to make sure you were okay."

She wrapped her arms around her waist and shifted uncomfortably from foot to foot. "I'm okay."

"You sure?"

"Yeah." She bit her lip and glanced toward the bed. "I should probably..."

She didn't move, though, and I studied her. "Want to talk about it?"

She shook her head, sending the long blonde strands tumbling around her shoulders. "No. I just... I can't seem to relax."

"That's understandable. You've been through a lot recently."

Nearly twenty seconds passed before she finally answered. "I just wanted to say thank you. For everything." She gestured between us. "I know we got off on the wrong foot, but I really do appreciate everything you've done for me."

I opened my mouth to tell her it was my job, but that was a lie. I wouldn't have let just anyone stay here, and I sure as hell never would have shown up at the hospital the way I did for anyone else. "I don't mind. I wanted to help."

She nodded self-consciously, her fingers drumming a nervous rhythm against her elbow as she lifted her gaze to mine. "Um... Do you want to come in?"

I stared at her for a second, weighing her words. Did she even know what she was doing to me? From what I knew of Sienna, the blush staining her cheeks told me she was only asking out of dire need, and I couldn't find it in me to refuse her. "Sure."

She backed away, keeping a healthy distance between us as I moved into the room. I took a seat at the foot of the bed, pulling one leg up as I turned to face her. Sienna sat a few feet away, legs curled to the side, and she pulled the sweatshirt tighter around her. Not for the first time, I wished I could read her mind. She seemed so closed off sometimes, and I couldn't help but wonder what had caused it.

After our failed date last week, I'd basically resigned myself to never seeing her again. But things had a funny way of working out, and fate was apparently conspiring to throw us together at every turn.

I could have asked Finn about Sienna's history, but I wanted her to open up to me. I wanted to hear it from her. I couldn't come right out and ask why she was so uptight, so I tried another tack. "How long have you been a realtor?"

Her gaze flicked to mine. "About four years."

"How old are you?"

She narrowed her eyes playfully. "A lady never tells."

I chuckled, and she smiled. "No, really. I'm twenty-six. How old are you?"

"Thirty-two."

She nodded a little and plucked at the hem of the sweatshirt. "How long have you lived in Cedar Springs?"

"All my life."

Her eyes flared wide with surprise. "I'm sorry, I didn't realize..."

I wasn't surprised she didn't know that. We came from entirely different walks of life. Sienna's father was one of the wealthiest men in town; my mother worked as a maid for men like him.

"It's no big deal. What did you do before you were a realtor?"

"I actually studied law."

My brows lifted. I knew she was smart, but I hadn't expected that. "You didn't like it?"

"I tried it for a while, but..." Her gaze dropped and she gave a little shrug. "I ultimately settled on realty. I'm actually up for a promotion."

I sensed there was more to the story, but I didn't want to press her. "Good for you," I murmured. "I'm sure you'll do great."

"Thanks." A tiny smile curled her lips, and her cheeks turned a delicate pink.

Everything about her fascinated me. I found I wanted to know everything there was about her. I shifted on the bed, lying down next to her and popping my head on my hand. "What else?"

Her gaze lifted to mine. "What do you want to know?"

"Everything."

The flush tingeing her cheeks intensified, but she slowly began to relax, mimicking my pose as she lay down next to me. "I'm a terrible cook," she admitted. "Like, really bad. I eat cereal most of the time or pick up food from the diner."

I laughed. "I wasn't very good when I first started out, either. But it's not so bad once you get used to it."

Talk turned to music and movies until her voice cut off and her eyes drifted shut. Careful not to wake her, I reached over and shut off the lamp, then stretched back out on the bed. For some inexplicable reason, I wasn't ready to leave her just yet. She lay next to me, like it was right where she belonged. Right where we both belonged.

TWENTY-TWO

SIENNA

I dreamed of Vaughn. My subconscious was apparently working overtime, because the images flashing through my brain were downright torrid.

I imagined his arms wrapped around me, his scent swirling on the air and stirring the embers of desire to life as he carried me up the stairs and into the bedroom. He settled me in the middle of the large mattress then crawled over me, his mouth and hands exploring every inch of my body. He kissed me slow and deep, each press of his lips against mine filled with possessive intent.

And I loved it.

For once I was able to let go and just feel. I didn't have to worry about rejection or having my heart broken or any of the myriad insecurities that plagued me. The walls I'd kept around my heart crumbled to dust under his touch, and I reveled in the way he made me feel cherished. Desired. Loved.

I didn't get to the good part. The images faded away as

the buttery glow of dawn penetrated my eyelids. I squeezed them shut, determined to hold onto the lingering pleasure for just a few more moments. Reluctant to leave the dream behind, I hovered on the cusp of sleep, Vaughn at the forefront of my mind. He was warm, soft and solid at the same time, and he made me feel... amazing. Even if it was just pretend.

I inhaled deeply, and his deliciously woodsy scent filled my nostrils. I wondered what it said about me that I smelled him, even in my dreams. Pushing the thought away, I yawned and snuggled closer to the source of the warmth—then froze.

Trepidation slithered down my spine as my eyes flew open. My nose was pressed against Vaughn's ribs, my right hand splayed over the taut muscles of his stomach. Ever so slowly, not moving a muscle, my gaze slid over his torso, watching it rise and fall on deep, steady breaths.

I lifted my head to glance at his face, and relief rushed through me when I found his eyes closed. Thank God. He was still asleep. One hand was tucked under his head while the other rested on his stomach, just millimeters from my own.

I closed my eyes tight, a grimace pulling at my lips. What the hell was wrong with me? He'd been a perfect gentleman, and I was practically feeling him up while he slept. Carefully shifting my weight, I removed my hand from his torso and edged away from him.

I had one foot off the bed when a low rumble from behind halted me in place. I tossed a look over my shoulder in time to see Vaughn stretch, his shirt riding up and revealing several inches of perfectly toned, deeply tanned flesh. My gaze snagged on the twin rectangular groupings of muscles, and my mouth went dry. My fingers twitched with the urge to trace them, and I curled my hand into a fist.

"Hey." At the sound of his deep voice, still raspy with sleep, my gaze flew to his face. Those icy eyes studied me intently, and I felt heat climbing into my cheeks.

I swallowed hard to clear my throat. "Hey."

"Sleep okay?"

The burning embarrassment intensified at the memory of being pressed up against him, and I managed a jerky nod. "Yeah."

"Want some coffee?"

God, yes. "That would be great, thanks."

I needed to get out of this room, away from his bed, before I did something completely reckless, like throw myself at him.

Would he even want that? I wanted to believe he did, especially after the way he'd stormed into the hospital room last night looking like he wanted to tear something—or someone—to pieces with his bare hands. Though his initial demeanor had been gruff, he'd obviously been worried about me. But worrying over someone was completely different than caring for them, let alone desiring them.

There were times that I thought I'd seen something more. Like the day of the accident. I swore I'd felt something crackling between us when he'd lifted me onto the car and stared deep into my eyes. I'd never been more tempted to kiss a man in my entire life. There was something in his expression, a dark glint in his silvery gaze that stirred my soul and twisted my stomach into knots.

But did he feel it, too?

He'd brought me to his home so I would be safe. The feel of his strong arms wrapped around me as he'd carried me inside tickled my brain and sent a little thrill of awareness through me. He'd cooked dinner, helped me shower... He'd even offered me his bed while he'd moved to the couch. And when my mind whirled restlessly, making me edgy and nervous, he hadn't hesitated to lie down next to me so I would fall asleep.

But he hadn't tried to kiss me. Or hold me. Or give any kind of indication that he was attracted to me. Hell, he probably wouldn't have even gotten this close to me if I hadn't asked him to.

Of course, that was my fault. Every time he got too close, I pushed him away. Terrified of being hurt again, I'd held myself back and built up the wall around my heart. Somehow, Vaughn had gotten past that. It was so ironic considering our disastrous first date. I never would have guessed he'd be the man who would touch my heart, but his actions over the past few days showed me exactly the kind of man he was—reliable and protective, strong and unyielding.

I'd never been into the alpha type before, but there was something about Vaughn that drew me to him. Part of it was because I felt safe with him. But more than that, I was comfortable around him. I didn't have to put on a show and pretend to be perfect. He'd seen me at my worst, yet he continued to stand by my side when I needed a shoulder to lean on.

I didn't like feeling helpless, but with Vaughn it was different. I couldn't explain why, but I didn't mind feeling vulnerable around him. He seemed to know when to push and when to back off, and the fact that he could read me so well was as reassuring as it was unsettling. I wished I knew how he felt, but I was reluctant to ask.

If he really wanted me, wouldn't he have made a move by now? I'd never met a man who controlled his emotions as well as Vaughn did. It made it nearly impossible to tell whether he was attracted to me the way I was to him. And that was the scariest part—I actually *wanted* him to make a move.

I should have pulled on my big girl panties and asked... I just wasn't sure I could handle being shot down again.

I slid from the bed, sneaking another peek at Vaughn as he did the same, hoping for another tantalizing glimpse of flesh. Unfortunately, his shirt stayed in place as he climbed from the bed, then gestured for me to precede him.

I traipsed downstairs, feeling the phantom sensation of his eyes on me the whole way. I made it to the kitchen first and made a beeline for the coffee pot in the corner. Vaughn held out a container of coffee as I flipped the switch to turn it on. "Should you be doing that?"

My hand actually felt a lot better today, and I stretched my fingers as if to prove it to him. "I'm good. I can handle the coffee."

A look of mild concern shadowed his eyes as he passed the container to me. I bit back a smile. It was kind of sweet how he was always checking on me, making sure I was okay. It made me feel even worse about the way I'd reacted last night.

I measured the scoops and poured in fresh water, then started the cycle. The potent scent filled the air, and I briefly closed my eyes. Though I was normally a tea kind of girl, there was something so incredibly fortifying about the smell of freshly brewed coffee.

The sound of cabinet doors closing drew my attention, and I swiveled toward Vaughn as he set two mugs on the counter. As soon as the coffee pot completed its cycle, I filled one mug then passed it to him. My fingers brushed his, and the contact sent a warm tingle down my spine.

Holding the mug in front of me, I glanced over at Vaughn. "I owe you an apology. For last night. And... before."

He shook his head. "It's no problem."

He didn't say anything else, and several minutes passed

in awkward silence, both of us sipping our coffees, but neither of us knowing exactly what to say. Finally, Vaughn cleared his throat. "I was hoping to ask you a few questions about last night."

I met his gaze and tipped my head to the side in question. "I told Officer Mackenzie everything last night."

He gave his head a little shake. "I'd like to check again, just to be sure. Sometimes details come back to you after your mind has had a chance to settle down."

That wasn't what I wanted to hear. In fact, the last thing I wanted was to deal with that this morning. I remembered every detail of the explosion yesterday—the sounds, the smells, the way the glass had cut into my hands and the pain searing my lungs. Those things were etched on my brain, but I knew nothing else.

I shrugged helplessly. "I don't know if I'll be able to help, but I can try."

"Better than nothing."

I turned to dump the remainder of my coffee, then left the mug on the mat to drain. I started to take a step backward when I collided with a hard body. The shock of having Vaughn so close threw me off balance, and I sucked in a breath.

For a second, neither of us moved. He was so close I could feel every inch of him from his large feet brushing mine to the broad chest pressed against my back. He felt so damn good, so solid and strong. I wanted to lean into him, absorb his strength and warmth.

So I did. Before I could think better of it, I reached backward, my fingers curling into the flesh of his hard thigh.

Vaughn jerked at the contact, and my cheeks flamed. "I-I'm sorry. I thought..."

I trailed off, mortified. I couldn't believe I'd done that. Taking a tiny step forward, I attempted to pull away from him, but he caught my hips in his two huge hands, halting my movement. Trapped between the counter and his huge body, I couldn't move an inch.

He dipped his head, so close I could feel his lips graze my ear as he spoke. "You thought what?" His voice was husky and deep, and it sent goosebumps sweeping along my flesh.

I bit my lip. Did I risk telling him? My heart twisted in my chest. If I brushed it off, I could still escape unscathed. But part of me wanted to know how he really felt. Was he attracted to me, too? Or was this just a job for him? Was he only looking after me because of what had happened yesterday?

"I was just wondering... I mean..." I stuttered over my words awkwardly, every cell of my body flaming with embarrassment.

His thumbs swept in gentle arcs over my lower back, causing me to shiver. "Tell me."

My heart threatened to beat out of my chest, and I swallowed hard before tentatively speaking. "I wasn't sure if you... wanted me."

His fingers curled into my hips. "You think I don't want you?"

I sucked in a breath as he pulled me flush against him, the ridge of his erection sliding between the cheeks of my bottom. My breath suspended in my lungs as his right hand slid around my front and splayed over my stomach, the slight pressure of his touch keeping us sealed together.

"You're all I can think about." His other hand coasted up my ribs then cupped my breast. My head dropped back to his shoulder as I arched into him. His mouth found the curve of my neck, and he left a trail of open-mouthed kisses in his wake as he trailed up the side of my throat. He gently bit down on the tender flesh, and desire coursed through my body, turning my legs to jelly.

"Christ, Sienna. You've been driving me crazy since the second I saw you."

I turned my head, and his mouth came down hard on mine. A sensation I'd never experienced rippled through me as his mouth slanted over mine. People talked about fireworks; this was different. Better. Stronger. The ground beneath my feet seemed to shift and shudder, and everything else disappeared until it was just the two of us.

I swayed and stumbled as he spun me toward him, and he yanked me against his chest. "I've got you," he murmured between kisses, his lips leaving my mouth to trail over my jaw and down my neck.

My head dropped back, giving him carte blanche, and I curled my fingers into his biceps as I fought to stay upright. Everything about him addled my senses; the taste of him made me so dizzy I could barely see straight. His hands slid downward, cupping my bottom before dragging me up his body and into his arms.

"Vaughn!" He latched onto my neck, and my vision blurred again. "What... what are you doing?"

"Kissing you," he returned before continuing his assault.

"Put me down," I complained without heat. "I'm too big."

He bit the space at the base of my neck, then licked the spot. "You're perfect."

A shudder rippled through my body. I felt hot all over, achy and tense, like my skin had shrunk two sizes. "I'm too tall."

"I love that you're tall. Means I don't have to bend halfway over to kiss you." He attacked my lips again, and I melted into him.

No one had ever picked me up before, let alone held me like this. His huge arms wrapped under my bottom made me feel dainty and desirable, and I shifted my hips. I wiggled against him, pressing my core against his erection until I felt the huge, hard head press at my entrance. I wanted him naked, wanted to feel his hot, hard flesh beneath my fingertips.

Shifting slightly, I managed to work my good hand between our bodies. A delicious rumble of sound broke from his throat as I cupped him through his sweats. He swelled under my touch, thrusting slightly into my palm, and sparks ignited in my belly.

"Fuck." He nipped my lower lip. "We should stop."

"Why?" Try as I might, I couldn't summon a single reason to not continue exactly what we were doing. I rocked my core against his pelvis, and he growled.

"I want you in bed the first time we have sex." He kissed me again, harder and more deeply than before. "And I need a hell of a lot more time to do it."

A whimper escaped as his erection nudged my folds again, covered only by the thin material of his sweats. "Vaughn... Please..."

An agonized groan left his mouth as he pulled away. "You have no idea how much I want to continue this." His hand fisted in my hair, forcing me to meet his gaze. "I've been waiting so damn long for you, but I don't want it to be like this. Not here, honey. Not like this. If you still want this later, I'll take my time, make it right."

"When?" I practically panted the word.

"Tonight." He kissed me again. "All night."

I pouted. "Okay."

He growled as he set me on my feet. "You better go before I change my mind."

I peered up at him, my mind still hazy with lust. "And if I don't?"

He gripped my chin and kissed me hard. "Trust me. I'll make it worth your while."

Though part of me was disappointed, I knew it was the right thing to do. Vaughn needed to get to work, and I had a statement to make. Sex on the kitchen table was most definitely not on the docket today. Still, I felt the irrational need to extract his assurance. "Promise?"

Stormy gray eyes stared into mine, seeming to look right into my soul. "You never have to question my word, Sienna. I always mean what I say."

It was as if his words had reached deep inside my chest and wrapped around my heart. I realized, in that moment, I did trust him—I trusted his word, trusted him to keep me safe. And that was the moment I fell a little in love with him.

TWENTY-THREE

VAUGHN

Though Mac had questioned Sienna briefly yesterday afternoon, I had a few questions of my own. "Walk me through what happened yesterday."

"I decided to go into the office for a bit—" I lifted a brow her way, and she had the good grace to blush.

"I needed something to do," she said quietly. Her gaze dropped to her hands, which fidgeted nervously in her lap. "I couldn't just sit around and think about what had happened."

I couldn't blame her. If I were in her shoes, I probably would have done the same thing. But she'd been in the office alone, completely without protection, and I had a huge issue with her putting herself in danger. I'd made my point abundantly clear last night, and she seemed to understand, because she lifted her regretful gaze to mine.

"Ashton had been pressuring me to get the paperwork signed, and I just wanted to get it over with. Calvin was in the office when I got there, and—"

"Calvin?"

"Christensen. He works with me."

Committing the name to memory, I gestured for her to continue. "I finished the deal with Ashton and saw him out. I noticed then that Calvin had left, so I locked the door. I was on my way back to my office when the window in the office to my left shattered. I didn't realize it was an explosion at first—not until I saw the flames."

She shuddered a little, and a wave of fury swept over me. She easily could have been killed; she was damn lucky she'd walked away with just a few minor cuts and bruises. It made the situation all the more dire, and I wanted to find the asshole who'd tried to hurt her.

"Molotov cocktail." She tipped her head in question, so I clarified. "That's what was thrown into the office. When you let Ashton out, did you see anyone else hanging around?"

She shook her head. "Not that I know of. I actually wondered if..." She bit her lip and trailed off.

"It wasn't Ashton," I said, reading her mind. "We've got him on camera. He was in the parking lot taking a call when the building went up."

I was more than a little disappointed to learn that, though it didn't surprise me. The man had accompanied Sienna to the hospital, and I wondered if he had feelings for her. He might be an asshole of epic proportions, but he wasn't responsible for the fire—at least, not directly. I hadn't yet ruled out the possibility that he'd hired someone to do it so he could swoop in and rescue her. Which led me to my next question.

"Is there anyone else you can think of who might hold a grudge or want to hurt you?"

She bit her lip. "Well... Remember that promotion I told you about? Calvin Christensen is vying for the spot, too."

Just like that, the man jumped to the top of my list. "Tell me about him."

As Sienna explained how he'd been colder to her lately, more resentful, I watched the play of emotions on her face, those pretty lips.

Christ, she was beautiful. I could still taste her on my tongue, still feel every soft curve of her body. I'd known she was gorgeous before, but after that kiss this morning... Damn. All I wanted was to take her home, climb into bed and sink deep inside her.

My groin tightened, and I shifted in my chair. Fuck. I had way too much shit on my plate to be getting turned on right now. Sienna was depending on me to find out who the hell was stalking her, and I was going to do it if it killed me. Which might be sooner rather than later, because if I didn't get inside her soon I was going to lose my damn mind.

"That's enough for now." I stood, then escorted Sienna to the car.

She climbed in without fighting me—for once—and I headed toward a quiet community on the south side of town. The homes were older, but the neighborhood was quiet and the people were kind. I parked in front of a small yellow house, and Sienna scanned it before turning to me.

"Where are we?"

"My mom's place." I unsnapped my belt and tipped my head. "You'll be safe here with her while I'm at work."

Sienna's eyes flared wide with surprise when they landed on my mother. Almost as quickly as it had come, the expression bled away, replaced with her usual sweet smile. "Hi, I'm Sienna."

She didn't wait for me to introduce her, just moved forward and offered her hand. My mother slid a quick look my way before she smiled back and tentatively took Sienna's hand in her own for a brief shake.

I knew this was a shock to both of them; I'd deliberately neglected to tell either of them about the other. I suspected from the look my mother had just thrown my way how she felt about me dating a white girl. And Sienna... I'd wanted to see her true, unfiltered reaction when she saw my mother for the first time.

Born in Haiti, her skin was a rich brown, her eyes as deep as coffee. My heritage had shocked more than one woman I'd dated. I knew the contrast was shocking. Though my skin was light brown, most people assumed I was just tanned from the sun.

Instead of inheriting my mother's dominant dark features, I'd apparently taken after my father. The man had run off before I was born, and I didn't know much about him except that I'd inherited his tall stature and silvery eyes.

Several women I'd dated had taken one look at my mother's dark skin and practically bolted. I'd dated mostly black and brown girls, but I didn't seem to fit in anywhere. Knowing I was mixed was a gamble they apparently weren't willing to risk.

Over the last couple of years, I'd stopped trying so hard to find a life partner and decided to just have fun. But watching Sienna with my mother gave me hope. It was too early to tell for sure, but we'd see if they survived the day together.

My mother was my litmus test; if they didn't get along, it was game over. Not that I bowed to my mother's every wish, but I needed them to respect each other.

I hugged my mother and bent low to whisper in her ear. "Give her a chance."

She nodded and offered a tight smile. I didn't say anything else; nothing I said would alleviate her concerns. I would just have to see how everything played out between the two of them.

I hated to drop Sienna and run, but I didn't have an option. At least she would be safe here. Whoever had been watching her would expect her to go somewhere familiar, like her father's house or the bed and breakfast. No one would think to look for her here at my mother's house. Sienna and I weren't even dating—an issue I hoped to rectify in the near future.

I felt far too possessive of her, but I couldn't help it. I had never felt a connection like this with another woman. Sienna was so strong, so determined to do things on her own, but she was letting me in by increments. Watching her walls fall as she let down her guard sent a thrill through me. I knew she had been hurt in the past, and the fact that she trusted me to care for her made me feel damn near invincible. She'd put her faith in me, and I wouldn't let her down.

I turned my focus toward the case as I walked into the police department for the second time this morning. I knew Finn was following up on leads, and I hoped he had something substantial. I made a beeline for his desk, and found him sitting behind his computer, a mountain of paperwork beside him.

His tired gaze flicked to mine as I entered. "Hey."

I tipped my chin in greeting. "Any news on the fire at TriStar last night?"

Finn scrubbed his hands over his face before leaning back in his chair. "Fire inspector ruled it arson. Just like we suspected, someone threw a Molotov cocktail through one of the windows on the back side of the building."

Anger, slow and hot, slithered through my veins. "Any idea who?"

He shook his head. "Calvin Christensen was in the building when Sienna arrived. According to her statement, he was gone by the time she finished her meeting with Ashton Reeves."

Those two men were currently at the top of my suspect list. "Sienna told me this morning that she and Christensen are up for the same promotion at work. Could be something there. Also, Reeves went to the hospital with her," I replied. "I wouldn't put it past him to have done something like that so he could swoop in and play hero."

Finn nodded. "I put in a request to get the tapes from the business next-door. TriStar's DVR system was destroyed in the fire, but I'll send it out to see if we can get anything off the hard drive."

"What about Christensen?"

Finn lifted a shoulder. "We questioned the man last night. He says he went straight home alone, so there's no one to back up his alibi."

My eyes narrowed. "Can we talk to a neighbor, see if anyone saw him?"

"Mac is handling that this morning. Hopefully we'll have an answer soon."

I nodded, still not appeased. We needed to see exactly who was at the realty office last night. We really needed that footage. "Let me know when you get the tapes," I said. "I'd like to take a look at them, too."

Finn tipped his chin in acknowledgment. "I'll keep you posted."

I headed to my desk, furious that we didn't have a single lead. It shouldn't have been surprising; cases like these often took weeks to solve. But this was Sienna we were talking about, and I wanted to get it wrapped up sooner rather than later, so she was out of danger.

For the next hour, I tackled the paperwork on my desk until Finn appeared next to me. "Footage just came in if you want to see it."

Hell yes, I did. "I'll be right there."

I finished inputting the last of the information, then shoved my chair back and headed to the conference room. Inside, Finn had his laptop hooked up to the large monitor for better visibility. My knee jiggled anxiously as I waited for him to rewind to yesterday afternoon. Finally, around 3:45 we saw Sienna's car pull into the lot next to a small BMW.

"Christensen's car," Finn pointed out.

I nodded, my gaze sweeping the screen for anything that might jump out at me. Fifteen minutes passed before another car pulled up, a Mercedes this time. I assumed it was Ashton, and my theory was confirmed thirty seconds later when he rounded the hood and entered the building.

Every cell of my body was tense as I watched the screen. In the periphery, people made their way up and down the sidewalks and through the adjacent parking lots of other businesses. No one looked out of place; no one appeared to have any sort of malintent. Though a few people passed TriStar, none of them slowed. None of them gave it any undue attention.

Five minutes after Ashton entered, the door swung open again, and Calvin Christensen stepped out. He closed the door behind him, then took a moment to lock it. His eyes were glued to his phone as he rounded the building and climbed into his BMW. He pulled out of the parking lot a moment later, heading toward the west side of town where he lived.

Finn and I both remained quiet as we watched the tape play out. Ashton exited the office less than ten minutes later and cut across the sidewalk toward his car. Though I couldn't see her, I imagined Sienna locking the door before going back to her office. Ashton climbed into the front seat of the Mercedes but didn't leave.

My eyes narrowed as I watched him pull out his phone

and apparently take a call. One minute passed, then two. I risked a glance at the timestamp in the lower corner of the screen, and I knew we were getting close. Ashton was still in his car, and no one else was visible in the parking lot of the realty office. The angle of the camera wasn't great, and we didn't have a clear view of the back window where the bomb had been thrown in.

I waited, watching, anticipation zinging through my veins. Ashton reversed, then started to pull out onto the main drag just as a window cracked. Though I was ready for it, it still caught me off guard.

Sienna's face appeared in the space, and the Mercedes whipped to the side of the road. Ashton clambered out at a dead run, already reaching for Sienna as she swung one leg over the sill. He scooped her up just as her body went limp, then carried her off screen, far away from the fire.

I couldn't help the flicker of jealousy I felt at seeing her in another man's arms, but I appreciated the fact that his actions more than likely saved her life. I didn't know whether I was relieved or disappointed that Ashton wasn't responsible.

Finn rubbed his chin. "Well, shit. Rules him out."

"But not Christensen," I said, glancing again at the timestamp. I pointed to the screen. "Rewind that."

When I saw Calvin leaving the lot, I made a mental note of the time. Just over thirteen minutes had passed since Calvin had allegedly left. It would have been easy enough to leave, park elsewhere, then double back. We needed to get a glimpse at the back of the building.

I glanced at Finn. "What about the back window? Anyone have eyes on that?"

"We're working on it," he replied. "The person working yesterday didn't know how the setup worked, so we're waiting on the owner."

A frustrated sigh escaped. I hated waiting on people. The footage continued to roll on the screen, and I watched idly as I racked my brain, trying to figure out the person's motive. According to Sienna, she and Calvin were vying for an important promotion.

Removing her from the picture would accomplish that goal, but if it was him, he wasn't very smart. It wouldn't look good for him to have been caught burning down his place of employment. Stranger things had happened though, I supposed.

Movement on the screen captured my attention, and I jerked upright in the seat. "Did you see that?"

I wasn't even entirely sure why it caught my eye—maybe because I'd been replaying every moment with Sienna recently. "Rewind that again."

Finn hit the button, and the footage reversed. "Right there."

The motion on screen resumed its normal pace, and I waited anxiously for it to appear. The car entered the screen from the right, headed down Main Street away from TriStar, and I gestured at it. "Pause that."

The screen froze, and I glanced at Finn. "Recognize that car?"

He enlarged the image and his eyes widened a fraction. "Holy shit. Is that...?"

The car was the exact color, make, and model as the one that had sideswiped our vehicles on the side of the road last week. Was it a coincidence? "It had a plate this time," I said warily.

Still, I had a bad feeling churning in my gut. Finn pulled up the LEDS database and typed in the plate number. I stared at the car, every instinct screaming that it was somehow involved.

TWENTY-FOUR

SIENNA

She hated me. Vaughn had disappeared out the door nearly an hour ago, yet his mother hadn't said more than a few words to me. Despite me trying to make small talk, she'd given me a bland smile and went about her day.

I glanced around the room from my spot on the couch, taking in the pretty caramel-colored leather furniture and newer flatscreen TV mounted to the wall. The place was tidy aside from a handful of knickknacks placed on the end tables and a beautiful antique-looking curio cabinet. Pictures filled an entire wall, and I rose to take a closer look.

From the frames, a young Vaughn stared back at me. His eyes were unmistakable, his grin infectious, and I couldn't help but smile as I studied each photograph. Sometimes he was alone; other times, he was photographed with his mother. But never his father. In fact, I didn't see evidence of the man anywhere in the house. Vaughn hadn't mentioned it, but I assumed his parents were divorced, and had been for quite a while.

Seeing his mother for the first time had caught me off guard. I'd never considered before that he might be mixed, but it made complete sense. His skin was a deep tan, which I'd attributed to the sun. I suddenly felt more than a little embarrassed that I hadn't considered the alternative. He must have thought I was a complete idiot.

The soft scuffle of footsteps behind me made me glance over my shoulder, and I smiled at Marjorie. I pointed to the pictures of Vaughn. "He was adorable."

She offered the same bland smile that didn't meet her eyes. "Would you like something to drink, Ms. Sienna?"

She obviously didn't want me here and resented my presence, but there was nothing I could do about that now. I was determined to get along with her for Vaughn's sake. "Please, call me Sienna. And I would love some tea if you have it, but I'm more than happy to get it myself."

Her gaze dropped to my injured hand. "I don't think my son would appreciate that. Besides, you're our guest," she said, grudgingly.

"Still, I hate to have you waiting on me," I said, keeping my voice soft and conciliatory.

She leveled a skeptical look my way, then finally nodded. She turned on her heel and headed toward the kitchen, and I quickened my pace to catch up to her. The hardwood floors of the living and dining rooms gleamed beneath my feet. It looked brand new, as did the Venetian tile in her kitchen. I glanced around the room, taking in the sparkling granite countertops and modern appliances.

"Your home is beautiful." It was small, but incredibly well-appointed. They were precisely the types of details I looked for when listing homes.

"Thank you." She gathered the teabags and sugar from the cabinet, then placed them on the table. "Vaughn has been slowly renovating for the past few years."

"He's done an amazing job," I replied, looking around.

"He's a good boy," she said as she put a pot of water on to boil.

I bit back a smile at her use of the word boy. Vaughn was hardly a boy. He was all man—and an incredible one at that.

"He's wonderful," I agreed. Two weeks ago, I never dreamed I would utter those words. Funny how things worked out.

For the first time, she seemed to give me her full attention. "Vaughn says you're a realtor."

I nodded. "That's right, I work for TriStar in town."

"Your face looks familiar. I must have seen it on your signs."

"Good possibility." I smiled. "My boss will be retiring in a few years, and if I'm lucky, I'll make partner so I can help run the brokerage."

Her brow furrowed the tiniest bit. "That's quite ambitious."

I couldn't tell if she was truly impressed or being condescending. I decided to take it as a compliment. "It's a lot of work," I agreed. "I'm looking forward to it, though. If things work out, I'll finally have something of my very own."

She studied me for a long moment, probably wondering why I even bothered to work. Before she could ask, I changed the subject. "Are you retired?"

She gave a brief nod. "I stopped working at Vaughn's request about five years ago."

I smiled at that. "He can be pretty persuasive."

A true smile tipped her lips. "Never could say no to that boy."

I understood that completely. Neither could I. "What did you do?"

Her gaze flitted away. "I was a maid for many years."

Oh. Now her reticence made more sense. I knew

firsthand how some of the wealthy people treated the help, and it wasn't good.

"Have you always lived in Cedar Springs?"

"Since I was a girl." She nodded. "I was born in Haiti but my father wanted a better life for us. We came to the States when I was five."

I knew I'd detected an accent earlier, but I hadn't been able to place it. "Was it a hard adjustment?"

She nodded slowly. "I didn't want to leave my friends or family, but I wanted my parents to be happy. My father met a businessman in Haiti who convinced him to come over. My father wanted us to fit in, so he took the man's last name —Allen—when we came across.

"We never had much money. No one wanted to hire a man with no skills, so my father worked any job he could find. We traveled all over the state until we finally made it to Cedar Springs. My father finally had enough money to rent a home, and he wanted us to have roots. My mother found work as a maid while my father continued to follow the crops. Eventually, I started helping my mother. Together, we managed to keep a roof over our heads and food in our bellies."

I couldn't begin to imagine. My family had always had money, and I couldn't remember ever wanting for anything. It was incredibly humbling to hear Marjorie's stories firsthand. I didn't think she would appreciate me saying that, though, so I changed the subject. "I'll bet you're enjoying your retirement, then. You certainly deserve it."

She smiled a little at that. "I would still be working if Vaughn hadn't begged me to stop. Now I just putter around the house all day. I wasn't sure what to do with my spare time, so I started making crafts to sell at the farmer's market."

"Really? What do you make?"

She shrugged self-consciously. "Wreaths, porch signs, and the like."

I'd noticed a few of the small plaques hanging on the walls, and I pointed to one. "You made that?"

She nodded, and I rose to get a better look. A scarf on the coat rack caught my attention, and I fingered the soft material. "This is beautiful. Where did you get it?"

She opened her mouth to speak but was cut off by the ringing of the phone. "I should get that."

I waved her off and turned back to the wall, inspecting the various pictures and wall plaques, listening with one ear as she answered the phone.

"Hello? No, no trouble." A pause. "Everything's fine," she replied, a tinge of exasperation in her tone.

I turned to meet her gaze and smiled when she rolled her eyes heavenward. "I will. Love you, too."

She gave her head a little shake as she hung up. "That was Vaughn calling to check in and make sure everything is okay."

"He's a good cop." He was a little overprotective, but I wasn't going to argue with that. I probably wouldn't be standing here right now if he weren't. "He's really helped me a lot."

Marjorie's expression sobered. "I'm sorry. That was thoughtless of me. I—"

"It's fine." I held up a hand to stall her apology. "I've been trying not to focus on everything too much either. Without Vaughn, I don't know what I'd do."

My cheeks heated as Marjorie's gaze slid over me. I hadn't exactly meant it to come out that way. It sounded like there was something going on between the two of us when there wasn't.

Yet, whispered my brain. My toes curled at the memory of the kiss we'd shared this morning. There was a definite chemistry between us, and I had a feeling that things would have gone a lot further had Vaughn not had to leave for work.

I felt like every emotion and thought was on full display, and I could only pray that Marjorie didn't read into it too much. Thankfully, the kettle on the stove began to whistle at that very moment, and she hustled forward to remove it from the burner.

She poured the hot water into the two cups on the table, then sank into a chair. I followed suit, my heart racing as I settled across from her. I'd never had a problem communicating with people. After all, I was a realtor—it was literally my job. But I was unaccountably nervous around Marjorie. I wanted her to like me, especially if things progressed between Vaughn and me.

She tipped her head my way. "You know, I don't think Vaughn ever told me. How did you two meet?"

I let out a little laugh. "It's kind of a funny story…"

TWENTY-FIVE

VAUGHN

Fury raced through my veins as I stomped away from the apartment building. If the motherfucker thought he could hide, he was dead wrong.

According to the system, the tan car was registered to Ryan Foley, who lived just outside of Dallas. Unfortunately, the man wasn't home. Maybe it was fortunate for him that he wasn't there, because I was ready to rip his head off his shoulders.

According to the manager, Foley was out of town and not expected to return for several days. His wife, however, was at work and due home later this evening. I'd left my number with the building manager, so hopefully I'd hear from her soon. Until then, I had to cool my heels.

We didn't have a warrant to enter the Foleys' apartment, but Gray was working on that to see if we could get a judge to approve it. I knew the evidence was circumstantial at best. The car that had sideswiped Sienna, though the same make and model, lacked the license plate tying it to Foley. So far there was nothing else to indicate that he was responsible.

Foley had lived in Dallas for nearly four years and seemed to have no direct connection to Sienna. Of course, that didn't mean he hadn't met or seen her at one point and developed some sort of fascination or obsession with her. It made me wonder how long he'd been watching her and what else we had missed.

It was ironic no one had noticed the vehicle if the driver was practically flaunting it. Was Foley stupid or just brazen as hell? By now we knew that the accident she'd been involved in was no accident at all, and Sienna was his target all along. The mutilation of her cat was incredibly personal, which bothered me immensely. It spoke of a man who held a deep-seated grudge and wanted to hurt Sienna.

According to the limited information we'd been able to dig up, there were no red flags in Foley's background. He'd studied computer science and obtained his bachelor's degree from the University of South Florida close to his hometown of Tampa before moving to Texas.

For the past three years he'd been working for a security company located in downtown Dallas. He had two moving violations, but nothing in his history that pointed to fits of anger or aggression. Not that that meant anything. Sociopaths were often adept at hiding their true emotions.

As I slid into the cruiser, I tossed one last glance at the apartment building. If the story about him being out of town was true, then he had to come back eventually. And I couldn't wait to speak with him in person.

My thoughts turned to Sienna as I headed back to Cedar Springs, and my body flushed with the heat of desire. That kiss this morning had been off the fucking charts. I'd never felt anything quite like it. Relief and a sort of triumph swept through me at the knowledge that she felt it, too. *Thank God.*

I knew she was still dealing with things from her past that she refused to talk about, but that was okay. She was coming around—fucking finally—and I couldn't wait to get her home tonight. She might still think all this was happening a little too soon, but not me. She was still fighting some demons, but I'd be right there beside her while she battled each and every one of them. Now that I'd had a taste of her, I wasn't letting her go.

Sienna had been a trouper over the past couple of days, and I headed toward the bed and breakfast to gather her things. In truth, I did feel bad that she didn't at least have her things with her. Of course, it wouldn't bother me in the least if she never wore another stitch, but I didn't think she'd appreciate me saying so.

Eden greeted me at the door, her eyes wide and anxious. "How is Sienna?"

"She's safe," I soothed her. "Until this is over, she's keeping a low profile."

She studied me for a moment before nodding. "After you called last night, I packed up all of her things. They're right here."

I followed her through the wide arched doorway into her office and gathered the suitcase and small duffel Sienna had packed two nights ago. "Thanks for doing this."

"No problem." She waved one hand. "Tell her to call me if she needs anything."

I wasn't going to involve Eden beyond what she'd already done, but I didn't say as much. "I'll let her know."

Eden must have guessed I wouldn't tell her where she was staying, or maybe she'd already suspected she would be with me, because her big blue eyes turned serious. "Don't let her get hurt."

I sensed a double meaning behind those few simple words, and I nodded. "I won't let anything happen to her. I promise."

With one last thank you and another promise to tell Sienna to call Eden, I climbed into my cruiser and headed into the station to wrap up for the day. Drew caught me as I walked past his desk. "How'd it go with Foley?"

"He's out of town on business, but his wife should be home from work soon. I'm hoping she can tell me something."

He nodded, a slight grimace pulling at his mouth. "I've got some bad news. The warden over at county just called about Adrian. He was stabbed this morning."

The shock of his words sent me reeling. "What the hell happened?"

Drew made a little face. "We're not sure yet. Apparently they were leaving the mess hall after breakfast when he was attacked by another inmate. The guy stabbed Hughes seven times, including once in the neck. They transported him to Mercy, but it doesn't look good."

"Jesus Christ." I shook my head. "What about the other inmate?"

"Transferred to solitary." Drew spread his hands wide. "And as far as how he got the weapon..."

Something clicked in my head. "You think it's an inside job. Just like Stratton."

Seth Stratton had escaped from the county jail, then abducted Drew's girlfriend, Emery, out of revenge for putting him away. It still wasn't clear exactly how he'd escaped, but we assumed someone inside had helped him out. The guards on duty at the time had been questioned, along with all other staff, but no solid evidence had ever been found. The jail supposedly had tightened its procedures—until now.

An escaped convict and an attempted murder on an inmate who'd just confessed to conspiracy was taking coincidence a little too far.

Drew's gaze darkened. "I don't want to think someone inside the jail is responsible, but..."

He trailed off. I understood exactly where he was coming from. There was nothing cops hated more than a dirty cop. It undermined the entire establishment and painted all of us in a bad light. If someone at the jail was, in fact, aiding the inmates, we needed to nip it in the bud.

"You talked to the warden?"

"Yeah." He nodded. "With everything going on I couldn't get many details, but he and Gray have a meeting set up for tomorrow."

Good. We needed to figure out what the fuck was happening and put a stop to it. "You on tomorrow?"

"Yep." His smile was lethal. "I wouldn't miss that for anything."

I tipped my head. "I'll see you in the morning."

Mind whirling, I headed to my mother's house. The closer I got, the more anxious I became. I knew my mother was wary of Sienna, but I wanted them to get along. They were the two most important people in my life, and I didn't know how I would ever choose between them.

Standing on the small front porch, I drew in a deep breath and braced myself before unlocking the door and stepping inside. The sound that greeted me nearly sent me stumbling backwards.

They were *laughing*.

And not Sienna's polite, sweet chuckle—but a deep, true laugh that reverberated through the house and wound its way through my heart. I followed the intoxicating sound toward the kitchen, where I found the two of them seated at the table, deep in conversation.

Sensing my movement near the doorway, Sienna's head snapped toward me, her eyes wide. The initial fear I'd seen in her expression quickly morphed to relief and... maybe pleasure?

"Hey." Her gaze roved over me before meeting mine again. "How was your day?"

Better now. "Same as usual." I glanced at my mother. "Everything good?"

"It was perfectly fine." She rose and pressed a quick kiss to my cheek. "Not even the slightest whisper that anyone knows she's here."

Exactly what I'd hoped to hear. My gaze slid toward Sienna. "Feeling okay?"

"I'm fine."

There was no missing the purple bags beneath her eyes, the exhaustion the emotional toll had taken on her. For the past few days. she'd been constantly on guard, and it was finally catching up to her. I could tell she was putting on a brave face, but I didn't comment on it. Once I got her to my place, I hoped she'd finally be able to relax.

"Smells good," I said to my mother, changing the subject.

She smiled as she stirred the contents of the skillet. "Made your favorite." She winked. "Sienna helped."

I turned to Sienna, who made a little face. "She's giving me way too much credit. I stirred it a few times. If she'd let me be in charge of anything else, it wouldn't be edible."

I grinned. The fact that she couldn't cook made her all the more attractive to me. I nodded toward my mother. "If you ever want to learn, she's the best."

My mother snorted. "You're biased."

"Maybe a little bit," I replied, shooting a wink toward Sienna and earning a sweet smile.

We traded small talk over dinner, and I reveled in the

way the two women talked openly, conversation flowing easily. Once Sienna was done, I gathered our plates and carried them to the sink. "Do you have everything?"

Sienna nodded, then glanced at my mother. "Would you mind if I used the bathroom?"

My mother made a shooing motion. "Go ahead."

As soon as Sienna disappeared I turned to my mother who met my inquisitive gaze, reading the silent question there. "She's not what I expected."

My heart constricted and my throat grew tight. They seemed to be getting along so well over dinner, and I'd hoped that they had found a sort of middle ground. I knew my mother was protective and didn't always take well to the women I dated, but I'd hoped this would be different. If that wasn't the case, could I let Sienna go? Everything in me screamed no, I couldn't do without her.

"What do you mean?" I asked cautiously.

"She's... not like her father."

"No." I shook my head. "She isn't."

My mother glanced toward the hallway. "She's a nice girl."

"She is." I studied her, waiting for the shoe to drop.

Silence stretched between us for several long moments before my mother's gaze found mine again. "She cares about you."

My breath caught. Did she really think so? It was almost too much to hope for. I knew the chemistry between us was insane, but the thought of her wanting me, falling for me... It seemed so far out of reach, yet I knew she was made for me.

My mother nodded as if answering my silent question. "I think she'll be good for you."

The vise around my heart released, and the tension I'd

been carrying all day lifted from my shoulders. "I think so, too."

The sound of footsteps rose on the air, and we turned almost in unison toward Sienna as she returned to the kitchen. Her steps faltered, and an uncertain smile curled her lips when she noticed both of us staring at her.

Before she could question anything, I moved forward and wrapped one arm around her shoulders. "It's been a long day. Let's head home."

Smile still fixed in place, she tipped her head up and nodded. There was a question in her eyes, but I wasn't ready to answer it yet. Not here.

I paused to kiss my mother's cheek. "See you soon."

Eager to get Sienna all to myself, I led her from the house and guided her into my truck. She went willingly, not saying a single word as I helped her inside, then buckled the seatbelt into place. My heart raced as I climbed into the driver's seat, acutely aware of the woman just a few feet away, a maelstrom of emotion swirling between us in the small space.

She trusted me. She cared for me—even desired me. But it wasn't enough. I was going to make her fall in love with me.

TWENTY-SIX

SIENNA

Something had changed. I wasn't sure what it was, but I sensed it wasn't good. I knew that they'd been talking about me. The second I stepped foot back into the room, they both clammed up, their eyes sliding toward me, then guiltily away again.

I stared out the passenger window, picking nervously at my cuticle. Vaughn hadn't said more than two words since we left his mom's house. It was completely uncharacteristic of him, and I didn't know what to do about it. Though my mind told me it could be a coincidence, my heart screamed to run fast and far away. All the old insecurities from the past swelled up, obscuring my perception.

Just like Derrick, Vaughn had measured me and found me lacking. The worst part was, I thought I was starting to fall for him, especially after this morning. I've never been kissed like that in my entire life. He held me like he never wanted to let me go, kissed me like he needed the breath in my lungs to survive. Yet in the span of just a few hours, everything had changed.

His mother and I, though we'd gotten off on the wrong foot, had developed a kinship of sorts. Or maybe I was just reading too much into things. Maybe she was being polite for Vaughn's sake. Maybe she didn't like me because of my heritage, or because of who my father was. I had a hard time believing that, because she had opened up so much, and seemed so accepting.

Of course, people said things they didn't mean all the time. Just like Derrick had told me he loved me and wanted to spend forever with me, that had been a lie, too. It seemed like no matter what I did, I would never be enough for some people. It shouldn't matter; I had told myself a thousand times that I didn't need someone else to validate my self-worth. For once in my life, I was just being me. And for Vaughn and his mother to reject me hurt more than I wanted to admit.

A lump formed in my throat, and I swallowed it down, blinking away the burning sensation that tingled across the bridge of my nose. It wasn't worth getting upset over. Vaughn and I weren't a real couple. He was just keeping me safe until they figured out who was after me and why.

My thoughts were drawn to a jarring halt when I felt the truck slow. I glanced around as Vaughn steered to the side of the empty stretch of road. "What's going on? What's wrong?"

I glanced in the side mirror as he put the truck in park. "Did something—"

My words were abruptly cut off as Vaughn reached across the cab and curled one hand around the back of my neck before hauling me against him. His lips crashed against mine, stealing the breath from my lungs. My vision swam as his tongue delved into my mouth, sliding across mine, leaving the faint taste of cinnamon behind.

A whimper escaped before I could stop it, and Vaughn clutched me tighter. The hand holding my neck tightened a fraction before sliding up into my hair. My muscles felt like putty as I allowed him to tip my head for better access, and he attacked my mouth once more.

His free hand dipped beneath the hem of my shirt, dragging it upward. I shivered as his warm fingers coasted from my hip, along the curve of my waist and up my ribcage. His thumb slid along the curve of my breast until it was cupped in his palm, and I instinctively arched into his touch.

His thumb slid beneath the band of my bra then swept upward, across my nipple. I sucked in a breath, and Vaughn nipped my lower lip. "Couldn't wait another second to touch you."

His mouth fastened along the side of my throat as his fingers tweaked and teased the tender nub. I shifted my legs, acutely aware of the pressure building between my thighs. The achy sensation intensified, and I wanted nothing more than to crawl into his lap and have him take it away.

The hand fisted in my hair tightened, tipping my head backward so he could better access my throat. His teeth sank into the soft flesh as he pinched my nipple, and I nearly came off the seat. I clutched at his biceps, my whole body tingling with need. "Vaughn!"

"Fuck." The single word was low and guttural, vibrating against my throat. "I knew it would be like this."

His mouth returned to mine as he slowly restored my shirt to rights. His kisses this time were much more gentle but still filled with need. I raked my fingers through his hair as he teased my mouth, loving the way his lips felt as they grazed over mine.

He swept the pad of his thumb along my cheekbone, his gaze caressing my face before meeting my gaze. His eyes glowed silvery in the moonlight, and the desire I found in the depths set my blood on fire.

"Every time I touch you..." He gave a slow shake of his head. "I never want to stop. I want to strip you down, kiss every inch of you."

One hand trailed down my thigh to my knee. "Starting with these long, gorgeous legs..."

He kissed me again, long and slow before he broke away, his lips grazing my jaw as he spoke. "Taste you..." His hand reversed directions, and my breath caught as his thumb stroked my center. "Everywhere."

God, yes. I nodded, even though it wasn't necessary. I would have done anything he asked in that moment. Never in my life had anyone ever made me feel the way he did.

Vaughn pulled back to look at me, his eyes dark with intent. My heart skipped a beat, and I dragged in a ragged breath. "Me too," I whispered.

His hand tightened a fraction, his fingertips burrowing into the flesh at the base of my neck. If it were anyone else, the power move would've sent me running. But I knew Vaughn would never hurt me, and his possessiveness sent a little thrill straight to my core.

Maybe it was stupid, all things considered, but the chemistry between us was undeniable. And while my head told me to be cautious, my heart was all in with Vaughn, and I could no longer deny that I was quickly falling for him.

He kissed me once more, then shifted the transmission into gear, and the truck began to move. I stared blindly out the windshield, a million emotions roiling inside me. I still hadn't caught my breath when Vaughn laced his fingers with mine, then rested our joined hands in his lap.

I could feel the heat of him through the coarse fabric of

his pants, and tingles of awareness shot through my body. I wanted to feel him wrapped around me. The solid, warm strength of him stretched over every inch of me.

Neither of us said a word until we pulled into the garage and parked. Lifting our hands, Vaughn pressed a kiss to my knuckles. "Why don't you head inside? I want to take a look at your hand."

His voice was thick and rough as it washed over me, and I nodded before reluctantly releasing his hand. I moved into the house and he followed a moment later, my suitcase in hand. The sight stopped me in my tracks. "You got my things." I was touched that he had remembered.

"I told you I would." He dropped the bag on the floor next to the bed, then pressed his fingertips to my lower back. "Let's check out those cuts."

Inside the bathroom, I leaned against the sink, and Vaughn deftly unwrapped the gauze to expose my wound. "How does it feel?"

I flexed my palm a couple of times. "Not too bad. A little sore, but nothing I can't live with."

"Good." He gave a decisive nod. "The doctor said to leave the bandage off tonight so the cuts can start to heal up."

His thumb trailed lightly over my palm. His silvery eyes met mine, and he lifted my hand, placing it on his shoulder. I arched into him as he gathered me close, and his mouth covered mine. I whimpered as his tongue slid over mine, sending my thoughts scattering and making my heart beat double time.

The arm wrapped around my waist pulled me closer until I rested at the edge of the counter. His firm erection pressed to the space between my legs, and I dug my nails into his back, urging him closer.

He yanked back from the kiss with a low growl. "Christ. You're so fucking sexy."

His mouth fastened on the sensitive cords of my neck and sucked hard. I knew I would have a mark tomorrow, but I didn't care. All I wanted right now was him. I wanted him to keep touching me, keep kissing me, wanted him to never let me go.

I grasped at his shirttail and yanked it from his waistband, then ran my hand over the hot, smooth flesh of his back. He caught my hand, stilling my questing fingers. "I've been working all day, honey. I need to shower."

I shook my head. I couldn't wait one more second to feel him against me.

Threading one hand into his hair, I yanked his head back down, and our teeth clashed under the raw force of the kiss. His large palms stroked up my back, down over my hips, lighting every inch of my skin on fire. I shifted, trying to get closer, needing to alleviate the ache between my legs.

I opened my mouth to him, and his tongue delved inside, sweeping over mine. His hands cupped my ass, and I sucked in a breath as he shoved my legs wider and ground his erection against my core.

His fingertips caught the hem of my shirt, and I lifted my arms, breaking the kiss just long enough for him to pull it over my head and toss it to the floor. I curled my fingers into the fabric of his shirt and pulled him back to me once more, needing to taste him again, unable to get enough. It'd been so long since I'd felt this way—so long I couldn't remember anything even remotely comparable.

One huge, warm hand slid over the curve of my hip and around my back. He expertly popped the clasp on my bra, then slid the straps off my shoulders, gently coaxing it down until my breasts were exposed to his view. A shuddering breath escaped my lungs as he cupped them in his huge palms, testing their weight, a reverent look on his face.

Suddenly, my head felt too heavy for my neck, and it lolled to the side as his thumbs flicked over the sensitive buds thrusting toward him. I let out a sigh as he rolled one tip between his thumb and forefinger, and I arched my back to get closer.

Eyes closed, I reveled in the sensations streaming through my body. I gasped and nearly hit the ceiling when his mouth latched on to one tight peak. His tongue flicked over my nipple, his teeth catching the tender bud and tugging. I whimpered as his free hand found my other nipple and tweaked it lightly, sending a current of electricity shot straight to my core.

Burying my hands in his hair, I held him close. My shoulder blades hit the cool material of the mirror as he pressed me backward, lavishing my breasts with attention. Each touch, each kiss stirred the fire in my belly until I could barely contain it.

Derrick's betrayal no longer felt as devastating as it had even just a few days ago. Vaughn had moved into my life so seamlessly that I didn't even realize the full impact of his presence. Whatever was happening with Vaughn was different, stronger... more potent.

He did something to me that I didn't understand, and I wanted his addictive kisses. I wanted him to keep touching me. I wanted him to never let me go.

TWENTY-SEVEN

VAUGHN

My blood felt like it was on fire, and I couldn't wait another second to have her. I wanted to touch every inch of her, use my lips and tongue to trace each curve—later. Right now, I just needed to be inside her before I exploded from wanting her.

Bending low, I put my shoulder into her midsection and flung her over my shoulder. She grabbed wildly at me, her gasp of shock turning to laughter as I hustled toward the bedroom. Inside, I tossed her in the middle of the mattress. Her eyes were wide and bright with anticipation, her smile wide as I quickly clambered over her.

"I've been thinking about this all day."

My mouth fused with hers as I grasped the waistband of the pants she wore and yanked them down. Her panties followed seconds later, and she was finally beautifully bare underneath me. The sight of her literally took my breath away.

Pushing off the bed, I shucked my clothes, my gaze

locked on her face the entire time. Her gaze dropped to my cock, and it swelled to the point of pain when her tongue darted out, swiping over her plump lips.

She flung her arms around my shoulders, yanking me back to her, and I went willingly. Our mouths crashed together, and I felt the scrape of her tight nipples against my torso as she wriggled beneath me in an attempt to get closer. I cupped her ass, bringing her more fully against me, and the tip of my cock nudged her soft folds. I sucked in a breath at the sensation.

"Vaughn!" Her teeth sank into her lower lip as her legs came up to frame my hips. "I need you."

Hearing her say those words—admitting that she felt the same way I did—made my heart swell with satisfaction. I kissed her hard. "I've been waiting forever for you. Since the second I saw you, I knew you were made for me."

"I'm yours." She lifted her hips and the head of my erection slipped an inch inside. She was wet, soaked and ready for me, and I had to fight the urge to drive hard and deep. I needed a condom—now.

"Honey, I—"

She didn't give me a chance to speak as she practically impaled herself on my cock. Stars danced before my eyes as I slid all the way in to the hilt, her soft warmth gripping me like a vise.

Holy Christ.

Sienna arched violently, her hips jerking upward at the sensation. Her inner muscles clasped me tightly, and desire spread throughout my body, my nerve endings tingling with awareness. The myriad of sensations were like nothing I'd ever experienced, the pleasure almost overwhelming. I'd never had sex without a condom before. Everything seemed more intense, and I felt my cock swelling in response.

Fuck it. We'd go slow next time.

Sliding one hand beneath her hips, I lifted her to meet each thrust, sinking deep inside, unable to get close enough, deep enough. I wanted to feel every inch of her wrapped around me, wanted her to feel me for days. I hammered into her hard and fast, claiming her mouth and drinking in her cries of pleasure.

Sienna dug her heels into the backs of my thighs, urging me on as she bucked wildly beneath me. I could feel her muscles clenching, growing tighter until she was practically strangling me. She pistoned upward, taking her pleasure with just a few short strokes. I grimaced as her nails cut into my back, every muscle locking up as she came with an unreserved passion I'd never witnessed.

Fuck, that was hot. Goosebumps exploded across her skin, and her body trembled as the aftershocks of her orgasm rippled through her. Her breaths came fast and uneven, her arms still tangled around my neck. I kissed her hard, and the electrical current sparking between us went straight to my groin.

Lifting her hips, I changed the angle so I could go deeper. She sucked in a breath, still sensitive from her orgasm. Her eyes fluttered closed as she focused on the sensations streaming through her body. I grasped the back of her head, drawing her gaze to mine. "Don't hide from me. I want to see everything."

She nodded, her cheeks flushed and looking incredibly sated. I pumped slowly, letting it build and grow, reveling in the way she placed her trust completely in me. It served only to turn me on even more and I drove deeper, harder, drawing out her orgasm until she came again. A wail drifted from her throat, and she tucked her face into the crook of my neck as if to hide.

The muscles across my lower back tightened as my cock swelled, and my release flowed from me with a low groan. My flesh tingled with remnants of desire, acutely aware of her body enveloping mine. Being inside her felt so damn good—so right. Her sweet scent, the feel of her skin, those breathy little gasps of pleasure... She was made for me.

Braced on my elbows over her, I dropped my head to her chest and fought to draw air into my lungs. My entire body shook with exhaustion, rattled by the knowledge that what we'd just done was far more than sex.

I should've expected it the second her lips touched mine. When she kissed me this morning, I felt an undeniable thrill, a shock of awareness I'd never felt with another woman. And if that wasn't enough, our lovemaking confirmed it for me—Sienna was the only woman I would ever want this way. She was the one.

Her grip on my shoulders had loosened, and I pressed a kiss to her chest just over her heart. Her pulse still thrummed wildly, matching my own rapid pace. I slowly withdrew and dropped to the mattress next to her. "Damn. That was fucking incredible."

Sienna didn't say anything, but I sensed her smile as she shifted next to me. Rolling to my side, I grabbed her hip and pulled her to me, so we were face-to-face. Luminous blue eyes stared into mine, and I felt my heart fall right out of my chest and into her hands.

It was far too soon to be thinking about love, let alone saying it, but I knew. Deep down, I knew that was exactly what I felt. "How do you feel?" I asked.

A secret smile played along her lips. "Perfect."

"Is your hand okay? I didn't hurt you, did I?"

She lifted it from where it lay between us and stretched her fingers a little. "You didn't hurt me," she replied quietly. "It was... amazing."

Her muscles finally began to relax, and I captured her

face in one hand. Big blue eyes, still glossy with desire, blinked up at me. "I wasn't wearing protection."

She bit her lip, looking incredibly embarrassed. Several seconds passed before she spoke, her voice a whisper. "I don't mind. As long as..."

I knew what she meant. I was clean, and I trusted that she was, too. No barriers, just two bodies coming together in complete unison.

I pressed a soft kiss to her lips. "I would never jeopardize you." I sifted one hand through her long golden locks as I studied her. "You're so beautiful."

Her gaze dropped to my chest, and even in the dim light I could tell she was blushing. I shook my head. She really didn't seem to understand or believe how incredibly amazing she was. "I like this look on you."

Her brows drew slightly together, and she scrunched up her nose the tiniest bit. "A sweaty mess?"

I smiled. She had no idea how sexy that was, too, but it wasn't what I meant. "You look like you're finally happy."

Her smile slipped away, her expression suddenly guarded. "What's that supposed to mean?"

I wondered why her first instinct was to get defensive. "Someone did a number on you, didn't they?"

Though her face was shadowed, I could practically see the fire flashing in her eyes. She scowled as she shoved to a sitting position. "I'm not some broken little doll who needs to be fixed."

"I didn't say that." I grabbed for her, but she evaded my grasp, swatting at my hands as she scrambled toward the edge of the bed.

"Just because we had sex doesn't mean you know me. Guys like you think—"

"Sienna, stop. Please." I caught her elbow and gently turned her toward me. "That's not what I meant. You know

I would never say that about you. I don't think you're broken, honey. I think you're one of the strongest people I know."

Her eyes narrowed suspiciously, but she didn't say a word, so I continued. "Have I ever given you a reason to not believe me?"

After a long moment, she finally gave a slow shake of her head. A relieved breath filtered from my nose, and I sank to the edge of the bed. Grasping her hips, I guided her between my legs. Her height put her head several inches above my own, and I peered up at her. I didn't want to tower over her; I wanted her to feel like she was in control for once. Because with me, she was.

"I hate when you shut me out," I murmured. "Just like our first date. Remember that?"

Her lips rolled together, as if stifling a smile. I couldn't hold back my own. "I was an asshole, and I'm sorry."

"It's okay. I..." She hesitated. "I wasn't exactly at my best, either."

"I know. I could tell you had your walls up, I just didn't know why. At first, I thought it was because you hated me." She opened her mouth to speak, but I lightly squeezed her waist. "Then after the car accident, I realized that wasn't it at all. Because you felt it, too. Didn't you?"

She licked her lips and nodded. "You know how they say women who experience traumatic things often develop a case of hero worship?"

I didn't bother to answer her rhetorical question as she continued, "At first, I thought it was just that. I tried to ignore it, tried not to focus on it. Every time I saw you, though, it was like... I don't know. Like everything around me changed the second you walked into the room. But..."

"But you've been hurt before and you were afraid to open up."

She stared at me, teeth buried in her lower lip before she gave a tiny nod. I suspected as much. "Your ex?"

Another small nod. I tucked a stray lock of hair behind her ear. "If you don't want to talk about it, that's okay. But you seem happier now. More confident."

Her gaze dropped, fixing on my chest for several moments before speaking. "Everyone always had expectations for me, and I felt like I had to do what they wanted. Not necessarily what made me happy. After he left, I had to do something for myself. I've spent my entire life making everyone else happy. I decided it was my turn."

"You deserve to be happy, too." I lightly grazed the soft flesh of her stomach with my thumbs. "I know I come off as pushy sometimes—"

She arched a brow, and I grinned. "Fine. Most of the time." I stared at her, my smile falling away as her pretty eyes met mine. "But it would kill me if something happened to you. I just want to keep you safe."

"I know." She stepped closer, and I looped my arms around her waist, pulling her in close.

I breathed deeply, dragging her unique scent into my lungs. "Come back to bed."

I slid under the sheets and a moment later she joined me. Her head moved to my chest, one leg sprawled over mine, and I smiled against the top of her head. Being with her was so easy. As different as we were, we just fit.

I loved the feel of her skin pressed to mine. It was so primal, so basic, but so perfect—exactly as nature had intended. I truly believed in soul mates—and every minute I spent with Sienna proved that she and I were meant to be.

TWENTY-EIGHT

SIENNA

Before the sound even registered in my mind, Vaughn was rolling out of bed. A blast of cold air hit me, and I shivered as I struggled to a sitting position. I blinked blearily, watching Vaughn as he quickly stepped into a pair of gym shorts, then yanked open the drawer of the nightstand.

My eyes widened as he pulled out a pistol and tucked it in his waistband. "What's going on?"

As soon as the words left my mouth, the pounding on the front door intensified. "Stay here. I'll be right back."

With just a few long strides, he was tearing out the bedroom door. Oh, hell no. There was no way I was staying here while he was dealing with whatever was going on downstairs.

I tossed aside the tangled sheets and stumbled from the bed. The clock on the nightstand read 6:05, and my stomach dropped to my toes. If the person on the porch was who I thought it was, we were going to have a huge problem.

I pulled on the closest thing at hand, which happened to be one of Vaughn's oversized shirts. I scrambled around in the dim light, looking for a pair of leggings, but finally grabbed a tiny pair of sleep shorts. I stepped into them as I hopped my way toward the door, then practically raced downstairs.

The dread in my stomach congealed as the familiar raised voice met my ears. I skidded to a stop just a few feet from where my father stood inside the doorway. His eyes, dark with fury, cut toward me, and his mouth twisted into a grimace. "What the hell is going on here?"

"I—"

Before I could explain, his gaze swept over me, and his expression darkened further. "And what the hell are you wearing? You look like a two-bit whore."

The words hit me with the force of a slap, and I took a tiny step backward. Half a second later, Vaughn was there, a solid presence behind me, his hands lightly grasping my upper arms to lend support. "With all due respect, sir," he said, his voice cool, "when you're in my home, you'll refrain from raising your voice to her. And you won't ever disrespect her like that again."

My father's gaze snapped over my shoulder to Vaughn, and I could practically see his body trembling with rage. "Absolutely not." My father gave a hard shake of his head. "I raised you better than this. I didn't spend my entire life giving you girls everything so you could shack up with someone like him."

"Dad!" I was absolutely mortified. The heat of embarrassment swept over me, and I dropped my chin a fraction. "I can't believe you would even say that. You don't even know him."

My father scowled. "I know—

"You know what? You should be thanking him right now for helping me. If it wasn't for him—"

"None of this should have ever happened," my father shot back. "Had you stayed at home where you belong, no one would have broken into your house. Which you lied about," he seethed, eyes narrowed. "I had to find out from Harvey that some lunatic butchered a cat and left it there for you. Now he tried to burn you alive!"

At the mention of Boots, my heart constricted. Vaughn seemed to understand, because he squeezed my arms. "Sir, if I may—"

"No, you may not," my father sniped. "You've done enough. We're leaving."

He reached for me, but I stepped away. Vaughn deftly tucked me against his side, placing himself between my father and me. "If she wants to leave, that's her choice," he replied, his tone steely. "But no one will tell her what to do."

Not even you. The unspoken words hung in the stunned silence that permeated the room.

Vaughn squeezed me a little tighter, a silent consolation. "Sienna is welcome to stay here as long as she likes."

I met my father's gaze. He looked shocked—and furious—that someone had stood up to him. I let out a slow breath. "I'm not a child anymore. I appreciate that you want to help, but I'm fine. The police are taking care of everything. We decided it would be safer for me to stay with Vaughn and not put anyone else unnecessarily at risk."

My father's mouth moved but I spoke up before he could come up with a retort. "You need to get used to this," I said softly. "Even after the police find whoever's responsible, I still plan to do what's best for me. I can't run home when something bad happens. I need to live my own life."

My father rocked back on his heels as he regarded me, his mouth set in a firm line. "I'm disappointed in you."

I took the words like a dagger to the heart. He'd always known his disappointment affected me more than anything. But I couldn't cave this time; I wouldn't. "I'm sorry," I murmured.

His gaze slid to Vaughn. "I hope you've enjoyed your time in Cedar Springs."

Without another word, my father spun on his heel and retreated from the house, slamming the door in his wake. For a moment, neither of us moved. We seemed to be waiting for something else to happen. But when the engine of the car roared to life outside then disappeared down the street, a collective air of tension seemed to rush from the room.

"Come on," Vaughn said. "I'll make coffee."

I trailed behind as he made his way into the kitchen and silently began to brew a pot of coffee. The silence lengthened and intensified, wreaking havoc on my already fraught nerves. I was still mortified about the things my father had said, and I felt compelled to apologize. "I'm sorry. For what he said. He's just angry, and—"

"Hey." Vaughn captured my face in his hands. "You don't need to apologize. It's not your fault."

He smoothed my hair away from my face. "And it's nothing I haven't heard before."

Tears pricked my eyes. I hated that he' been disrespected like that. He didn't deserve my father's disdain. My lungs tightened as I tried to hold back my tears, and I slid my arms around his waist, anchoring myself to his sturdy frame. Part of me was terrified he'd pull away, that he would want nothing to do with me now.

"Shh..." He rubbed my back in sweeping circles. "Don't be upset, sweetheart. I can take it."

"You shouldn't have to," I said fiercely. "It's rude and, and I won't speak to him until he apologizes."

One large hand cupped the back of my head, then turned me so I was forced to look at him. "He's your father, honey. He cares about you. He just wants to make sure you're not making a mistake."

At that, I recoiled. "You think this is a mistake?"

Had I read him completely wrong? I started to step away, but Vaughn caught me back to him.

"You could never be a mistake." He shook his head and tightened his hold on me. "You're the best thing that's ever happened to me. You're the first person who's truly seen me and accepted me for who I am."

"I like who you are."

My words were timid but honest, and Vaughn smiled. "I know, honey. I love that about you."

"You won't really lose your job, will you?" My heart stuttered in my chest. He loved what he did. I would never forgive myself if he was fired because of me.

"No, honey." He squeezed me tight. "It would take a hell of a lot more than this to get me fired. And if they want to make me choose between you or them, they can go to hell."

My heart thumped hard in my chest at his words, and it felt like the ground had disappeared from beneath my feet. No one had ever said anything like that to me before.

Vaughn's gaze slid over my body. "It's no wonder he jumped to the conclusion he did though." His palm swept over my hip, then under the hem of his shirt. One brow lifted as he encountered the flimsy shorts I wore underneath. "Maybe next time we see your father you should not look like you've just been fucked."

My cheeks went up in flames, but I couldn't help the smile as the memory of last night flooded my mind. "He was the one who showed up at six in the morning." I ruffled my messy hair. "And this is just bed head. We technically haven't had sex since last night."

He grinned wolfishly and lifted me to his chest. "You're right. We should probably fix that."

TWENTY-NINE

VAUGHN

A voicemail from Foley's wife greeted me as soon as I sat down. After spending most of the day on patrol, I wasn't in the mood to deal with any more shit. I hoped to hell she had good news for me. I'd just picked up the phone when a voice behind me stopped me cold.

"Dallas PD found your guy."

I dropped the phone back in its cradle before giving Chief Thorne my full attention. "Davies?"

"Yep." Gray reached behind him and plucked a sheaf of papers off the printer. "Just got word of it this morning."

He tapped the papers a few times on his desk to straighten them, then extended the stack my way. "I knew you'd want a first look."

My gaze quickly scanned the header from the medical examiner's office, and I flipped through the pages until I found the official police report. According to DPD, a man had been found in an abandoned warehouse downtown. Rather, the man's remains had been found.

Six days ago, two kids had broken into the facility and stumbled upon a dead body. Shaken, they'd called it in, and the police secured the scene to investigate. Thank God the minors had called it in; otherwise, who knew how long it would've taken to find him. The kids had been released with a warning to stay out of condemned properties, but they were probably scarred for life.

Apparently, the damage inflicted to his body, coupled with the intense heat inside the warehouse, had done Davies no favors. The victim would've had to be identified by dental records except for the fact that his teeth had been pulled.

The killer had been kind enough to leave Davies's driver's license tucked into the back pocket of the victim's jeans, indicating the man's identity. While they were still officially waiting on the DNA test to come back, they were almost certain the victim was Chester Davies. I was certain we would get confirmation any day now.

"Did you look at this?" I flicked a look at Gray, who shook his head.

"I saw it had come through as soon as I got back from the meeting with Darwin."

I nodded as I flipped back to the medical examiner's report and skimmed the page. "Official cause of death was exsanguination."

The corners of his lips dipped into a frown before he spoke. "Same stab wounds as victim one?"

I shook my head. "Apparently not. According to the medical examiner, his body was covered in shallow lacerations."

"That shouldn't be enough to kill someone," he murmured as I continued to read.

"That's true, except when you hit a major artery.

According to this, several of the cuts had begun to heal over. Those were the minor ones."

Gray grimaced. "Someone tortured him."

"Sounds like it. Looks like the killing blows were twin lacerations to the femoral arteries." He would have slowly bled to death, but that wasn't even the worst of it. My stomach twisted as I read the next notation. "When Davies was tortured and left for dead, the scent of the blood drew the rats living in the warehouse. They apparently consumed a good portion of him before the boys entered the building and scared them off."

I passed the report to Gray, fury simmering in my veins. Who the fuck did something like this? Davies wasn't exactly a standup citizen, but he sure as hell didn't deserve this.

Gray skimmed the portion I'd just read and his face twisted. "Christ. What the fuck is wrong with people?"

The killer was escalating—growing bolder and more depraved.

"How'd your meeting with the warden go?"

He scowled. "About as good as expected. Internal Affairs is investigating the incident, but... you know how that goes. Darwin was pretty dodgy about the whole thing."

Figured. No one ever wanted to admit they were wrong or had a traitor in their midst—especially not in law enforcement. If it was discovered that someone at the jail was covering up crimes, the news would have a fucking field day.

"And Adrian?"

"He's in a coma at the moment." Gray grimaced. "That's good news and bad, I guess. Security has been appointed to his room 24/7, but it's a waiting game."

"Jesus." Everything was a tangled mess. "Well, hopefully we'll find out more soon."

He rolled his eyes as he pushed off the desk. "Wouldn't count on it."

Yeah, me either. Turning my attention back to the situation with Foley, I dialed the number his wife had left and waited impatiently for the call to connect. She answered a moment later, and I introduced myself. "Mrs. Foley, this is Officer Vaughn Allen with Cedar Springs Police Department. I was hoping to speak with your husband."

"Is everything okay? He's not in trouble, is he?"

Not yet. "Nothing like that," I soothed. "We placed him near the scene of a crime, and I was hoping he might be able to answer a few questions for me."

"I'm sure he'd be happy to help, but he's out of town right now working with a client."

"Your building manager did mention that," I replied. "He works for Callaway Logistics, is that right?"

"That's right," she confirmed. "He's scheduled to fly in tomorrow evening."

"If you could have him give me a call when he gets in, that would be great."

By the time she'd promised to have Foley contact me, I was already pulling up the contact info for Callaway. I ended the call and immediately dialed the number for their main reception. A woman answered after three rings. "Callaway Logistics, Corinne speaking."

"Hello, Corinne." I introduced myself. "I was hoping to speak with Mr. Foley, but I believe he's out of the office this week."

"That's correct. I can send you to his voicemail, if you'd like."

"That's okay," I said. "Can you tell me when he'll be in?"

"He'll return from vacation next Monday."

Vacation? "I was under the impression he was on a business trip."

"No, sir," she replied. "He's taking some personal time off."

Interesting. So, he wasn't with his wife, and he wasn't at work. Where the hell was he? "Thanks, Corinne. I'll touch base with him on Monday."

I hung up the phone and rubbed my eyes. What a clusterfuck. I couldn't wait to get home to Sienna. But first, I had one more thing to do.

THIRTY

SIENNA

I had just sat down when the sound of a car pulling into the drive drew my attention. The sound of the garage door opening reached my ears, and my heart lurched in my chest, sending a flurry of excitement steaming through my veins.

Though I'd only known him a short time, I couldn't deny my attraction to Vaughn. I craved the sight of him, craved his attention. I loved the way he looked at me, the way his hands felt as they slid over my skin.

I practically vibrated with restless energy as I waited for Vaughn to come inside. I was rewarded a moment later when the door swung open. His eyes widened with surprise then pleasure when he saw me waiting for him. "Hey, beautiful."

His bag hit the floor seconds before his arms looped around me and his mouth came down on mine. The pressure forced me backwards, bending me over his arm. I looped my arms around his neck, clinging to him as I was swept away by the kiss.

Finally Vaughn lifted away, a seductive smile curling his lips. "Hi, baby."

"Hi," I managed breathlessly, my head still spinning with desire.

"How was your day?"

"Better now," I said before I could think better of it.

"Me too." He kissed me once more, then squeezed my waist. "I have a surprise for you."

"You do?"

Before I could say anything else, he grabbed my hand and hauled me toward the living room. "Come here."

He guided me toward the couch and gently pushed me down. "Close your eyes."

"What? Why?"

He smirked at me. "You don't want your surprise?"

I wrinkled my nose. I hated surprises. "Am I going to like it?"

"I hope so," he said, tipping his forehead against mine. "Give it a chance. Please?"

I pushed my lower lip out. "Okay. If you say so."

"I say so." He captured my mouth once more in a quick, sweet kiss. "Close your eyes, and I'll be back in just a second. No peeking," he warned as his footsteps receded from the room.

The outer door opened then closed as he went into the garage, then returned. Anticipation swirled in my stomach. What was he doing? His steps neared. "Keep your eyes closed and hold out your hands." I did as he asked, and he cupped both of mine in one huge palm.

At the first soft, furry contact I jerked, and my eyes flew open. Vaughn's huge hands cradled mine, preventing me from dropping the tiny kitten he'd settled in my lap.

"Oh!" My heart practically spilled out of my chest at the

sight of it curled into a tiny ball. I lifted my gaze to Vaughn. "Is he yours?"

"Hardly. I'm not a cat person." Vaughn snorted. "He's yours."

Shock rippled through me. "You got him... for me?"

"I thought you could use some cheering up," he said by way of response as he rubbed the space between the kitten's ears with one fingertip.

Tears burned my eyes at the sight, and gratitude swelled inside me, along with something a lot more potent. My heart felt too big for my chest, like it was going to beat right out of the confines of my rib cage.

Vaughn hooked a finger under my chin and lifted my gaze to his. "Don't cry, honey," he murmured. "I know you miss Boots."

"That's not it." I shook my head. "I mean, it is, but..."

"But what?" he prompted softly as he settled on the couch next to me.

I swallowed down the emotion clogging my throat. "Thank you. This is the most thoughtful thing anyone has ever done for me."

Vaughn studied the kitten for a moment. "This little guy needed a home, and I couldn't think of anyone better to take care of him."

He looped an arm around my shoulders, and I snuggled into him as he pressed a kiss to my temple. "Where did you get him?"

"Funny story." Vaugh stretched his legs out in front of him. "I was on a call this morning when I heard this guy crying. I found him beneath a dumpster behind the pharmacy. I checked inside to make sure he didn't belong to anyone, but no one claimed him."

"He's so little." The curious kitten began to explore, climbing awkwardly over my lap first, then Vaughn's before hopping onto the couch. "He can't be more than a few weeks old."

"The vet guessed him to be around seven weeks." Vaughn shrugged. "Otherwise, he seems healthy."

"Are you sure you don't mind having a kitten here? It should only be a few more days," I added hastily. "I'll take him to my house as soon as everything is clear."

He lifted his free hand to cup my face and met my eyes. "You're welcome to stay here as long as you like. Both of you." His thumb swept over the apple of my cheek, and heat swirled low in my belly. "I like seeing you when I get home from work."

Liquid pleasure melted through me. "Me, too."

"How was your day?"

Though Vaughn had texted me constantly throughout the day to make sure I was safe, I'd barely moved from the couch. I'd watched a movie on Netflix, but surprisingly, I'd slept a good portion of the day. My body was probably still catching up from the stress of the past couple of weeks.

"Boring," I responded honestly. "I feel so lazy."

"You need the rest. And it won't be much longer." Vaughn ran his fingers through my hair. "We have a couple leads we're following, so hopefully one of them will pan out and you can get back to normal."

I wasn't entirely sure what normal entailed. I liked spending time with Vaughn, liked being here with him. What would happen once this was all over?

"Are you okay?"

I lifted my gaze to his and pasted on a smile. "Of course. Why wouldn't I be?"

His head tipped a little to one side as he studied me. "You looked sad for a second."

"Just thinking of everything I'll need for the kitten," I lied. "I have a bunch of stuff at my house."

"I already got it." My eyes flared with surprise as Vaughn pushed to his feet. "It's all in the car."

I followed him into the garage and held out my hands as he passed me a large pizza box.

"Dinner," he explained with a grin before reaching back into the truck to gather the kitten's things.

Back inside the house we got the kitten settled, then carried the pizza to the living room. Surprise rippled through me when Vaughn extracted a candle from the bag and lit it. "I picked it up at the pharmacy today. It reminded me of you—something in your perfume."

He'd bought it because it reminded him of me? That was the sweetest thing I'd ever heard. I felt my insides go all gooey.

"I know it's not much." He looked embarrassed, and my heart swelled in my chest. I couldn't help but lean in and kiss his cheek.

"It's perfect." To a normal person, pizza on the couch probably wasn't a lot. But to me, it was everything.

THIRTY-ONE

VAUGHN

The ringing of the doorbell startled us both. I glanced at the screen of my phone, noting that it was nearly 8:30 at night. Who the hell could be here?

I turned to Sienna, who peered up at me. "Think it's your dad again?"

"Could be, though I don't know why he would be here again so soon." She offered a little shrug. "At least he used the doorbell this time."

I grinned as I pushed to my feet. "I'll be right back."

Pushing aside the curtain over the window, I peered out into the driveway. In the faint glow of the streetlamp, I saw my mother's sedan illuminated in the driveway. I quickly unlocked and yanked open the door, my gaze roving over her. "Is everything okay?"

My mother smiled tentatively. "I know it's late. I hope you don't mind me stopping by."

"Of course not," I replied, my voice tinged with concern. "You know you're welcome here anytime."

My mother stepped inside, and I closed up behind her. Sienna had stood as soon as she heard my mother's voice, and she offered a polite smile and a wave. "Hi, Ms. Allen. It's good to see you again."

"You too," my mother returned.

I rested one hip against the arm of the couch as I regarded my mother. "What brings you by?"

"Actually, I have something for Sienna." She opened her large tote bag and withdrew a small package wrapped in silver paper.

Sienna's brows drew together, her expression showing her surprise. "You got something for me? You didn't have to do that."

My mother shrugged self-consciously as she passed the small box to Sienna. "It's nothing big. But I thought you might like it."

Sienna carefully peeled away the paper and extracted the hand-knit scarf from within. Her mouth formed a tiny O, and her gaze flew to my mother. "Are you sure?"

My mother smiled. "I made a second one for you since you seemed to like it."

Sienna hugged it to her chest. "I love it. Thank you so much."

She moved forward and pulled my mother into an awkward hug. Watching the two of them together, a strange sensation swelled in my chest. It was the first time I'd seen anything like it; my mother had certainly never acted this way with any of the other women I dated. Both women looked like they might cry, and I felt suspiciously off-balance myself.

In an attempt to break the tension, I fingered the woolen material with a grin. "Do you need a scarf?"

"Your mother has one just like it," Sienna explained. "I

saw it when I was at her house the other day, and I asked her where she got it. I didn't realize she had made it herself."

"When are you ever going to wear it?" I grinned. "We live in Texas, honey. It's seventy-five on a bad day."

Sienna lightly backhanded me. "Not all the time. Besides, I'm always cold."

I did know that, and I loved being the one to warm her up. She seemed to read my thoughts, because her cheeks turned bright pink, and her gaze dropped to the scarf in her hands.

"Thank you again," she said as she turned to my mother. "I really appreciate it."

"It was my pleasure," she returned with a smile. Her gaze switched to me, and I sensed she wanted to talk about something.

Sienna must've picked up on the vibe too, because she dipped her head. "I should go get ready for bed. It was really good to see you again, Ms. Allen."

I watched her go, a small smile playing along the corners of my lips. When I turned back to my mother, I found her watching me intently. I lifted my brows in question, but she spoke before I had a chance to say anything.

"I'm sorry." She pointed in the direction Sienna had disappeared. "I had my reservations at first, but I was wrong. She's a wonderful young woman."

"She is," I agreed.

My mother smiled a little. "You love her."

It was a statement, not a question, but I didn't bother to dance around the subject. I nodded. "I do. She's just..."

"Special?" my mother supplied.

"I know it sounds crazy," I said, but my mother held up one hand to cut me off.

"It's not crazy. You can't help the way you feel about

someone, even if you've only known them for a short time. Sometimes you just know that someone is meant for you."

Her words troubled me. My mother had never married —had never even come close, to my understanding—yet she spoke like she'd experienced it firsthand. Maybe with my father? "Were you in love with someone?"

It was the first time I had asked her, and I kicked myself for not doing so sooner. My mother gave a gentle smile. "I thought so, but after I got pregnant with you, he decided we were no longer suited."

She looked like she wanted to say more, so I stayed quiet. "I never told you the whole story about your father, but you deserve to know." She tipped her chin toward the couch. "Do you mind if we sit?"

I gestured for her to make herself comfortable, then seated myself at the opposite end of the couch and draped one arm over the back. A nervous anticipation sluiced through me as she took a moment to gather herself before speaking.

"Obviously, you know you weren't planned. Not that I would ever take it back," she said fiercely. "You are the best thing that ever happened to me. But the circumstances... They weren't the best."

My stomach swooped as her expression turned sad. "You were so curious about him when you were young, but I couldn't bear to tell you the truth. I allowed you to believe it was an affair, but that's not what really happened.

"When we first moved to America, things were tight. My parents took any job they could get, and your grandmother worked in a very prominent household. When I got old enough, I started working alongside her. The man had a son who was a bit older than me. I had just turned fourteen, and their son was home on break from college."

The hair on the back of my neck prickled as the dread in

my stomach congealed. Every cell of my body screamed that this wasn't going to have a good ending, but I forced myself to stay calm.

"The boy made it a point to talk to me, and he made me feel special."

Bile rose in the back of my throat, and I swallowed it down. My fists clenched as I leaned forward a tiny bit. "Did he...?"

My mother's gaze fixed on her hands which tumbled in her lap. Finally, she nodded. "I told my mother what had happened, but there was nothing we could do."

Had she accused their son of rape, she would've lost her position. "That's bullshit," I seethed.

My mother lifted one shoulder. "It was a different world back then."

My entire body vibrated with anger at the situation. For years, my mother had told me that my father was an important man who traveled a lot for work. I'd held out hope when I was younger that he eventually would come home, but he never did. Never in a million years would I have dreamed it was because he raped my mother.

"Who was it?"

My mother bit her lip and hesitated so long I thought she wouldn't answer.

"Ma..."

"It doesn't change the past, Vaughn," she responded. "What's done is done, and I prefer to leave him in the past."

I wanted to understand where she was coming from, but I didn't think I was big enough to do so. Part of me wanted to find the man and make him take responsibility for what he had done. I waited anxiously as she wrestled with herself before finally blowing out a breath.

"Your father is Matthias Kingsley."

For a moment, it felt as if the world had disappeared. I

was in a freefall and only my mother's apologetic expression grounded me. She couldn't have shocked me more if she had tried. Matthias Kingsley was literally the last person I ever would have expected to be my father.

Richer than God, the man was a real estate mogul who made his money swindling properties from owners who had fallen on hard times. He'd built an empire off the backs of hard-working people. The man was cold and calculating, the very definition of entitled elite.

His son, Bennett, on the other hand, was his polar opposite. Bennett had worked as Lieutenant on the police force until about six years ago. He'd quit following the death of his partner and decided to take up the reins in the family business.

People had once joked that Bennett and I looked so similar that we must be brothers from another mother. I'd never considered it at the time, because it was so outlandish. Now it made perfect sense.

I wondered if Bennett knew the truth. Almost immediately, I discarded the thought. Had Bennett known, he certainly would've said something. He was incredibly noble despite his corrupt father's influence, and I was positive he would have said something.

I couldn't figure something out though. "Why did you stay here?"

"I wanted him to see you," she said simply. "I hated what he had done, and I didn't want to let him off easy. I wanted him to see you every single day and know what he had given up."

I'd never taken my mother for the vindictive sort, but I silently congratulated her choice. Though it wasn't a popular opinion, especially in the South, I was sure her parents would have understood if she'd wanted to terminate the pregnancy.

Thankfully, she hadn't. Instead, she'd lived right beneath Kingsley's nose, forcing him to watch his by-blow grow up while he married and fathered another son. Not that it seemed to bother him much—Kingsley didn't seem to have much of a conscience.

My train of thought derailed, coming to a shuddering halt when something else occurred to me. Kingsley was good friends with Sienna's father. My stomach felt like it had fallen straight out of my body, and a buzzing noise filled my ears.

My mother laid a gentle hand on my arm. "For what it's worth, I think she loves you, too."

I nodded, feeling sick. What would Sienna say if she knew the truth? Cold spread from my heart all the way to my outer extremities. I had to tell her; she had a right to know. As I let my mother out, I couldn't help but feel like this new revelation might just be the end of us.

THIRTY-TWO

SIENNA

My heart leapt into my throat at the sight of Vaughn sitting at the end of the bed. Those arresting silvery eyes lit on me, causing my steps to falter as I entered the bedroom.

He moved with the lithe gracefulness of a large cat as he pushed to his feet, his long stride easily devouring the short distance between us. His face was set in a hard line, his expression filled with a mixture of desire, and... something that looked almost like regret.

His huge arms banded around my waist, pulling me into the hard wall of his chest. His head dipped, and he trailed his mouth along the side of my throat. My pulse leapt wildly out of control, and I clutched his biceps to stay upright. "Vaughn..."

His mouth fastened over the sensitive cords of my neck, and I sucked in a sharp breath as a bolt of pleasure spiraled through me. I arched shamelessly into him, my nipples peaked and aching as they brushed against the fibers of the towel.

Vaughn nipped my ear. "I need you."

Before I could blink, he stripped the towel away and dropped it to the floor. His hands roamed my body, his touch firm and possessive. His hands moved to my bottom, and he easily lifted me as his mouth covered mine. The kisses were urgent, driven by some deep-seated need I couldn't define.

I broke the kiss as he spun us toward the bed. "Is everything okay?"

Instead of answering, he lay me in the middle of the mattress, caging me with his huge body. His mouth found my nipple and he sucked hard, making me arch shamelessly against him. I sank my hands into his hair, clutching him close as he licked and teased his way across my chest to the other side.

One hand moved between my thighs and parted my folds, testing my readiness. I whimpered as he sank one finger deep inside before swirling it around my clit. His mouth covered mine again, the kiss hard and rough as his tongue slid over mine. It held a desperate quality, and fear spiked through me.

He leaned away briefly to strip his shirt over his head, and I placed my hands on his chest. "Vaughn, you're worrying me." His gaze was locked on me as he stripped out of his pants, his eyes filled with fire of desire but also a hint of worry. "Is everything okay?"

He prowled back over me, his face only inches from my own. He studied me intently, his gaze sweeping over the contours of my face, taking in every detail before meeting my eyes again. "You are perfect."

As he lowered himself once more, and his mouth brushed over mine, achingly tender this time. I looped my arms around his shoulders, sliding my hands over the smooth skin of his back as the head of his cock brushed my center. He rolled his hips, sliding deep in one smooth thrust, and I curled my nails into his back at the sensation.

Heat spiraled through me at the feeling of us coming together, and tingles danced along my nerve endings. He held me close, one hand wrapped around my shoulder to keep me in place as he slowly began to move. His gaze stayed locked on mine as he thrust slow and deep on measured strokes.

The sensation was exquisite, the emotion like nothing I'd ever experienced. Everything with Vaughn was heightened. He made me feel treasured, and I wondered if I had mistaken the look in his eyes earlier as sheer need.

His huge body enveloped me, pressing me into the mattress, and I soon tipped over the edge. Vaughn followed a moment later, pouring his heart and soul into me. His hold on me tightened, and his face turned into the curve of my neck, where he nestled my throat and teased me with soft kisses that seemed to go on forever.

Finally, he lifted away, shooting me one last longing glance before climbing from the bed. My chest rose and fell rapidly as I tried to draw in oxygen to calm my sated body and spinning mind.

Vaughn's movements caught my attention, and I watched warily as he pulled a pair of gym shorts from his dresser and stepped into them, then tugged on a T-shirt. I bit my lip as I pushed to a sitting position, suddenly uncomfortable being naked while he was fully dressed. He refused to look at me, and cold prickles of wariness spread over my skin.

I hurriedly gathered the comforter around me like a shield, waiting for him to say something—anything. Instead, silence stretched between us, thick and tense until I was ready to tear my hair out. There was no denying it now; something was most certainly wrong.

"Are you going somewhere?" I asked, not entirely certain I had hidden the jealousy in my voice.

Vaughn shook his head, and his gaze met mine before sliding quickly away again. I nodded, reading between the lines. My entire chest tightened as I stood and began to gather my clothes.

"Sienna..."

I shook my head. "You don't have to say anything else. I understand."

His reticence hurt worse than I thought possible. The love I felt for Vaughn had snuck up on me, seeming to come out of the blue. It was stronger than what I'd ever felt for my ex, and to have him throw it back at me broke my heart.

"It's not what you think," he started, but I held up a hand.

"Really, you don't have to say anything. In fact, it's better if you don't. Let's just pretend this never happened." I reached down and snatched up my clothes off the floor, tears blurring my eyes and burning across the bridge of my nose.

Vaughn reached for me, but I shrugged away from him, steeling my spine as I turned toward the door. I refused to let him see me cry; I needed to hold off just long enough to get out of here and away from him.

He caught up with me in two long strides, and his arms came around my waist, halting my progress. "Don't go, honey," he murmured against the back of my neck. "Please."

I couldn't figure out what he wanted. He'd flipped a one-eighty on me, pulling away emotionally then begging me not to go. I started to shake my head, but Vaughn gave me a gentle squeeze. "Please just hear me out. If you still want to leave afterward, I'll understand."

Confusion washed over me at his words. He seemed to sense my hesitation and gently turned me in his arms until I was peering up into those steely gray eyes. Silently, he took my hand and led me to the bed. He popped himself on the edge and patted the mattress next to him, indicating I should sit. I settled gingerly next to him, mentally pulling a cloak of armor around my emotions.

"My mother stopped by to talk about my father."

I nodded, not knowing how to respond to that. Vaughn had never spoken of his father, but I sensed their estrangement.

"I used to wonder about him when I was young," Vaughn said, a tinge of wistfulness in his tone. "I used to imagine where he was and what he was doing, why his work kept him from us."

"Did he not visit often?" I asked softly.

He shook his head. "I never knew my father."

Shock rolled through me at his pronouncement. "You never once saw him?"

His lips tipped into a sort of sad smile. "I saw him, I just didn't realize at the time that he was my father."

My brows drew together in confusion, and Vaughn dragged in a deep breath before continuing. "My mother worked for his family when she was young."

He recited the story about the young man taking advantage of his mother, then leaving her to deal with the consequences alone.

Fury caused my chest to expand. "I can't believe his parents didn't force him to step up and do the right thing."

Vaughn lifted his shoulder. "My grandparents probably didn't want to lose their positions in the household. I doubt they ever said anything to them."

I shook my head. "That's wrong."

He reached out and trailed his fingers along my forearm. "It feels like it was a lifetime ago. His opinion doesn't matter to me anymore."

I tipped my head to one side. "Then how did he come up in conversation?"

Vaughn sighed. "He still lives around here. He's wealthy and powerful, and he would just make my mother's life miserable if I said anything. Besides, I'm more worried about how it'll affect you."

"Me?" My mind raced to put together the pieces of the puzzle.

"Your father doesn't like me already, and to know this..."

I stared at him, a sinking sensation in my stomach. "Who is it?"

He opened and closed his mouth, but nothing came out. I turned to face him more fully. "Tell me."

"Kingsley."

The name fell between us with the force of a lightning bolt striking the earth. Holy shit. Kingsley was so proper, so pretentious. I couldn't imagine him doing such a thing.

On the other hand, he was awfully narcissistic, so he probably felt it was within his rights to take advantage of a young woman from the wrong side of the tracks. Anger bubbled in my veins as I regarded Vaughn. "You need to tell him."

"I'm sure he knows about me," he said wryly.

"This isn't 1950 anymore," I said firmly. "After everything he's done to your mother, he needs to acknowledge what he's done."

Vaughn studied me for a second. "You don't mind?"

"That he left a teenager pregnant and alone, forcing her to raise her son by herself? Of course I mind," I snapped. "What he did is despicable. He—"

Vaughn reached over and grabbed my hand. "Not that. Me. You don't mind that I'm his son?"

"It wasn't your fault. He knew better."

One hand reached out and wrapped around the back of

my neck, pulling me so close our noses almost touched. We stayed like that for several long minutes, breathing each other in.

Neither of us said a word, but we didn't need to. The bond we'd formed couldn't be broken.

THIRTY-THREE

VAUGHN

Footsteps echoed behind the door, and I braced on the balls of my feet, anticipation zinging through me. A judge had granted a warrant to search the vehicle, and I was hopeful we'd find something to nail Foley's ass to the wall.

Drew shifted restlessly next to me, and my heart gave a hard thump as the footsteps on the other side halted on the other side of the thick slab of metal.

I could practically feel the man's eyes studying me through the peephole, and I resisted the urge to slam my fist against the door. The tumbler clicked as the lock turned, and the door opened a scant few inches before catching on the chain. A single eye peered warily around the edge of the door, sweeping from the top of my head all the way down to my toes, then back again. "Can I help you?"

"I hope so," Drew replied. "I'm Detective Drew Thorne from the Cedar Springs Police Department. I was hoping to ask you some questions."

"I was just on my way out," the man hedged.

I stifled the urge to roll my eyes. He may as well just confess his guilt now.

"I can always come back with a warrant," Drew offered, steel lacing his tone.

The man let out a harried sigh. "What do you want to know?"

"Do you mind if we come in?"

The man hesitated for several seconds, and I was sure we'd hit a dead end. Finally, he nodded. The door closed, and I heard the chain slide free before he opened the door again and stepped back. "Just for a few minutes," he warned.

How gracious of him. I scanned the room as I walked inside. Clothes spilled out of a suitcase sitting just inside the bedroom, and the bed was unmade. A pizza box and two soda cans littered the coffee table, and the living room seemed to be in a state of general disarray.

Considering how clean the scene was during the break in at Sienna's house, I was a little surprised to see such a mess. But I couldn't rule anything out. Even the most meticulous killers got sloppy. I was hoping that was the case with this guy.

Drew and I settled on the couch, and the man took the recliner adjacent to us.

"We're investigating a recent string of crimes in Cedar Springs," I began. "We're hoping you might be able to help us."

The man blinked at me. "Cedar Springs?"

"That's right." I nodded. "It's about an hour west of here."

He gave a little shake of his head. "I've never been there, so I'm not sure how much help I'll be."

"Do you recognize this woman?" Drew held up a picture of Sienna. "A man matching your description was seen leaving the TriStar realty office building where she works."

The man lifted his shoulder. "Never been there."

"You sure? Because your vehicle was seen fleeing the scene just moments after she was attacked."

Though she hadn't technically been attacked, I knew Drew was testing the man.

But Foley just shook his head. "I don't know what you're talking about. I've never been anywhere near Tri-Star, and I have nothing to do with this woman."

"Mind if we take a look at your car?" I asked.

His wary gaze turned to me. "Why?"

"The car we saw had some damage to the right front fender. If it's not yours, we can rule it out pretty easily."

"Whatever." He huffed as he pushed to his feet. "If it'll make you feel better."

"It would." I offered a tight smile, then stood and followed him out of the apartment, and down to the elevator. He hit the button for the parking garage, which was located underground.

"We tried to stop by a few days ago," I said. "But you weren't home."

He shook his head but didn't meet my gaze. "I was traveling for work."

"You go places without your car?"

"I don't like to pay to leave it in long-term parking. I had my wife, Katy, drop me off instead."

Though what he said made sense, I remained skeptical. His secretary had told us he was on vacation last week, so if he was traveling, it wasn't for work.

"Where did you go?"

He flicked a quick look my way. "Chicago. I was working with a client."

"Oh yeah? I was thinking about taking my girlfriend

there for our anniversary," I lied. "Any special places I should check out?"

"Uh…" The elevator doors opened, and he quickly stepped out. "I didn't really get a chance to check out the city."

"Shame. Maybe next time." I slid a quick look at Drew, whose expression told me he didn't believe a word, either.

"My spot is over here." Foley pointed to the far corner of the parking garage. From here, I could see the rear bumper of the tan sedan, and I mentally confirmed the license plate.

The car was pulled forward into its corner spot, and I tossed a look his way. "How long was your trip?"

"I left last Monday. Just got back last night."

I nodded as I rounded the car—and stopped dead. Drew lifted his brows my way, and I gave an almost imperceptible nod before gesturing toward the front fender. "Mr. Foley, could you take a look at this?"

He stepped forward and immediately froze, his eyes going wide. "What the hell?"

He was a hell of an actor, I'd give him that.

He glanced between Drew and myself, eyes wild. "This is the first time I've seen that!"

"Hmm…" I gestured toward the vehicle. "Could you unlock this for me, please?"

His hands shook as he used the fob to unlock the sedan. Drew stood near Foley, keeping an eye on him as I slipped on a pair of gloves and opened the door. A quick scan of the interior showed nothing significant. Damn it.

I popped the trunk, fighting a scowl as I rounded the car. We needed something solid. Something like—

A gleam of silver caught the light as I lifted the lid of the trunk and peered inside.

Something like that. I turned to glance at Foley, whose face was devoid of color. I lifted the bloody knife from the trunk and held it up for his inspection. "Care to explain this?"

He shook his head, his whole body shaking violently. "Th-that's not mine! I've never seen it before!"

Drew's mouth turned down as he reached for the man's hands. "You have the right to remain silent..."

A buzzing filled my ears, drowning out the Miranda rights as I bagged the knife. The handle sported the exact same logo as the ones from Sienna's collection, and dried blood covered the blade. Anger swirled in my stomach, turning my skin hot. How the hell could he have done this to her? And why?

I battled down my anger. All that mattered now was that Sienna was safe. She could rest easy knowing the man who'd killed Boots and targeted her would soon be behind bars, exactly where he belonged.

It was finally over.

THIRTY-FOUR

SIENNA

A smile tugged at my lips as I watched the kitten prance happily around the living room. In the blink of an eye its posture changed, turning predatory. Its tiny body wiggled for a moment before pouncing on the toy mouse. They rolled and tussled for a moment before the kitten leapt to its feet with a hiss, back arched.

I couldn't help but laugh. "You silly little thing." I scooped up the kitten and cradled it to my chest. "What am I going to do with you?"

The kitten bumped my hand with its head, silently asking to be petted. I obliged as I pushed to my feet and carried the kitten toward the litter box. Instead of buying a new one, Vaughn had picked up the one in my house, along with the few toys I'd purchased for Boots. The kitten pawed at the litter for a moment before doing its business, then leapt from the box, off to see what other mischief he could find.

The thought that Vaughn had picked up the kitten for

me despite his obvious dislike of cats never failed to warm my heart. I was discovering new facets of his personality every day, and falling for him a little more.

The sound of a key turning in the lock startled me, making my heart jump with a combination of fear and excitement. Nothing had happened over the last couple of days, and I knew that I was safe here, but the memories were still fresh in my mind. Logically, I knew whoever had set the fire wouldn't be using a key to enter the house, but the fact that I hadn't heard Vaughn pull in surprised me.

I'd been so lost in thought watching the kitten that I had completely lost track of time, not paying attention to my surroundings. I checked on the kitten, who was currently tussling with a toy, then started toward the front door to meet Vaughn.

A smile lifted the corners of his lips as his gaze landed on me. "Hey, beautiful." He dropped his bag on the floor, simultaneously reaching behind him to close and re-lock the door. "I have some good news for you."

"Oh?" I tipped my head to the side. "What's that?"

"Remember the car that swiped yours on the side of the road?"

I nodded as he looped an arm around my waist and tugged me toward the couch. "Yeah. What about it?"

"Well..." He dropped to the couch and pulled me down beside him. "After the explosion at TriStar, we pulled footage from some of the local businesses. We found the same car in the background."

My heart gave a hard thump. "Seriously?"

"Yeah." Those molten eyes stared into mine, studying me. "Do you know Ryan Foley?"

I searched my memory for the name but came up empty. "I don't think so. Was it him?"

Vaughn nodded. "We just got confirmation today. His

car showed damage from the accident, and..." He paused for a second, watching me intently. "There was a knife in the trunk."

My brows drew together. A knife? But—

"Oh." Suddenly it hit me. The man had killed Boots, and Vaughn had found the weapon in the trunk of the car. Tears stung my eyes, burning across the bridge of my nose.

I found myself enfolded in Vaughn's arms before I formulated a response. "I'm sorry, honey."

Though I hadn't had Boots all that long, the loss still stung, exacerbated by the viciousness of the attack. I hoped his death had been quick, and that he hadn't felt any pain.

Vaughn tucked my face in close to his chest as my tears fell free. "We've got him. We have all the evidence we need to put him away."

I nodded but couldn't speak over the lump in my throat. It just didn't make sense. I'd never met this man. How could he feel such hate for me? It was good news. I was glad he'd been caught. But I needed to know *why*.

I opened my mouth to speak, but nothing came out. I cleared my throat and tried again. "W-why? Why would he do this?"

"I'm not sure, honey." Vaughn petted my hair away from my face, gently wiping away the tears that clung to my cheeks. "He wasn't exactly cooperative. But we'll find out."

Meow. The kitten's plaintive cry drew my attention downward, and I couldn't help but smile. It stood on two legs, his paws pressed to my calf. His small head tipped to the side as he peered up at me and meowed again, almost like he could sense my despair.

I lifted him up and cuddled him to my chest, his tiny furry body tucked between myself and Vaughn. His small paws opened and closed as he purred contentedly, and I lifted my face to smile at Vaughn. "I guess I should give him a name."

I'd been putting it off, and now I understood why. Subconsciously I'd been trying to keep my distance, fighting the attachment in case I lost him, too. And even though Boots was gone, Vaughn had found the man responsible. It was like a weight had been lifted off my shoulders, and the last sliver of reservation slipped away.

"What do you think?" I looked at Vaughn. "Any suggestions?"

"Something ferocious." He stared down at the kitten and rubbed his thumb over its tiny paw. "Those claws are small but deadly. I can already see the havoc he's going to wreak on this couch."

I grinned. "We can get him declawed when he gets bigger."

Vaughn's gaze flicked to mine, and I suddenly realized what I'd said. "I mean—"

But he didn't let me finish. "That's a good idea. We can talk to the vet about it."

Heat swept up my cheeks as happiness spread through me like warm maple syrup. "What about Oliver? Ollie for short?"

He swept a stray lock of hair off my cheek and tucked it behind my ear. "If you like it, that sounds good to me."

I dipped my head, heat flaring over my face. "So, um... What happens next?"

"With the case?" I lifted a shoulder, and his hand slid up the back to my neck, directing my gaze to his. He waited until I met his eyes to speak again. "Or us?"

I rolled my lips together, heart threatening to beat out of my chest. "Us," I whispered.

He leaned in closer, his fingers tracing along my jaw,

then over my lower lip. "We do this. Meet after work. Your place or mine—anywhere you want, as long as I get to see you. We'll have dinner, watch TV, then..." Dipping his head, he rubbed his nose along mine. "Go to bed."

His lips feathered over mine and he bit down lightly, causing me to suck in a breath. He chuckled then met my gaze. "Sound good to you?"

I nodded, unable to speak.

"Good." He leaned in, gaze fixed on my lips. A hairsbreadth away, he jerked back with a stifled shout.

I jerked in surprise as he jumped up and swiped at his left leg. "Damn it!"

Laughter bubbled up and I covered my mouth with my hands as I watched Vaughn attempt to pry the kitten away from where he was attached to his thigh. The tiny claws finally retracted as Vaughn peeled the kitten away and held him up.

"Little shit." He looked into the kitten's eyes. "I should have left you under the dumpster."

I couldn't help but laugh as Vaughn handed the kitten off to me. Despite his grumbling, I knew Vaughn would never have left the animal to fend for itself. Clutching the kitten to my chest, I stood, then stretched up on my toes and pressed a kiss to his cheek. Vaughn turned his head, and his lips found mine for a hard kiss that melted my insides and caused my pulse to skitter wildly.

A moment later he pulled away, leaving me breathless and more than a little lightheaded. How did he always do this to me? He had to have some sort of magic touch.

Releasing me, Vaughn rubbed the kitten's head. His gaze flicked to mine, and a wry smile tugged at his lips. "Maybe you should call him Rambo instead. Might be more appropriate. I won't have to worry about you with him here to take down any bad guys."

I grinned. "Between the two of you, I'd say I'm plenty safe."

His silvery eyes met mine and held. "Always, honey. Always."

THIRTY-FIVE

VAUGHN

Foley's hands shook, causing the water to slosh over the lip of the cup. The droplets splashed over the table, leaving small dots on the photographs laid before him.

"I was out of town, like I told you. There's no way I could have done this." He stared at the still shots of Sienna's car parked on the side of the road, the tan sedan swiping the left corner of the bumper, then fleeing the scene.

Drew slid a picture of Sienna forward. "Do you recognize this woman?"

Foley glanced at it, then shook his head. "Like I told you last time—she doesn't look familiar."

"You sure? This is Sienna Holt. Does that name ring a bell?"

Again the man shook his head. Drew extracted another photograph, this time from TriStar, Foley's vehicle in the background. "You see this?"

He pointed to the car. "Can you verify that the license plate matches your vehicle?"

The damage to the right front fender wasn't visible in the picture, but we all knew it was the same car.

Foley glanced at the photo and swallowed hard. "Y-yeah. That's mine."

Drew stared at the man across from him. "This photo was pulled from a camera near TriStar Realty. It was taken just a few moments after the building exploded."

Foley's eyes widened. "I swear I didn't do that. I've never even been there. And that lady"—he pointed to Sienna—"I never heard of her before. Never seen her in my life."

From behind the two-way glass, I studied the man's posture. Beside me, his wife shook her head. "Don't you understand you have the wrong person? He didn't do this."

"Mrs. Foley, I understand you're upset," I said slowly. "But this is a very serious allegation."

She threw her hands in the air. "How could he possibly have done this? He was out of town the whole time."

I didn't bother to respond. She either didn't want to believe he was capable of it, or she was covering for him. I knew from speaking with Mr. Foley's assistant that he wasn't in the office, but I was holding that card close to my chest for the moment.

We'd questioned Katherine Foley as soon as we'd arrived at the station, but she didn't appear to be aware of her husband's deception. She herself had been at work during all three incidents, so it was easy enough to rule her out. I'd allowed her the opportunity to witness the interview, hoping her reaction would give me better insight on how to proceed.

"Mr. Foley, you understand your vehicle has been photographed at the scene of both crimes? How do you explain that?"

"I... I don't know. It wasn't me, I swear."

"I'm going to call our lawyer," she seethed.

I tamped down the urge to roll my eyes. I was honestly surprised she hadn't lawyered up already, but she'd insisted they had nothing to hide. "Mrs. Foley, I would absolutely advise you to seek legal counsel. As Detective Thorne mentioned, your husband has been placed at the scene of several crimes."

Inside the interview room, Drew changed tacks. "Mr. Foley, can you tell me where you were during the incidents?"

Drew rattled off the days and times, and I watched Foley's face pale. "I was out of town."

"For business, is that right?"

"Yeah." He picked up his cup again, hands shaking violently.

"And you still work for Callaway Logistics?"

He paused, his gaze fixed on the photos in front of him. "That's right."

"That's interesting." Drew shuffled some papers. "Because when we called and spoke with your assistant, Corinne, she told us you'd taken the last two weeks off."

Beside me, Mrs. Foley sucked in a shocked breath. Her body went utterly still as she stared at her husband. Foley's gaze slowly lifted to the window, his expression full of guilt and regret.

"We know you weren't working," Drew pressed. "Where were you?"

As if sensing her presence behind the glass, Foley's face twisted. "I'm sorry." He dropped his face into his hands for a moment before meeting Drew's eyes again. "I was... I was with my girlfriend."

Mrs. Foley's hand flew to her throat, and she swayed on her feet. I shot out a hand, ready to catch her if she fell. Gripping the ledge of the wall so tight her knuckles turned white, she stared through the glass at her wayward husband.

"Where were you?" Drew asked again.

"We drove up the coast a little." He let out a resigned sigh. "We spent the first week in New Orleans."

"You were there the entire week?"

"Yeah. On Monday we headed back and stayed at a Ramada Inn over in Ft. Worth."

"Walk me through what happened—start with last week."

Foley flicked another look at the window before speaking. "My wife…" His voice cracked, and he cleared his throat to start over. "Katy dropped me off at the airport last Monday morning. I had Dina come pick me up as soon as she left."

I slid a look at Mrs. Foley, who didn't even seem to be breathing. She hadn't moved a muscle, had done nothing except stare intently at her husband.

"We… we drove her car up to New Orleans and stayed in a hotel there. Dina had never been there before, so…" His voice broke, and he cleared his throat before starting again. "After that, we spent some time in Ft. Worth."

Drew made a little motion for him to elaborate. "What did you do there?"

Foley shot Drew a wry look. "We… you know."

Mrs. Foley closed her eyes. Reaching behind me, I snagged the box of tissues from the table and held them out. She extracted one, but her eyes remained dry.

Foley took a deep breath. "We stayed mostly in the room. Went out a couple times for dinner. Went to a club one night."

Mrs. Foley clutched the tissue tightly, her fingers crushing the fine material as she clenched her fist over and over.

"I told my wife I was flying in night before last. I had Dina drop me at the airport, then…" He sighed. "I called Katy to come pick me up."

He glanced up at the window again, and Mrs. Foley closed her eyes before turning to me. She met my gaze, back straight, chin up. "I believe I'll need a lawyer after all. If you'll excuse me."

I nodded and held the door for her, then escorted her from the station. As she started to cross the lobby, I stopped her. "Mrs. Foley? I'm sorry."

She tipped her head in acknowledgment, then disappeared.

Drew was just exiting the interview room when I caught up to him. "Did he confess?"

"No." He shook his head. "He's adamant that the girlfriend will alibi him. What do you think?" He leaned a shoulder against the wall. "Ft. Worth isn't too far. Definitely could have driven to and from without raising any red flags. The wife would have been at work, so she never would have noticed."

I'd had the same thought. "I'll check with the girlfriend and see if I can find anything."

Drew passed me her info, and I headed back to my desk. Even if she did alibi him, there was a lot stacked against him. Unless something drastic happened, the case was pretty tight. We'd gotten our guy, and now we could finally rest.

THIRTY-SIX

SIENNA

The melodic tone echoed through the lower level, and it took me a moment to realize it was the doorbell. Today was my first day back home, and it felt familiar yet not.

I'd spent the morning getting Ollie settled in his new home, doing laundry and unpacking the things I'd kept at Vaughn's. After they'd found the owner of the tan car, he'd deemed it safe to return. It was a relief, yet I'd become comfortable in his home. We'd decided for now to split time between his place and mine, and he was coming over after his shift tonight.

True to his word, he'd cleaned up the kitchen, and all of the blood had been removed, like it was never even here. I appreciated his help more than I could say. He'd been absolutely amazing over the past couple of weeks, and I practically floated on air as I made my way to the front door. Things between us had moved quickly, but in so many ways, it just felt right.

The whole debacle with Derrick felt like it had

happened a lifetime ago. The hurt and betrayal had diminished, replaced by Vaughn's unconditional love and support. I wasn't sure what the future held for us, but what I did know was that this thing between us was special. I loved him in a way I'd never loved anyone else, and I had a feeling no one would ever touch my heart the way he had.

Surprise rippled through me as I checked the peephole. I wasn't expecting anyone, least of all Sophia's fiancé, Ethan. Did something happen? I yanked open the door, my gaze sweeping over his face. "Ethan. Is everything okay?"

"Hey." He grinned. "Everything's good. I saw you were home, so I just wanted to stop and check on you."

I stepped back and gestured for him to enter. "Yeah, it's my first day back, actually. Come on in."

"Thanks." He stepped into the foyer and jumped a little when Ollie stealthily attacked from the side. His eyes widened. "You got another cat."

"I did." I scooped up the kitten, detangling his claws from the hem of Ethan's dress pants. "Actually, Vaughn got him for me. After... You know." I waved a hand in the air and pasted on a smile. "Anyway. What brings you by?"

His gaze lifted from the kitten and met mine, a sheepish smile curving his lips. "I kind of have a favor to ask."

"What's that?"

"I wanted to do something special for Sophia. My grandmother passed down her ring to me, and I was hoping you could take a look at it and see if Soph might like it."

"Of course." I smiled. "That's so sweet. I'd love to see it."

He rubbed the back of his neck. "I actually don't have it. I saw your car and decided to stop. The ring is at my family's cabin where they used to stay. If you're free, we could go pick it up, take it to the jeweler."

I bit my lip. There was still so much to catch up on, but the pleading look he sent my way had me reconsidering.

"It would mean a lot," he said. "We'll be quick, I promise."

Damn it. He obviously adored my sister, and besides, Vaughn wouldn't be home for several hours yet. I couldn't find it in me to deny him, so I nodded. "Let me grab my purse."

Ethan brightened. "Thanks. You're a lifesaver."

I smiled. "I'm happy to help."

I put Ollie in the laundry room so he wouldn't damage anything while I was gone, then gathered my purse and phone before meeting Ethan at the front door. I locked it behind us, then followed him to his car, my heart feeling surprisingly light as I climbed inside.

He threw a quick look my way. "Sophia is really excited about the wedding."

"Good. I'm glad." And I meant it.

I found the idea of my baby sister getting married didn't bother me nearly as much as it once had. Now that Vaughn was in my life, it was as if a spark of hope had flickered to life in my heart. He made me feel beautiful, like he truly treasured me, infused me with confidence that Derek had slowly stripped away. I wondered if someday Vaughn and I would be planning our own wedding.

I couldn't help the smile that curled my lips, and Ethan tipped his head to the side as he studied me. "Everything good?"

"Perfect."

He nodded, a little smile forming on his own lips. "You look really happy."

"I am. Now that we finally put everything behind us, I feel like I can finally move forward."

Ethan steered the car toward the south. "The world is crazy. You never know what can happen these days."

"Too true." The thought prompted me to take my cell phone from my purse. Vaughn always liked to know where I was and that I was safe, so I wanted to let him know that I would be gone with Ethan this afternoon.

I quickly typed out a message and hit send, waiting impatiently for it to show as delivered. Ten seconds passed, then twenty, but the message still didn't go through.

"What the heck?" I held the phone up like doing so would get better reception.

"No service?" Ethan asked.

I shook my head. "It shows I have service, but it's not going through."

"Must be a glitch," he replied. "Could just be an issue with the tower or something. Give it a minute and I'm sure it'll go through."

I drummed my fingers on my thigh as I waited, but the message still wouldn't go through. I made a low sound in my throat, and Ethan flicked a look my way. "It's okay. You can borrow my phone if you need it, or there's a landline at the cabin."

I nodded absently, still staring at the screen, a flutter of unease taking up residence in my stomach. Something felt off. I just couldn't put my finger on exactly what it was.

THIRTY-SEVEN

VAUGHN

Something didn't feel right.

There was still no correlation between Foley and Sienna that we could find, and he swore up and down during his interview that he'd never seen her before. I didn't know what to make of it. The damage to the car spoke volumes, and the knife... It was like a literal smoking gun.

Foley insisted he had nothing to do with the attempts on Sienna's life, and crazy as it was, I was beginning to question it myself. It all seemed too... easy.

There was an alternative that I was reluctant to consider. Maybe he really was telling the truth. But if he wasn't responsible, who the hell was?

I glanced across the coffee table at Dina, the woman Ryan Foley claimed to have spent the past two weeks with. "Ms. Schneider, can you tell me where you were last week?"

She crossed one leg over the other. "I was traveling with a friend. Why?"

"We're investigating a series of incidents that occurred in Cedar Springs. Ever been there?"

Her brows drew together. "Not that I'm aware of."

"Do you know Ryan Foley?"

Her lashes flickered the tiniest bit before she nodded. "We met last year at Callaway's holiday party."

"Is that where you work?"

"No." She sat up a little straighter, sensing the shift in questioning. "I was dating someone he worked with at the time."

"Have you seen Mr. Foley recently?"

She was silent for a moment. Her gaze darted over my shoulder to the window, and I could practically see the wheels turning as she debated whether to lie or not. "I've seen him," she finally replied.

"Was he the friend you were with the last couple of weeks?"

She opened her mouth to speak, but decided against whatever she was about to say and snapped it closed again.

"Ms. Schneider, I'm not here to judge you. Whatever happened is between you and Mr. Foley. But I need to ask you about last week. Okay?"

She swallowed hard before nodding. "Sure."

"You said you were traveling. Where, exactly?"

"New Orleans for a while." She licked her lips. "We spent the past week in Ft. Worth."

Exactly as Foley had claimed. I nodded. "And you were there all week?"

"That's right." She folded her hands tightly in her lap and shifted uncomfortably. "I'm sure you know about his, um... About Katy?"

I dipped my head in acknowledgement, and she blew out a breath. "Does she know? About... me and Ryan?"

"She does now," I replied softly.

She momentarily closed her eyes, and a quiet epithet fell from her lips. "She seemed so nice at the party. I felt so bad at first, but Ryan was always saying how unhappy he was. We started talking a few months ago, and it just... happened."

She turned her pleading eyes on me, and I held up a hand. "Ms. Schneider, you obviously care about him. Mr. Foley has been accused of a very serious crime, and I need you to help me establish a timeline. Tell me about when the two of you headed up to New Orleans."

Her eyes rolled toward the ceiling as she contemplated her answer. "Katy dropped Ryan off at the airport around nine, and I picked him up around nine-thirty. It took us a while to get up to New Orleans, and we didn't check in until late. We ordered room service that evening and the next day. The desk clerk of the hotel should be able to confirm that he was with me."

"I'll speak with him, thanks." I decided to start at the beginning, when Foley's vehicle had sideswiped Sienna. "Can you tell me where you were last Tuesday?"

"We didn't do much that day. We were both pretty exhausted from all the driving. We did go out to dinner— some restaurant in the quarter."

I jotted down the info. "And when did you leave New Orleans?"

"Monday morning," she replied. "We got into Ft. Worth around eight or so. We mostly stayed in the hotel—so we wouldn't be recognized," she explained needlessly. "Most of the time we stayed in the hotel, um..." Her cheeks went bright pink, and her voice dropped a fraction. "Hooking up."

"Why not spend the two weeks in New Orleans?" I asked.

"It was cheaper," she replied simply. "The idea was kind

of to hide in plain sight. We were close to home, but far enough away that we wouldn't run into too many people."

It made sense in a twisted sort of way. If they'd checked in on Monday as she stated, they would have been back in the area when Sienna's house had been broken into and Boots mutilated. "How about this past Tuesday?"

"Tuesday..." She tapped her lips. "Tuesday we went to a cute little café downtown for brunch."

"What time was that?"

"Eleven, maybe?" She shrugged. "I still have the receipt if you want it."

"That would be helpful, thanks."

"That night we went to a club—Excelsior."

"And Wednesday? Specifically around dinnertime." I was even more curious to know where the hell Foley had been during the explosion at TriStar.

"We went to a sports bar to watch the game."

I jotted down the info. "Would you happen to have the receipt for that, also?"

"I do. Oh!" Her face brightened, and she sat up straight. "I have pictures—and a video!"

"May I see them?"

She quickly snatched up her phone and pulled up a string of pictures. The camera roll was filled with images of her and Foley in the French Quarter, watching the parades and taking selfies at some of the major landmarks.

Finally I got to the video. The timestamp read 4:04 Wednesday afternoon—the precise time when Sienna had been at TriStar. I glanced at Ms. Schneider. "May I have a copy of this?"

"Whatever you need."

I sent the video to my email, a heavy feeling in my gut. I passed the phone back to her. "Thanks for your help. I'll let you know if I need anything else."

I silently swore as I made my way out of the apartment building. Foley was our only suspect—and the photographic evidence had effectively exonerated him.

If he wasn't responsible, who the hell was?

THIRTY-EIGHT

SIENNA

The cabin was completely blocked from view by towering, dense pines that seemed to rise straight up to the sky. The car slowed, and Ethan scanned the area. "I know the driveway is here somewhere."

He chuckled sheepishly, and I smiled. "I don't blame you. I don't know how people find anything around here. Your grandparents must have really wanted their privacy."

Ethan laughed. "I'll say." He pointed to a dirt and gravel road on the right. "Here it is."

The car bounced along as we climbed the steep incline, and the log cabin seemingly appeared out of nowhere as we crested the hill. "It's beautiful."

Ethan slowed to a stop and gestured to the house. "Come on in. You can take a look around while I get the ring."

"Sure, if you don't mind."

I followed Ethan up the wide porch steps and waited for him as he looked for the key. He checked under the mat, then over the lintel of the door. His cheeks flushed red, and he mumbled something under his breath.

"Can't find the key?"

His lips pressed into a firm line. "It has to be around here somewhere."

He hunted behind the patio furniture, and I finally found it beneath a flowerpot. "Here it is."

His eyes filled with relief. "Thanks."

He unlocked the door, then put the key back into his hiding spot. "Come on in."

He gestured for me to precede him, and I stepped into the living room. It was dim inside, the floors and furniture covered in a thin coating of dust. A musty smell permeated the air, causing my nose to twitch, and I fought back a sneeze.

"We don't come here much," Ethan said by way of apology.

I waved him off. "No problem. I'll just wait here."

I checked my phone again as Ethan went upstairs, but my message to Vaughn still hadn't been delivered. That was strange. My phone showed only one bar of service inside the cabin, so I decided to head outside and try again.

"Ethan," I called up the stairs. "I'll be outside."

"Be there in a second," he yelled back.

I stepped out onto the front porch and clicked on the option to resend the message to Vaughn. A notification came through a second later, telling me it had failed once more. What the hell was going on?

The tread of steps on the front porch drew my attention to Ethan. His hands were empty, and I tipped my head at him. "Did you find it?"

"Yep. I'm all good."

The way he stared at me sent alarm bells pinging in the back of my mind. "Do you want me to take a look at it?"

He shook his head. "That's okay, it can wait until we get to the jeweler."

I nodded slowly, my mind whirling. He was acting strange. "Is everything okay?"

He nodded. "Of course."

Every cell of my body felt hyperalert as I studied him. His demeanor had changed, his expression bordering on aloof, his voice cold.

My pulse kicked up, and I swallowed hard. "Ethan, what's going on?"

He took a step toward me, and my muscles twitched with the urge to flee. "You seem to be extraordinarily lucky. Saved from that car accident, then the fire." My stomach clenched as he took another step forward, his icy gaze locked on me. "What will it take to get rid of you?"

The words sent a shock through my system, and I recoiled. "What?"

Ethan couldn't possibly mean what I thought he did. He was marrying my sister. He was going to be my brother-in-law. But the way he glared at me told me none of that mattered to him. "W-why?"

He shook his head as he descended another step to stand on the ground just a few feet away. "One accident. That's all it should have taken. But you couldn't make it easy and just die, could you?"

Bile rose up at the animosity drenching nod tone. "I've never done anything to you."

"I know." A cruel smile twisted his lips. "That's what makes all of this so perfect."

Goosebumps broke over my skin despite the heat of the day. "Why do you hate me?"

"I don't hate you. But I have my future to think about. I need to provide a good life for Sophia, and the money will go a long way."

"What money?"

He cocked his head. "Your inheritance. With you gone, everything will go to Soph. With your share, we won't have to worry about anything ever again."

"And you don't think my sister will be upset if you kill me?"

"You've had a lot of accidents lately. No one will question it when you disappear."

I stared at him. "You do realize that if I just disappear, insurance will never pay out."

A muscle twitched in his jaw as he stared at me. I knew I probably should've kept my mouth shut, but the whole thing was so absurd. I wasn't able to help myself.

"I can arrange for you to be found eventually."

There was no doubt in my mind that he would do it too. Ethan was completely unhinged. He'd been plotting for weeks to kill me. How had none of us seen this side of him? "He'll find you," I said.

"The mutt you call your boyfriend?" His lips twisted with disdain, sending fury coursing through my body.

"His name is Vaughn. And he's twice the man you'll ever be." Ethan's eyes narrowed, but anger spurred me on. "The police will know that I was with you, and they'll come looking for me."

He laughed, and the sound sent goosebumps rippling over my spine. "Good luck with that."

Ethan had lost his damn mind. I needed to get the hell out of here. I still held my cell phone, and I squeezed the two buttons on the side of the phone. After a few seconds, it would automatically summon emergency services. All I needed to do was bide my time and distract him long enough for them to show up. "Ethan, I—"

"Haven't you figured it out yet? No one knows where

you are, and they sure as hell aren't coming for you. Did you ever wonder why your cell phone isn't working?"

He pointed toward the car. "I've got a jammer on there that blocks the signal. So that stupid emergency protocol you're trying right now..." He arched a brow my way. "That's not going to work, either."

Shit. I loosened my grip on the buttons, fear settling over me as the last of my hope dissipated into thin air. I couldn't give up yet. He said there was a jammer in the car. That just meant I had to get far enough away and the phone could get a signal again.

My face must've given away my thoughts, because Ethan chuckled as he threw his arms wide. "Where do you think you're going to go? The trees alone would block the reception."

I had to get away from him, but running on foot would be futile. I had no idea where I was, let alone what the terrain around the area looked like. My luck, I would do Ethan a favor by falling off a cliff and breaking my neck. He had mentioned before that there was a landline inside the cabin, but, even if that were true, I would have to find it and make a call before he got inside the house. My options were limited, and my window for opportunity was rapidly closing. Ethan took another step forward.

I edged toward the car to put some distance between us. I couldn't remember if Ethan had taken the keys with him or not. As close as he was, I more than likely wouldn't have enough time to get inside and lock the doors, even if the keys were inside, which I doubted they were.

Ethan tracked me, his body tense, his eyes watchful. I had to get away from him; I at least had to try. I took several steps backward before whirling and making a break for it. I heard the sound of footsteps on gravel as Ethan gave chase. I changed directions suddenly, veering around the car and back toward the cabin.

The sharp rocks dug into the soles of my thin ballet flats, But I shoved the pain away as I raced toward the house. Instead of rounding the car as I had, Ethan reversed directions and bolted over the hood, costing me precious seconds. I watched in my periphery as he quickly gained on me, and I forced my muscles to move faster.

The lattice of the porch came into view up ahead, and just beyond that, a narrow sliver of bright yellow. *A shovel.* It was propped against the side of the cabin, and I lunged for it, wrapping both hands around the bright yellow handle just as Ethan caught up to me.

I turned and swung with all my might, but the motion was hampered by our close proximity. The shaft of the shovel connected with his shoulder and sent the vibration back to my hands, causing my grip to loosen.

Ethan grunted but didn't go down. We were too close; I had no advantage. Ethan wrapped a hand around the handle and ripped the shovel from my grasp. I held onto it a second too long and stumbled toward him. I tried to change directions, but I was too late. He swung the shovel in a wide arc, and the flat of the blade caught me in the middle of the back.

A strangled cry of pain ripped from my throat as I stumbled forward. It felt as if the air had been torn from my lungs, as I tried to drag in much-needed oxygen. The world careened wildly around me as I fell, and I managed to shoot out my hands at the last second. My fingers dug into the grass, and I clawed at it, fighting for traction. I had just managed to get my feet under me when agony ripped through my right leg.

I screamed in pain and hit the ground, clutching at my thigh. Blood saturated my pants and seeped through my fingers, and tears blinded my vision. My body convulsed in pain, and I could barely make out his hazy form as Ethan stepped over top of me, one foot on either side of my torso.

He lightly dug the tip of the blade into my stomach, and I automatically sucked in a breath in an attempt to get away from it. He pressed down harder, until the blade left a crescent in the sensitive flesh of my stomach. Releasing my leg, I grabbed the handle of the shovel to keep him from impaling me. My hands were slick with blood, and my grip slipped.

A horrible smile curved his mouth. "I'm impressed. You've put up one hell of a fight. It's almost a shame I have to kill you."

I almost couldn't focus as pain radiated through my body.

Ethan dropped to his haunches, so he hovered just inches from me. His dark brown eyes bore into mine. "Close your eyes, Sienna. You don't want to watch this."

More like he didn't want to have to look me in the eyes while he killed me. Anger spurted through me. "Fuck you! You're nothing but a coward."

His eyes flashed with fury, and he leaned so close our noses almost touched. "I'm not a fucking coward."

Sucking in my cheeks, I took a breath and spit in his face. His face went slack with shock before rage exploded over his expression. "You fucking bitch!"

Taking advantage of his distraction, I drove my left leg upward as hard as I could. Ethan howled in pain as my knee connected with his groin. His grip on the shovel loosened, and I drove the heel of my hand up into his nose. Blood spurted from the orifice, splattering both of us, and I shoved him off as he fell to the side.

"You cunt!" One hand covered his groin, while the other

wiped blood from his nose, but I refused to feel bad. "I'm going to kill you!"

Grabbing up the handle of the shovel, I reared back and swung it as hard as I could. The flat of the blade connected with a side of his head, and Ethan went down hard. He landed face down on the ground, and everything suddenly went deathly still.

The blood rushing in my ears gradually slowed as I stood over him, waiting for him to regain consciousness. Several long moments passed, but he didn't move. I wasn't going to waste any more time. My head felt woozy from the loss of blood, and I knew I had to get help before I bled out.

Keeping the shovel close by, I patted down Ethan's body, searching for the keys. I found them in his right front pocket but they snagged on the material, refusing to come free. Blood trickled steadily from the wound in my leg, and I ground my molars together as I shifted positions so I could roll Ethan to his back.

He was heavier than he looked, and it took several tries to get him turned over. I finally worked the keys free, then clambered to my feet and dragged myself toward the car as quickly as I could. My right leg didn't want to function, so I used the shovel as a makeshift cane as a hobbled forward.

I was halfway to the car when a low groan met my ears. I threw a look over my shoulder and my heart went into a tailspin as I watched Ethan roll to his side, then push up onto his hands and knees. His head lifted, those deep eyes locking on me.

Shit.

Digging the tip of the shovel into the ground, I used it as leverage to push myself forward. My hands shook, and the keys slid through my fingers, slippery with blood. After two tries I finally managed to get inside the car and lock the door. I shoved the key into the ignition and cranked it just as

Ethan reached the driveway. My right leg refused to cooperate, so I stepped on the brake with my left foot and shifted into reverse.

Shards of glass rained down around me as the window to my left exploded, and a huge set of hands wrapped around my neck, cutting off my scream. I let go of the steering wheel, grasping at his hands, trying to get him to release me. With my only thought to escape, I stomped down on the accelerator.

The car swerved wildly on the gravel, and Ethan's hands slipped away. Relief and hope bloomed inside me but it faded just as quickly as the rear end of the car slammed into something. My head snapped backward at the impact, sending stars dancing before my eyes. Just a few feet away, Ethan was walking toward me again.

Fear and anger in equal measure welled up, and I shifted the transmission into drive before hitting the gas. The tires spun for a moment before catching, and Ethan's eyes widened as the car shot forward, heading straight for him. He tried to leap out of the way, but there wasn't time. The emblem of the hood ornament caught his midsection, throwing him face down on the hood.

The sharp crack of wood splintered the air as the car launched into the porch, trapping Ethan between the house and the vehicle. His head lifted, dark eyes filled with surprise and fear. He opened his mouth to speak, but blood poured out instead, choking off his words.

I closed my eyes against the macabre site, wishing I could cover my ears and block it all out. Thoughts ricocheted through my head, and I finally forced myself to focus. My hand shook as I shifted the car into reverse. But instead of moving, the engine gave a rough cough, then went silent.

I stared stupidly at it, uncomprehending. I tried to crank

the engine again, to no avail. My gaze lifted to Ethan, whose lips twisted into a rueful grin. A horrifying laugh left his throat, washing over me.

This couldn't be happening. I turned the key again, and though I tried several times, it refused to turn over. I grabbed the steering wheel and shook it, a long, loud scream resonating from my throat.

Blood covered the seat, and I managed to drag myself out of the car and up the steps into the cabin. I could only hope to God that they had a landline somewhere inside. Every cell of my body hurt, and it felt like an hour had passed before I finally found an old white cradle-type phone in the kitchen. I grabbed the headset and punched in 911, then slid down the wall to sit on the floor.

"911. What's your emergency?"

My lips parted to speak, but they were stalled as black began to seep into the edges of my vision. I dimly heard the operator's voice on the other line before the phone slipped from my hand with a clatter, and everything went black.

THIRTY-NINE

VAUGHN

Before the elevator doors had opened the whole way, I'd already launched myself into the hallway, weaving through the visitors gathered there, my gaze scanning the plaques on the doors.

The woman at the desk downstairs told me Sienna was in room 416, and I followed the increasing numbers. At the end of the hallway, a familiar face caught my attention, and my breath halted in my lungs. Near the door of a hospital room, Spencer Holt stood, his face stoic, his arms wrapped around Sienna's sister, Sophia, as she sobbed into his chest.

Oh, God.

The lights overhead suddenly seemed too bright, and the floor felt like it was spinning beneath my feet. A vise tightened around my lungs as cold swept over me. Spencer met my gaze and held, a bleakness in his expression that ripped my soul to shreds.

"Hey." A hand clamped down on my shoulder a

moment before Mac's voice penetrated the dizzying fog of fear. "You're all good."

Was I? I couldn't tear my gaze from Sienna's father where he stood comforting Sophia just a few yards ahead. He held her close, one arm wrapped tightly around her waist while the other made slow, comforting sweeps up and down her spine. Her pitiful sobs pierced my ears. Those were the tears of utter devastation—of loss.

Emotion clogged my throat, and I forced one foot in front of the other as Mac led me forward. As we neared the door to Sienna's room, dread swirled in my gut. I needed to see her, but no one had been able to tell me anything when I called. I was going in blind, and I fucking hated it. I had no idea how badly she was hurt, or what had transpired. All I knew was that I hadn't been there for her when she needed me most.

Swallowing hard, I cleared my face of every emotion and steeled my spine. The door stood wide open, the lights turned down low, and I drew in a deep breath before crossing the threshold. It took my eyes a moment to adjust, and when everything finally came into focus, my heart cracked wide open at the sight that greeted me.

Sienna lay in the narrow bed, her face turned slightly to one side as she reclined on a pillow. The blanket was pulled up to her chest, leaving only her arms and upper torso exposed. But what I found there sent fury streaming through my veins.

Her face and neck were splattered with dark liquid that I could only assume was blood. Several scratches stood out against her pale skin and the pristine white bed linens.

I closed the door to block out the sounds beyond the room and approached silently, not wanting to disturb her. Whatever she'd been through today, her body needed rest.

But I couldn't help the urgent need to touch her, to make sure she was truly okay.

I sank into the stiff chair next to the bed, my gaze sweeping over her as I did so. She looked so small and frail, and I suddenly realized how easily I could have lost her—could still lose her.

Reaching out, I slid my fingers lightly over the back of her hand. Her fingers twitched in response, and her lashes fluttered before her big blue eyes opened. I couldn't help the smile that stretched my face. Those pretty eyes were the most beautiful thing I'd ever seen.

"I'm sorry, honey," I whispered. "I didn't mean to wake you up."

She licked her lips. "It's okay. I'm glad you're here."

"Me, too." My heart constricted as I stared at her. "I'm glad you're okay."

Her hand twitched, seemingly searching for me, and I wrapped her fingers in mine. Her chest rose and fell on a deep breath, and she squeezed my hand tight, like she never wanted to let go.

Still grasping her hand, I shifted onto the bed next to her, careful not to jostle her too much. "Am I hurting you?" I whispered.

I wasn't sure why I kept my voice down; the situation just seemed to call for it.

"No. I..." Sienna swallowed hard before shaking her head. "I want you here."

The vise around my heart clenched tight, and my eyes felt suspiciously damp as I leaned forward and touched my forehead to hers. To see her like this tore at my soul. My girl was hurt, and I couldn't even hold her.

"I'm sorry I wasn't there." My lips brushed her cheek as I spoke. "I'd give anything to go back in time and be there for you."

"I shouldn't have..." She squeezed my hand again, her grip not nearly as strong as it was a moment ago. I could tell she was tiring again, and quickly. "I didn't know. And now..."

She drew a ragged breath, and a tear slipped from the corner of her eye.

"It's not your fault, honey." I swiped away the tears that trickled down her cheeks. I wanted so badly to tell her how much she meant to me. How much my life had changed since she'd roared into my life.

How much I loved her.

But I did none of those things. In the end, I just held her as she faded into a deep sleep. I enveloped her with my body as best I could, lending my strength and support. She needed to know I was here for her—that I would always be here for her—no matter what.

I lay there with her even as her breathing turned even and deep, not wanting to let her go. I would have stayed there longer, but the touch of a hand on my shoulder drew my attention to Mac. He gestured toward the door, and I kissed Sienna's forehead once more before gently extracting my hand from hers and laying it on the bed. I slipped from the mattress and met Mac in the hallway.

Mr. Holt and Sophia were gone, and I assumed they'd moved to the waiting room. I turned to my friend. "Thanks for being here."

"Of course." He dipped his head. "Why don't we go grab some coffee?"

I tossed one last glance Sienna's way, feeling like my whole heart was in that bed.

"We won't be long," Mac said. "But I figure it's better to discuss this somewhere else."

I nodded and fell into step beside him as we made our way to the elevator and down to the bottom floor of the hospital. I hadn't asked for details when he'd called me an hour ago. All I could remember was him telling me Sienna was hurt and been taken to Mercy Hospital. Everything after that was a blur.

Once we were settled in a corner table with coffees in front of us, I met his gaze. "Tell me everything."

"The local police are still investigating, but Sienna was apparently in an altercation with her sister's fiancé, Ethan. She was hurt pretty badly but managed to call 911."

How the hell could he do this to her? "Where the fuck is he?"

"He's here."

Fury burned through me. "Where? I'm going to—"

"Downstairs."

Downstairs? But...

Mac speared me with a look, and I sat back hard in my chair.

The morgue.

I wasn't entirely certain whether I was relieved that he was dead or not. "What happened?"

"I'm not sure. Ethan's car was at the scene when they arrived, so they're assuming they rode together."

"Where the hell were they?"

"Some cabin. Belonged to a coworker of his, I guess." Mac shrugged. "According to the officers who got there first, it looked like they got into a fight. Sienna ended up with a huge gash on her leg, and Ethan had a pretty good welt on his head."

He explained how the local police found a shovel covered in blood, and how the driver's seat of the car was covered in blood, apparently from the wound in Sienna's leg.

Mac rubbed the back of his neck. "They found Ethan

pinned by the car. He bled out before they got to the hospital."

Jesus Christ. I dropped my face into my hands. I couldn't begin to imagine what she'd been through.

"She's okay." I lifted my head and met Mac's steady gaze. He leaned in a bit as if to emphasize his point. "And she's got you. It's going to be rough for a while, but you two got a second chance. Don't be afraid to tell her how much you care about her."

His eyes were haunted, and my heart twisted a little. Mac knew the pain of loss firsthand. "I'm sorry. About…"

He waved me off. "Sienna is good for you. And I know you love her. You'll get through this."

I nodded. Mac was right. She needed to know how I felt —how I'd felt since the moment we met.

Sienna was my entire world, and I didn't want to spend a single day without her.

FORTY

SIENNA

From my spot in the corner of the couch, I watched as Vaughn prowled restlessly around the room. "Sit down. You're making me nervous."

He threw an incredulous look my way. "I'm making you nervous? Seriously?" He snorted. "Says the woman who took ten years off my life. I'm not sure my heart has slowed down since I got that call."

Less than twenty-four hours had passed since I'd been released from the hospital, and I knew Vaughn was still keyed up. He'd barely left my side during the past few days except to work, and only when he knew I had someone with me.

My hospital room felt like it had a revolving door. My father had visited frequently, as had Marjorie, Eden, and various friends and coworkers. Despite that, Vaughn had called to check in on me nearly every half hour, making sure I was safe and sound, ensuring I wasn't experiencing any complications.

The cut on the back of my thigh had resulted in seventeen stitches, and they pulled a bit as I shifted my weight. My grimace wasn't lost on Vaughn, and he was kneeling by my side before I could blink. "What's wrong? Is everything okay?"

I eased my weight to the side and grabbed his hand. "I'm fine. The stitches just pulled for a second."

"Does it hurt? Do you need—?"

"I'm okay. Really." I tugged on his hand again, pulling him up so he sat on the edge of the couch next to me. "I don't need anything except you."

His expression softened, and he slipped a hand around the back of my neck. His gaze roamed my face, taking in the assortment of scratches and colorful bruises. His lips turned down, and his hand flexed the tiniest bit. "I'm so sorry, honey." His voice cracked. "I knew something was off. If I'd only figured it out sooner..."

I shook my head. "It was exactly what Ethan wanted. To distract you, to keep you busy."

"I shouldn't have left you alone," he said fiercely. "I'll never forgive myself."

"It's not your fault," I quietly admonished. "I made the choice to go with him."

And I'd regretted it every moment since I climbed in the car.

"You didn't know." Vaughn leaned in and pressed his forehead to mine. "He took advantage of you. He knew you would trust him. And I..."

"You couldn't have known. None of us did." The man was preparing to marry my baby sister; who better to trust than him? But he'd fooled all of us.

His steely eyes met mine and held. "Sienna... I—"

The doorbell rang, cutting off his words, and he growled. "Damn it. I'll be right back."

He pushed off the couch and I watched him go, a warmth suffusing my chest. I rubbed at the space just over my heart. I loved him so damn much.

The soft murmur of voices drifted toward the living room, and shock hit me a moment later when Vaughn reentered the room, my sister at his side.

My heart nearly broke at the sight of her, eyes red from crying, her face splotchy and lined with emotional turmoil. Her expression was guarded as she stared at me. "Hey."

Seeing my sister immediately brought to mind all the memories of that last day with Ethan. The crazed look in his eyes as he'd come after me... Watching the life drain from him...

I cleared my throat, forcing down the emotion and blinking away the tears stinging my eyes. "Hey. Want to come in for a sec?"

She nodded but didn't say a word as she silently drifted closer. She glanced around before perching on the opposite end of the couch. Her gaze landed on Oliver, playing with a stuffed mouse, and a tiny smile curled her lips. "He's cute."

"Thanks." He'd been a good distraction since being home, though he was absolutely fascinated with Vaughn. The man who swore he wasn't a cat person was slowly coming around. I even caught him cuddling Ollie and sneaking him treats when he thought I wasn't paying attention.

My gaze moved back to my sister, and my smile fell. Sophia stared at her feet, looking like she'd aged ten years in a matter of days. Despite what he'd done, she'd loved and trusted him. She'd been absolutely devastated by Ethan's duplicity, and I knew she was still reeling from his loss. "How are you holding up?"

"I... I don't know." Tears glazed her eyes. "It doesn't seem real. I still can't believe..."

She drew in a ragged breath as a tear slipped free. "I'm sorry. I'm so sorry."

She crumpled in on herself, face buried in her hands as she sobbed.

"Soph..." I pushed my palms flat on the couch as I struggled to sit up. Vaughn was there a moment later, strong hands lifting me so I could move to her side. Pulling her close, I wrapped her in my arms. Tears slid down my cheeks at the injustice of it all. I was furious with Ethan for hurting me, but also my sister. She'd placed him on a pedestal and he'd destroyed her dreams and her trust.

For several minutes we sat there, silently crying and soaking up comfort from the other. Sophia shook her head against my shoulder. "I didn't know."

"Of course you didn't," I soothed. "None of us did. I'm sorry you have to deal with this. You don't deserve it."

She peeled away and swiped at her tears. "I can't believe he would hurt you. It's just..." She shook her head. "Why? I just don't understand."

"I'm not sure," I murmured. "He made it sound like he wanted the money."

"What then?" she asked angrily. "Would he have killed Dad, too?"

I bit my lip, unsure what to say. Honestly, I wouldn't put it past him. Ethan was driven by greed, and he wasn't likely to stop. "Soph, he made some bad choices." That was a hell of an understatement. "But he loved you. I know he did."

"If he really loved me, he wouldn't have done this," she snapped.

I understood why she was lashing out, not that I blamed her. "Maybe he was under a lot of stress and just... snapped."

The thought had hounded me ever since I'd woken up in the hospital. Nothing else really made sense. Ever since I'd known him, Ethan had been kind and well-mannered. He'd either hidden his true self or he'd recently had some sort of psychotic break.

Sophia shook her head as another tear slid down her cheek. "I'm so mad at him."

"I know." I rested my head on her shoulder. "All that matters is we have each other."

She grabbed my hand and laced our fingers together. I squeezed her hand. Neither of us said another word; we didn't need to. In the silence, two broken souls began to heal.

FORTY-ONE

VAUGHN

My knee jiggled nervously, and I fought to bring my racing pulse under control as I scanned the interior of the swanky lobby. Bennett Kingsley was located on the 34th floor, and the view from the large plate glass window was incredible.

Afternoon sunlight sparkled off the nearby buildings, turning them gold. I wondered what it would be like to work in a place like this. I felt a moment's jealousy before it quickly bled away. I couldn't handle being cooped up in an office all day long, even one as nice as this.

Sienna might appreciate it though. Her father definitely would. Not that I gave a fuck what he thought. The only person who mattered was Sienna. It wasn't lost on me that I was considering our future and the type of life I could offer her long term. Neither of us had spoken of it, seemingly afraid to jinx it.

After what Sienna's ex had put her through, I didn't blame her in the least. No wonder she was so skittish. But what I'd told her the other night was true. It was thrilling to see her true self emerge. She fought with herself for so long, determined to find her own way through life, and I respected the hell out of her for that. She was so smart, so damn strong, and I wanted her by my side for as long as she chose to stay. Which hopefully would be a long damn time.

The leggy blonde positioned at the desk stood, pulling my attention back to her. "Mr. Kingsley will see you now."

She flashed a bright white smile my way, but it didn't reach her eyes. She was pretty and polished but utterly fake. "Thank you." I nodded her way as she pushed open the heavy wooden door, gaining me entrance to Kingsley's office.

The man rose and rounded his desk, one hand outstretched. "Mr. Allen."

The door clicked quickly closed behind me as I gripped his hand. "Mr. Kingsley."

We shook, then he extended a hand toward a chair in front of his desk. "Please have a seat."

I did so, and he followed suit, dropping into his own chair. "What can I do for you?"

I stared into his bright blue eyes, my stomach churning. Was it really possible this man was my brother? The features were similar enough. His skin was naturally a few shades lighter, his hair a touch more brown instead of black. His eyes were more blue than gray, but he had the same jawline, the same broad forehead.

I cleared my throat. "You probably don't remember me, but we worked together at the PD."

Recognition lightened his expression. "That's right. You were a rookie then."

I smiled. "I admired the hell out of you and Brandt. You were some of the best officers I've ever worked with."

"I appreciate that." His lips lifted in a polite smile, but his eyes dimmed at the mention of his late partner.

I sensed that the loss still weighed heavily on him, so I quickly changed the subject. "Looks like business is going well."

"Can't complain." He spread his fingers wide. "You looking to get into real estate?"

"Hell no. My girlfriend is better suited for that. She's a realtor for TriStar."

His head tipped slightly to the side. "Anyone I know?"

"Sienna Holt."

"Ah." He nodded a little. "I'd steal her, but she likes being a shark in a small pond."

I grinned. That was incredibly apt. "I'm probably biased, but I think she's pretty amazing."

"Nothing wrong with that. Besides, I'm inclined to agree with you."

He leaned back in his chair. "Cedar Springs treating you well?"

"Very. It's been a little chaotic recently. You've probably heard about the murders."

"I have." His brows lowered. "What a shit storm. I won't ask questions because I know you can't say anything, but I hope for your sake you find the asshole."

"Me too. It pisses me off to think he's running around out there."

"I can imagine. Some days I think the whole damn world has gone crazy."

It definitely felt like my world had been tossed upside down. The tension between my shoulder blades came back full force, and I straightened in my seat. "I learned something the other day, and out of respect, I wanted to speak with you first. It's kind of... personal."

"Whatever you need."

His expression turned serious, the intense blue of his eyes fixing me in place. Though I'd rehearsed it in my head several times over the past few days, I wasn't even sure exactly how to broach the subject. I decided just to jump in.

"My grandparents were exceptionally poor. They came from Haiti and moved to the US for a better life and ended up in Cedar Springs. My grandfather was a migrant worker and my grandmother cleaned houses for many of the wealthy residents. As soon as she was old enough, my mother started working alongside my grandmother."

I blew out a breath. "I never knew my father. My mother got pregnant at fifteen, and the idea of terminating a pregnancy back then was..."

I met his gaze, and Bennett nodded. "I'm sure."

"My father wasn't interested in me, and my grandparents didn't want to say anything."

"They didn't want to risk her being fired," he said quietly.

I nodded. "She kept the secret for years, never said a word. When I was young, she told me that my father traveled a lot and couldn't see us."

"I'm sure that was difficult for both of you."

His brow was slightly furrowed, and I was certain he was trying to figure out what I was getting at. I decided to just get it over with. "My mother was working for one of those families one summer when their son came home from college. Apparently he seduced her, and... I'm the end result of that."

Bennett's lips pressed into a firm line. "And by seduced, you mean he forced himself on her."

My heart rate kicked into overdrive as I inclined my head. "My mother likely never would have said anything, but since Sienna's father moves in the same circles..."

Bennett blinked, and I could practically see the wheels turning in his head. "I'm sorry. You think...?" That icy gaze swept over me, more intently this time, taking in every inch of my face.

He expelled a breath and sat back heavily in his chair. "Shit."

My thoughts exactly. "You think it's possible?"

He studied me again. "I mean... Different eyes, but... yeah. I can see the resemblance."

I grimaced a little as I studied him. "You're taking this better than I expected."

He steepled his fingers and touched them to his mouth before speaking. "To be honest, I'm not as surprised as I probably should be. If it's true, it was a shitty thing for him to do, and I'm sorry for that. If you want—"

I held up a hand. "I'm not looking for anything. With all due respect, I've lived my entire life without him. I don't need anything from him now. I just wanted you to know."

"I appreciate you coming to me." Bennett eyed me. "What are you going to do now?"

"I don't know," I admitted. "Request a paternity test, maybe? I'm not sure it even matters anymore."

"If you're my brother, I would say it matters a hell of a lot," he pointed out.

Part of me felt relieved. But the other part of me was angry. I was furious with Matthias for what he'd done—the way he'd treated my mother, the way he'd ignored me. It wasn't fair. I'd spent my entire life without a father. Now that I knew who he was, I felt conflicted. I couldn't go back in time and change things, but I could at least get some sort of justice for my mother. She'd been little more than a child then, and she deserved more than that.

"Whatever you need, you let me know." Bennett sat forward. "He's going to try to pay you off, keep you quiet. Don't let him. Make him accept responsibility for what he did."

A lump formed in my throat at the vehemence in his tone. "I will."

He stared at me for a second, then slowly shook his head. "Still can't quite wrap my head around it."

I'd had several days to stew over it, and it hadn't quite sunk in for me yet, either. "It might not be true," I said, though there was no reason for my mother to lie, especially not after all this time.

Bennett seemed to think the same thing, because he shook his head. "My father has had people try to extort or blackmail him before. But I never believed it... until now." His stare intensified. "What about a DNA test? Yours and mine," he said at my confused look. "If it shows we're possibly siblings..."

"Are you sure? It's a lot to ask, and I've already done enough by coming to see you."

He sliced a hand through the air. "I want to make things right, at least as much as I can."

"I appreciate it. I've taken up enough of your time, but I'll stop back soon."

He snatched a card from the holder on the desk, scribbled something on it, then passed it my way. "My cell."

I nodded and tucked the card into my pocket. "I'll keep you posted."

I left the office, my mind whirling. I didn't know what the future held or how it would affect all of us, but I was glad it was out in the open. No more secrets. No more lies. Sienna and I could move on, free of baggage.

We could finally look forward to a future—together.

FORTY-TWO

SIENNA

Despite Vaughn's insistence that I stay home to recuperate, I decided to go to TriStar to speak with Tristan. My boss had stopped in to check on me a few days ago, and he'd told me to take my time before coming back to work.

Part of me was nervous to leave the house, but the larger, more rational part of me knew the sooner I got back to normal, the better off I'd be. Besides, there was something I needed to take care of.

"I'll be fine." I settled my hands on Vaughn's chest. "I promise."

Stormy eyes peered down into mine, fraught with worry. "Are you sure you're up to it?"

Over the past week and a half, the lacerations on my back and leg had begun to heal, and the intense aches I felt initially had dimmed to a dull discomfort. "I need this," I said quietly.

After everything that happened with Ethan, I refused to hide. I needed to get back out there and move on.

A few days after his death, the police had searched his house and found keys to Ryan Foley's house and car. Having those allowed him to come and go undetected while Foley was out of town. Apparently, Katy Foley, who was a personal assistant to a partner in Ethan's firm, mentioned that Ryan would be out of town for a couple of weeks. It presented the perfect opportunity for Ethan to carry out his plans.

A camera from the parking garage at Foley's apartment had captured images of the vehicle coming and going, but the man's face was obscured. We knew now it had been Ethan all along. He'd also had a key to my house, which I assumed he'd made a copy of when he asked to borrow my car on Thanksgiving. I wanted to kick myself for being so damn trusting.

Vaughn tucked a lock of hair behind my ear. "I know, honey. I don't blame you for that. I just worry about you."

I clutched his hand and nuzzled my cheek against his palm. "I'll be okay. I just need something to take my mind off everything…"

I trailed off, and Vaughn cupped my face as I shivered. His thumb stroked over my cheekbone. "Do you feel guilty?"

I contemplated his question. The hospital had offered counseling, and though I'd spoken with the therapist twice since the incident, it felt so much more personal with Vaughn. He understood what I'd been through, and he hadn't pressed me to talk about it. I licked my lips. "I do and I don't. I know," I said as his mouth parted to speak. "I know he would have killed me. That's why I don't feel bad. I would have preferred he been arrested, but…"

I shrugged, my chest tight with a combination of remorse and resignation. "He never would have stopped. We know that now."

Vaughn's hand slipped around the back of my head and pulled me close. The tension in my muscles slowly seeped away as he pressed a lingering kiss to my forehead. A moment later he pulled back to study me. "Don't hesitate to call if you need anything. Doesn't matter what it is, I'll drop everything and be there in a heartbeat."

His words made me melt a little inside. There was nothing he wouldn't do for me, and I loved him for that. His support gave me the strength and confidence to move on. "I'll call if I need anything," I promised.

His thumb slid lower, over my bottom lip, his eyes following the movement. His expression was so serious, I could swear he was about to say something. But he didn't. He dipped his head and captured my mouth in a possessive kiss.

My senses reeled as he pulled away, and my fingers itched to pull him into the bedroom. I suddenly realized that was precisely what he'd intended—to take my mind off the topic at hand, even if only for a moment.

He winked at me as his hand trailed down my arm. His fingers found mine for a light squeeze. "See you tonight."

Then he was gone. My pulse raced wildly as I watched him retreat from the house and climb into his truck. I wasn't sure how I'd gotten so lucky to find a man like Vaughn, but one thing was for certain—I damn sure wasn't going to let him go.

I gathered my purse, then headed into TriStar. Inside, the smells of charred wood and fresh paint assaulted my nose. It felt like the explosion had happened just yesterday. I could still feel the ground rock beneath my feet, feel the heat of the flames, the smoke filling my lungs.

Goosebumps raced over my skin, but I forced the dark memories away as I turned down the hallway. Nerves twisted my stomach into a knot as I knocked on Tristan's door.

His head snapped up, and he grinned at the sight of me. "Sienna!" He pushed to his feet and rounded the desk, arms outstretched. "How are you feeling?"

"Much better, thanks." I returned his hug, then gestured to the chairs in front of his desk. "Do you mind if we sit for a minute?"

"Of course." He closed the door as I settled into a seat, then he claimed the one across from me. "I'm glad you stopped in. There's something I want to discuss with you."

"Oh? What's that?" I asked the question though I had a pretty good idea what he wanted to talk about.

"I want to start off by saying how much I appreciate your hard work around here. You always give 100%, and your clients adore you."

At that, I smiled. "They're the best part of my job."

"And that's precisely what we need here at TriStar," Tristan replied. "I'm proud to have you here, and I hope you'll consider becoming a more permanent part of the team." He grinned. "The promotion is yours if you'd like it."

I couldn't help feeling flattered. This was exactly what I'd worked for over the past few years. But I needed to know something. "Do you mind if I ask you a question first?"

"Anything." He crossed one ankle over the opposite knee as he reclined in the chair, his focus on me.

"When I started working here... Did you give me the listings you did because of my father?"

His brows drew together. "Are you asking if your job was a result of nepotism?"

I bit my lip. "I know that sounds bad, and I'm sorry. I just—"

He leaned forward. "Sienna, let me tell you something.

I'm not the kind of person who bows to others. If I were, I wouldn't be in the position I am now." He spread his hands wide as if to encompass the brokerage. "You're sitting here today because of the work you've put in and the rapport you've built with clients. Nothing more."

That was a huge relief. "I'm glad to hear that," I said honestly. "And as much as I appreciate the offer, I'm afraid I'll have to decline."

His eyes widened with surprise. "Are you not happy here? We can negotiate the terms of the promotion if that's what you're concerned about."

I held up a hand and shook my head. "It's not that. The promotion is very fair. I just feel like Calvin would be a better fit."

His head tipped slightly to one side. "Are you planning to stay on?"

"I'm not sure," I said slowly. "I love what I do, but it's never been my dream."

"I can respect that," he replied with a nod. "Well, I'm disappointed you won't be partner, but I hope you know you're welcome here as long as you like."

"I appreciate that." I smiled and pushed to my feet. "And thank you again for the offer."

"It still stands," he said good naturedly as he extended a hand my way.

I laughed and slipped my palm into his. "Give it to Cal. Trust me—you won't regret it."

I left Tristan's office feeling much better than I had when I'd shown up. Until we'd spoken, I wasn't entirely sure what I was going to say. But declining the promotion was the right choice. As much as I loved my job, I knew I wouldn't be happy here forever..

My heart jumped in my chest, and I sucked in a breath as a man stepped directly in front of me, bringing me up short. My pulse hitched when I recognized Cal, and I offered a tiny smile. "Hey."

"Hey." He dipped his chin, his gaze sweeping over me from head to toe.

I shifted uncomfortably as he took in the bandage wrapped around my leg, the bruises and myriad cuts on my arms that had begun to heal.

He met my eyes. "How are you doing?"

"I'm okay, thanks."

"Good." He leaned one shoulder against the doorjamb as he studied me. "I was sorry to hear about what happened."

"Me, too." Who could have predicted that my soon-to-be-brother-in-law would go crazy and try to kill me?

"I, um..." He ran a hand through his hair. "I wanted to apologize for the things I said before. And say congratulations—on the promotion."

"Thanks." He sounded sincere, which I appreciated. "But I actually declined Tristan's offer."

His eyes widened. "What? Why?"

I lifted a shoulder. "I just don't think it's the right fit for me at the moment. I think you'll make a much better partner than I would."

His mouth opened and closed before speaking. "What are you going to do?"

"I don't know yet, but I'm sure I'll figure it out." I started toward the lobby, but the sound of my name halted me in my tracks. I turned toward Cal, who stared at me, his gaze intense.

"You should stay on. You're a hell of a realtor."

His praise brought a true smile to my lips. "Thanks."

FORTY-THREE

SIENNA

I entered the bedroom and found Vaughn already in bed, his broad shoulders reclined against the headboard, the sheet pooled around his hips. The sight of all those taut muscles made my mouth water, and my steps faltered as my gaze drifted over his sculpted pecs then across his shoulders and down to his thickly corded forearms. Jeez, the man was absolute perfection everywhere.

"Whatcha looking at?"

At his question, I reluctantly dragged my eyes up to his. "Just you."

"Yeah?" The corner of his mouth quirked up, and he patted the bed. "Come here, beautiful."

My heart did a funny little flip, and the ground seemed to disappear beneath my feet as I practically floated across the room. He threw back the sheet then reached for me, pulling me into his arms. I curled into him, loving the way his entire body seemed to envelop me. It was like we'd done this a thousand times, like we were made for each other. We fit like two halves of a whole.

One hand moved to my hair and began to rhythmically stroke through the long strands. I snuggled into him and closed my eyes, reveling in the sensation. Being with Vaughn was different in so many ways. He was always attentive, always attuned to my thoughts and feelings, always touching me. I loved it. I loved *him*.

With everything that had happened over the past few weeks, we hadn't discussed it. But I suspected he felt the same. I opened my mouth to speak, but Vaughn beat me to it.

"Do you think your dad likes me?"

Every cell of my body went cold at his words. It was too close to my past. My ex had wanted to impress my father, cared more about his image than me. I thought Vaughn was different; had I misjudged him?

Vaughn's hand stilled in my hair. "What just happened there?"

"What do you mean?" I tried to keep my tone light despite the fact that I felt like crumbling to pieces inside.

Using my hair as leverage he gently tipped my face up to meet his. He studied my eyes for a long moment. "I said something that upset you. What was it?"

I hated that he could read me so well. "I'm just surprised you care what my father thinks. You don't strike me as the kind of guy who cares about others' opinions."

"When it comes to your family, I do." His brow furrowed the tiniest bit. "It would be nice to be on good terms with them, if only for your sake."

The tension began to seep from my muscles at his earnest expression. He wasn't trying to impress my father. He was trying to make life easier for me. Again. "I think he'll warm up to you in time," I said diplomatically.

Vaughn smirked. "So he doesn't like me."

I couldn't help but smile. "Like you? Maybe not at the moment. But he does respect you."

His fingers massaged my scalp before sliding through my hair again. "Do you value his opinion?"

I bit my lip. "I used to, and I still do to a point, but I won't let anyone have that kind of control over me anymore. Why?"

"Just curious. I'd like him to like me."

I could sense there was more. "Why do you want his approval so badly?"

He stared at me. "Because one of these days I'm going to ask you to marry me, and I'd like you to say yes."

My heart practically tumbled out of my chest, and the words lodged in my throat. He continued to peer up at me, those intense eyes unblinking. "I just need to know if I'm going to need your father's permission first."

I managed to move my mouth. "I'd like you to get along... but you don't need his permission."

His smile started slow, then grew. He cupped the back of my head and leaned in, sealing his mouth over mine in a slow, tender kiss. Neither of us said a word. But I couldn't help the happiness that billowed up inside me.

"For the record," I whispered in his ear, "if you asked me to marry you... I'd say yes."

His hands tightened before pushing me away slightly so he could better see me. His eyes scanned my face, sending a flurry of butterflies battering against my ribcage. Nervous anticipation bubbled in my veins, swelling with every second that passed. Silence stretched between us for nearly a moment before he spoke again. "Do you have any idea how much I love you?"

I was both shocked and exhilarated by his words. It felt

like the air had been sucked from the room, and my mind spun deliriously as my heart beat too fast.

"I never thought I'd find someone like you." He trailed his fingers over my face. "You're so beautiful, so smart... You're leagues beyond me."

"I am not," I protested, embarrassment prickling over my skin. I hated hearing him compare himself to me. The fact that I'd grown up in a wealthy household was nothing more than luck. Vaughn worked every day to protect the people of Cedar Springs, yet he couldn't see how much I loved him for that.

"You are." He smiled. "I don't deserve you, but I swear, Sienna—I'll show you every day how much you mean to me. Your father may never like me, but—"

"Vaughn—"

He continued as if I hadn't spoken, "I'll try my best to make you happy, and—"

"Shut up." That got his attention. I framed his face in my hands, my gaze searching his shocked eyes. "You've done more for me in just a few weeks than anyone else has—ever. Your past doesn't matter to me, or how much money you make. You take care of me—of everyone. You make me happy, and I'm so damn proud of you. I love you so much it hurts."

Hope shone in his eyes as he pulled me closer. "Sienna—"

"Shut up and kiss me."

He grinned. "Don't need to tell me twice."

He dedicated himself to the task, stripping us both until we were bare. His kisses were tender and deep, his touch slow and reverent. He made love to me with a passion that touched me all the way to my soul.

Once we'd both come down, he lifted his head and

peered at me, his eyes glowing silver in the moonlight. "Marry me. Be mine, forever."

Elation rolled through me, and I threw my arms around his neck. I crashed my lips to his, pouring my answer into the kiss.

He was my lover. My hero. My future.

My whole life.

EPILOGUE

VAUGHN

Our break in the murder case came in the most unlikely of forms. Cloistered in the small observation room adjacent to the interrogation room, I faced the deputy. "When did he come in?"

"Last night. Picked him up for possession outside of a seedy motel downtown."

I nodded a little. "You said he mentioned Chester Davies."

"Not directly," the deputy corrected. "Once the drugs wore off and he realized where he was, he threw a holy fit. Started screaming, trying to shake the place down."

I rolled my eyes. Sounded about right.

"Something he said caught the officer's attention. He started going on and on about some warehouse, about how the guy screamed and screamed, and how he was going to end up just like him."

"You think he saw something?"

"Not sure," he replied, "but we'll find out for sure."

The deputy had called me this morning to let me know that Joshua Blum had been brought in for questioning regarding Chester Davies's murder. I didn't think the man was in any way responsible.

According to the deputy, Blum was a hardcore user. It wasn't uncommon for addicts to rob or kill someone for their next fix, but those crimes were often messy and impulsive. Whoever had killed Davies was methodical and precise. He'd wanted him to suffer.

I watched through the two-way mirror as the door swung open and a man entered, escorted by a female officer and a man in a suit. The man, who I assumed was a detective, gestured toward the chair. "Have a seat."

The man trudged toward the table, shuffling along as if he had all the time in the world. The orange jumpsuit combined with the glaring overhead lights made his pale skin look even more sallow, highlighting the huge, dark bags beneath his bloodshot eyes. His hair was stringy, hanging in greasy clumps around his face, and his shifty gaze flew around the room, taking in every detail.

"Sit down." The officer squeezed his shoulder, guiding him into a chair.

"Ow!" He shrugged her off and rubbed dramatically at the spot. "That hurt!"

The officer ignored him and disappeared from the room, leaving just the inmate and the detective. "Mr. Blum, I'd like to ask you some questions."

Blum wrapped his arms around his waist but didn't respond, his eyes still flickering around the room.

I grimaced as I watched the tremors rack his body, early signs of withdrawal. This wasn't looking promising.

"Mr. Blum?" the detective prompted.

Blum shook his head. "I wanna go home."

"I'm sorry, I can't allow that to happen yet. You'll be

transferred to a rehab facility, but I need to ask you some questions first."

Blum shook his head. "I didn't do nothin'."

"No one is accusing you of anything," the detective replied. "But you said last night that you frequent a warehouse on the west side, is that right?"

When Blum didn't respond, the detective continued. "A man was killed there a couple weeks back. What do you remember about that?"

Blum's eyelids flickered. "Dunno."

The detective extracted a photo from the manila envelope on the table, then slid it toward Blum. He didn't even look at it before shaking his head. "Got nothin' to do with any dead man."

"But you saw him, didn't you?" Blum slanted a look toward the detective before glancing away again. He knew something, I could feel it.

"I just want to find the person responsible," the detective said, "and I don't want any more innocent people to die."

Blum twitched violently but still didn't speak. The detective braced his elbows on the table and leaned forward. "If you know something, you need to tell us. We can keep you safe."

"Don't know 'im," Blum said.

"Did you see the person's face?" the detective pressed. "Was it a man?"

Blum scratched at the cuffs of his jumpsuit, then jerked a shoulder. "Dunno. Maybe."

Blum went silent so long that I thought he would refuse to answer. When he did, the vehemence in his tone startled me. "Ashley! This is for Ashley!"

My brows drew low over my nose, and I narrowed my gaze at the inmate. Was he still high? I couldn't tell. Who was Ashley, and what the hell did she have to do with this? Another violent shudder racked his body, and Blum rubbed at his temples.

"Who is Ashley?" the detective prompted.

"Ashley. He said he was doing it for Ashley," Blum reiterated.

The detective gave a slow nod. "Did he say anything else?"

"I want to leave." The trembling of his limbs intensified, and I recognized the early signs of withdrawal. Shit. We were losing him.

"Wanna go home!" Blum shouted, his gaze flying around the room, his eyes wild and unfocused.

The detective pressed once more, but Blum grew more agitated with every passing second. Knowing that he wouldn't be answering any more questions today, the detective rang for the guards, who escorted an agitated Blum from the room just a moment later.

I dragged a hand over my face and waited for the detective to join us. There had to be some correlation there. Maybe a girlfriend or wife? I couldn't recall any next of kin by the name of Ashley in either man's files, but I would need to go through them again to be certain.

Davies had sustained twenty-three lacerations to his body from which he'd slowly bled out. Our first victim had been stabbed twenty-three times. The MO was slightly different, but the message was the same. The number was significant, I just wasn't sure why. Yet.

But I was damn well going to find out.

———

Don't miss the next book in the Rescue & Redemption Series!

When two strangers break into Eden's bed and breakfast, Nick rushes to her rescue. Between battling the brewing storm and evading the intruders, it becomes a fight for survival as danger closes in from every side...

Turn the page for a sneak peek of Cold Justice!

COLD JUSTICE

PROLOGUE

The car rumbled slowly along the dark country road. Tonight the moon was full and bright, its silvery glow filtering down through the trees. The driver steered the car carefully, no headlamps to guide his way.

At the end of the lane a large home came into view, and the driver slowed to a stop then parked.

"That it?" asked his passenger.

The first man nodded. "Christmas is just a few days away. It should be empty then."

The second man nodded slowly, his mind spinning. There were so many things that could go wrong. They had to be careful. "You sure?"

His accomplice scoffed. "There's no one here half the time anyway. That's what makes this place perfect. Trust me —everyone will be long gone."

It was almost Christmas, after all, and who there hell

came to a tiny place like Cedar Springs around Christmas? No one.

He nodded. "Let's do it."

Neither man said another word as the car slowly reversed down the road, no one the wiser.

————

CHAPTER ONE

NICK

Beady eyes stared at me from every direction, making the hair on the back of my neck stand on end. It was... horrifying.

Everywhere I looked, festive paraphernalia covered the space, and the soft strains of Christmas music filled the air. Worst of all was a seven-foot-tall artificial tree in the corner of the foyer that had been covered in white fluff and decorated to look like a giant snowman.

I tipped my head in contemplation. It vaguely resembled the Stay-Puft marshmallow man from the movie and looked almost as evil. The twin snowmen at the base of the tree mocked me, and the longer I looked at them, the more their smiles resembled sinister sneers.

A shudder rippled down my spine as I closed the front door of the bed and breakfast I'd been referred to, then marched past the hoard of holiday horrors. Garland and bright red bows had been wrapped around the banister of the large, curving stairs in front of me, taunting me with their cheery vibrance. A headache pulsed at the backs of my eyes, made worse by the ridiculous, gaudy decor that filled the space.

The rustle of papers came from my right, and I followed

the sound through a large arched doorway. Scowl fixed firmly in place, I entered the small but brightly lit room. If I thought the monstrous decor would have been relegated to the foyer, I was bound to be disappointed. A large nutcracker stood sentinel next to the fireplace, and I shuddered. God, those things were creepy. I couldn't begin to understand the fascination with them; I thought people had stopped using them centuries ago.

One of the few uncluttered surfaces was a large mahogany desk situated in the center of the room. A woman sitting behind the desk rose when she saw me, and a bright smile curved her lips. "I thought I heard someone come in. Welcome!"

Holy shit. The first thing I noticed was the sweater. I winced as the lights blinked merrily, nearly blinding me. The second thing I noticed was her eyes. They were the brightest blue I'd ever seen, rivaling that of the sky on a cloudless day. It threw me off balance, and it made me that much more uncomfortable. I lifted a brow her way. "Did they run out of decorations at the store?"

She stared at me for a moment as she processed my quip, then burst into laughter. "It's a bit much, I know, but I can't help it. I just love it so much."

"Yeah. I got that." My tone was dry, and her lips compressed into a tight smile as she regarded me.

"You must be Mr. Ginsley."

I nodded briskly as I dug out my wallet from the breast pocket of my jacket and presented my card. "Correct."

"My name is Eden." I studied her as she swiped it through the card reader on her desk. Her hair was the color of burnished gold, the mass of wild curls falling down around her shoulders. "I prepare breakfast and lunch each day, and offer room service as requested. Will you be needing dinner tonight?"

"No. I'll be going out." My gaze drifted down her torso, enveloped in the huge sweater. "Ugly sweater party after work?"

Her head jerked up, that bright blue gaze clashing with mine. "What?"

"Your sweater." I tipped my head toward the atrocity. "Is that for one of those ugly sweater parties?"

"Nope." She gave me another of those ridiculously sunny smiles. "I just wanted to wear something festive."

All right, then. I shifted on my feet, not sure what to say.

The machine beeped, and she returned the card to me. "Would you like a receipt?"

"That won't be necessary. However, I'd prefer a room facing East so I can wake with the sun."

Her expression didn't change one iota as she gave me a single, slow blink. "I've put you in room three, top of the stairs to your right."

I lifted a brow. "Nothing on the ground floor?"

"Not at the moment." She passed me an old-fashioned key, then folded her hands in front of her with a serene smile. "Have a wonderful stay."

I eyed her for a moment, wondering if that was the southern equivalent of telling someone to piss off. I knew things were different down here, but I didn't have the patience to care right now. I was already on edge with the upcoming holiday, one I had dreaded all year round. It brought back so many memories better left buried.

Curling the key in my hand, I strode up the wide staircase. My lip curled as I took in the garland wrapped festively around the rails, tiny golden bells dangling from the bright red bows. I found room three easily enough, and I unlocked the door. I had one foot across the threshold when I froze in my tracks. Oh, hell no.

I stomped back down the stairs and stopped beneath the archway of the office. The woman didn't bother to look up, and I sent a glare her way. I cleared my throat. Loudly. "Excuse me."

Her blonde head slowly lifted, those bright blue eyes clashing with mine. The force of them, combined with her sweet smile, threatened to throw me off balance. "Yes, Mr. Ginsley?"

I steeled my spine. "Could you come with me, please?"

"Of course." She rounded the desk, curvy hips swaying gently as she moved toward me. "How can I help you?"

Ripping my gaze away, I spun on my heel without a word and trudged back upstairs. I pushed the door open with hand and gestured for her to enter. "I'd like you to remove this."

Her brows drew together. "This...?"

I swept an arm around the room, indicating the Christmas decor placed around the room. "All of this. It needs to go. Now," I added firmly.

I watched as she slowly began to gather the decorations, almost as if it pained her to do so. Well, too bad. I had no desire to be reminded of the upcoming holiday right now. "I have work to do while I'm here, and I don't want to be bothered."

"Of course not." There was no missing the derision in her voice, or the way it dropped before she quietly added, "Prick."

I narrowed my gaze at her. "What?"

She snatched up the small Santa figurine from the dresser and held it up with a beatific smile. "St. Nick. Can't forget him."

I knew I hadn't misheard her, but I didn't have a chance to say anything as she moved toward me, arms full of decorations. "Anything else?"

"No." I held the door wide open, indicating for her to leave me in peace.

She moved into the hallway and smiled my way. "Have a nice evening, and I hope you have a *wonderful* holiday."

I didn't miss the emphasis on that, either, and I rolled my eyes as I slammed the door.

A wonderful holiday? Not likely.

———

Don't miss Cold Justice, now available everywhere!

ALSO BY MORGAN JAMES

QUENTIN SECURITY SERIES

Twisted Devil – Jason and Chloe

The Devil You Know – Blake and Victoria

Devil in the Details – Xander and Lydia

Devil in Disguise – Gavin and Kate

Heart of a Devil – Vince and Jana

Tempting the Devil – Clay and Abby

Devilish Intent – Con and Grace

Quentin Security Box Set One (Books 1-3)

Quentin Security Box Set Two (Books 4-6)

*Each book is a standalone within the series

RESCUE & REDEMPTION SERIES

Friendly Fire – Grayson and Claire

Cruel Vendetta – Drew and Emery

Silent Treatment – Finn and Harper

Reckless Pursuit – Aiden and Izzy

Dangerous Desires – Vaughn and Sienna

Cold Justice – Nick and Eden

Rescue & Redemption Box Set One (books 1-3)

RETRIBUTION SERIES

Unrequited Love – Jack and Mia, Book One

Undeniable Love – Jack and Mia, Book Two

Unbreakable Love – Jack and Mia, Book Three

Pretty Little Lies – Eric and Jules, Book One

Beautiful Deception – Eric and Jules, Book Two

Hidden Truth – John and Josi

Sinful Illusions – Fox and Eva, Book One

Sinful Sacrament – Fox and Eva, Book Two

Retribution Series Box Set 1

Retribution Series Box Set 2

Retribution Series Box Set 3

The Complete Retribution Series

STANDALONES

Death Do Us Part

Escape

BAD BILLIONAIRES

(Radish Exclusive)

Depraved

Ravished

Consumed

ABOUT THE AUTHOR

Morgan James is a USA Today bestselling author of contemporary and romantic suspense novels. She spent most of her childhood with her nose buried in a book, and she loves all things romantic, dark, and dirty. She currently resides in Ohio and is living happily ever after with her own alpha hero and their two kids.

Made in United States
Troutdale, OR
12/10/2024